REA

ACPL ITEM
DISCARDED

ALLEN COUNTY PUBLIC LIBRARY

3 1833 04671 0568

P9-EDY-366

AUG 1 0 2004

OUTLAWS

Other Five Star Titles
by T. T. Flynn:

Hell's Cañon: A Western Quintet
Reunion at Cottonwood Station: A Western Quartet
Death Marks Time in Trampas
The Devil's Lode: A Western Trio
Long Journey to Deep Cañon
Night of the Comanche Moon
Prodigal of Death: A Western Quintet
Rawhide
Ride to Glory: A Western Quartet

OUTLAWS

A Western Quartet

T.T. FLYNN

Five Star • Waterville, Maine

Copyright © 2004 by Thomas B. Flynn, M.D.

Additional copyright information on page 224.

All rights reserved.

No part of this book may be reproduced or transmitted in any form or by any electronic or mechanical means, including photocopying, recording or by any information storage and retrieval system, without the express written permission of the publisher, except where permitted by law.

First Edition
First Printing: July 2004

Published in 2004 in conjunction with
Golden West Literary Agency.

Set in 11 pt. Plantin.

Printed in the United States on permanent paper.

Library of Congress Cataloging-in-Publication Data

Flynn, T. T.
    Outlaws : a western quartet / by T.T. Flynn.—1st ed.
        p. cm.
    Contents: Blood of the Dons—Bandit of the Brindlebar—
    Valhalla—The fighting breed.
    ISBN 1-59414-040-5 (hc : alk. paper)
    1. Outlaws—Fiction.   2. Western stories.   I. Title.
PS3556.L93O87 2004
    813'.54—dc22   2004047082

OUTLAWS

• TABLE OF CONTENTS •

BLOOD OF THE DONS

T.T. Flynn completed "Blood of the *Dons*" on November 18, 1935. It was the twenty-seventh story he had written that year. It was accepted immediately upon submission by Popular Publications' *Dime Western*. But as would occasionally happen, it was in another Popular Publications magazine that this story would be published. The title of "Blood of the *Dons*" was changed to "Fighting *Dons* of San Saba" when this short novel appeared in *Star Western* (4/36). The author was paid $400.

I

"Man from the North"

Don Mike O'Grady's mother had been Antonita del Grazar of that ancient clan whose lands, a thousand miles to the southeast, formed an empire. In his dreams *Don* Mike could see her yet, that lovely woman, black-haired and vivid, small, dainty, and proud, always a stranger among the blunt, blond Americans of the Oregon country.

Before he was six *Don* Mike sensed the faint sadness that walked always with his smiling mother. Perhaps, too, Antonita O'Grady did not know that her son was absorbing more than words those nights under the clear bright stars when she talked to him a bit wistfully of that distant country where she had been a girl—the country of *caballeros* and *peónes*, of fighting Apaches and Navajos, of vast sheep flocks and herds of cattle, and mines of gold and silver.

They were fabulous tales that his mother told him of that mighty land of mountains and deserts, where the farthermost horizons could not contain the vast del Grazar land grants. He listened spellbound to her stories of the del Grazar men who rode blooded horses bearing silver-studded saddles, proud that they were del Grazars, whose very wish was law.

At seven, *Don* Mike, called so by his mother, squirmed at her knee and asked: "But, Mother, why are we here, where Daddy doesn't own much land?"

Antonita O'Grady smiled in the moonlight, and gently said: "We are here, *Don* Mike, because I loved your father very much. Oh, *very* much. Never forget, silver and land are not love. When you are a grand man like Big Mike, *hijo mío*, never forget that love is enough . . . if it is love."

So the picture shaped in young *Don* Mike's mind—of a daughter of the proud and haughty del Grazars, who had given her love to a rollicking Irishman whose fortune was his horse and saddle, and his prospects only his heart. She told of how the del Grazar clan had unbendingly opposed her marriage to this outsider. But he had fought for her and won her—he had married her and taken her to this cold and new land of the Northwest.

Antonita O'Grady was content that it had been so. She loved the big husband who would never own an empire, but who never forgot to tell her that he loved her. Yet always a part of her reached back to the Río Grande and her own people. She would never go back, she told *Don* Mike, a little sadly, but without bitterness. The del Grazars were proud and unforgiving. If they would not have Big Mike, she would not have them. She, too, was proud.

But *Don* Mike grew up with that heritage of del Grazar pride, crossed with the gay wildness of his father. Irish and Spanish—quick fire and hard steel—ready laughter and an occasional tear—quick pride and quick gentleness. *Don* Mike O'Grady y del Grazar he was, speaking Spanish and English, with black hair and blue eyes, the smile of a fawn and the smoldering pride of a grandee. He could throw a rope, draw a gun or knife, and ride with the dexterity of one who had been born to such accomplishments.

When Big Mike O'Grady was rolled to death by a man-killing horse, Antonita O'Grady did not weep—much. But to *Don* Mike, who was twenty, pale and stunned by this unjust thing that had happened, she said: "We do not belong here any more among these good people. We will go back where there is land that should be mine, and yours, from my father, and make them proud of the name of O'Grady. *¿Qué no, hijo mío?*"

"You bet," said *Don* Mike.

Antonita O'Grady sold the ranch. It did not bring much. Big Mike had been a better husband and father than a moneymaker. They took the railroad east to Denver, and south to Las Vegas, and the stagecoach from there to Santa Fé. *Don* Mike marveled as the blond Americans grew fewer and he came into country where Spanish was spoken on every side. It was all strange, and yet somehow familiar.

In Santa Fé, where the streets were narrow and little burros stood patiently under big loads of firewood in the dusty plaza, Antonita O'Grady touched her flushed cheek and said: "I am sick a little, *Don* Mike. I think we will stay here for a day or two."

They stayed a week. The last four days, Antonita O'Grady spent with the quiet nuns in the hospital beside the church, and then one morning the sun burst up over the green Sangre de Christo Mountains to the east and found *Don* Mike riding alone over the bare, open mesas to the south.

The doctors had been baffled by the little fever that had taken Antonita O'Grady, in spite of everything they could do. But the soft-voiced nun who had been with her at the last had quietly said: "She died of a broken heart."

Through the tears that blinded him and dry sobs that caught his throat as he rode south alone, *Don* Mike knew it was so. Antonita O'Grady could not live without that rollicking Irishman who had been her life.

Mike O'Grady rode into San Saba, on the Río Grande, as the sun was slipping behind the mountains to the west. Back of him were dry mesas and dry arroyos, barren, dry mountains to the west and to the east across the river. The dust of the long, hot day's ride lay faintly gray over man and horse.

He was surprised now to find in San Saba a seething bustle of life. There had been freight wagons back along the rutty road, and a surprising number of riders, but Mike had only nodded to the men he passed. Now here was a crowded plaza with saloons running wide open, horses lined at hitch racks, freight wagons, ranch wagons, and buggies standing about.

His questing eyes saw brown-skinned Mexicans, lighter American and Spanish cowmen, men with laced boots who looked like miners, and other men, Spanish and American, who looked as if they were more at home in towns than out on the range.

He left his horse at the second livery stable. The first was full. And of the stocky, bearded man in charge, Mike asked: "How far to the Circle Half Moon Ranch?"

The stocky man spat. " 'Bout twenty-three miles, if you mean the headquarters. The Circle Half Moon runs a hundred an' twenty-five miles to the west, I hear. Never rode out that far myself. Too damn' many Apaches snoopin' around lookin' for what they can pick up."

Mike nodded and talked as he rolled a cigarette. "I've heard they're pretty bad. How come the town's so crowded?"

The stocky man stared at him. "You ain't from around here?" he said.

Mike grinned faintly. "Never been here before."

"Huh. I thought so. But you mean to tell me you drifted in here an' never heard about the place? By God, you must've, or you wouldn't have asked me." The stocky man spat tobacco juice against the nearest stall post. "You must've come in with blinders on your eyes an' your ears stopped up. Don't head too fur west o' here like that. The Apaches has been licked plenty, but they still snoop around to see if they can lift a little hair now an' then, an' the Mexicans are mighty surly." The liveryman's voice grew slightly sarcastic. "I reckon you know San Saba's the county seat?"

"Yep, I know that," Mike agreed.

"Well, son, there's nine new mines in this end of the county, an' more on the way. They're throwin' new cattle onto the grass all around here an' be damned to anyone. San Saba is on the way to be the sweetest little puddle of hell you ever dirtied your boots in." The liveryman spat again and eyed the gun and sheathed knife that Mike wore at his waist. "Looks like you come primed fer trouble. Can you use that gun?"

It was *Don* Mike O'Grady, half Irish, half grandee, who smiled back under half-closed eyes. "Why not?" he asked. "But I didn't come here to kill anyone."

The liveryman chuckled. He found himself liking this tall, dark-haired young fellow. "I suppose," he said, "you came here to make your fortune?"

"No," Mike denied mildly. "I came here to take my fortune."

13

The liveryman stared. "Mister," he said, "you're talkin' like trouble *now*. Anyone who comes to San Saba to *take* his fortune is mighty apt to have to shoot for it."

Mike sobered. It sounded like an omen, which he was quick to deny.

"I think not," he said. "I'll get my horse in the morning. *Buenas noches, señor.*"

Don Mike wandered about the plaza, taking in the sights. So this was San Saba, where young bloods had fought with pistols for the favor of their ladies at the *bailes*, and life had been lazy and rich with peace. Now San Saba smacked of the boom wildness of Denver. American energy pulsed on every side. There was little here, so far, to match the del Grazar saga his mother's memory had pictured for him.

Across the plaza activity boiled out of a saloon. Men's voices shouted angrily. A gunshot snapped through the somber dusk. From all directions men ran toward the spot.

Mike went with them, and, when he stood on the outskirts of the crowd, he heard a big, bearded cowman snort: "It was only a Mex he kilt! By God, the sooner we run 'em all outta here, the better we'll get along."

At the man's shoulder Mike spoke calmly: "They've been here a long time, mister. Couple of hundred years, haven't they?"

The big cowman wheeled on him, saw who had spoken, and snorted angrily again. "What of it? *We're* here now, an' they git under our feet. If we don't like 'em, we'll run 'em out. How long you been around here?"

"One hour," Mike said mildly.

"I thought so. You'll learn better before you've been here long."

"Perhaps," Mike said civilly.

14

The crowd began to break up. Mike drifted along to the next saloon, and ordered a whiskey and drank it thoughtfully, and ordered another as the bar began to fill up with customers who had run out to watch the fracas.

At Mike's right elbow a lean man in the forties, with a drooping blond mustache over a thin-lipped mouth, called down the bar to a friend: "I hear there's eight hundred head of Swallerfork cows comin' over from Pecos, Dave. You meetin' 'em?"

"Not this trip, Blondy," the fourth man along the bar answered. "I've got too many things to do."

He was thick-chested and deep-voiced, that speaker. His dark-tanned face was broad and solid, and a heavy black mustache covered his strong mouth. His sombrero, black shirt, and buckskin vest were dusty, as if he had ridden hard through the day. Mike noticed particularly the man's powerful, stubby hands that looked as if they had always known work and power. Even the band of gold about one finger was broad, thick, massive, and Mike noted, too, that, when the man spoke, the others listened respectfully.

A few minutes later Mike spoke to the lean man beside him. "Are the del Grazars moving in more cattle?"

His answer was a loud, incredulous "Huh? The del Grazars movin' in more cattle?" The speaker laughed loudly, called down the bar. "Dave, here's a young feller wants to know if the del Grazars are movin' in more cattle! Guess he's talkin' about the Swallerfork bunch you're bringin' over."

Others laughed. There was a general turning of heads to scan Mike. He smiled faintly at them, unabashed. "Must be something wrong about that," he said. "I don't savvy it."

From farther along the bar he got again: "How long you been around these parts, mister?"

"I just rode in."

15

"You sound like it," the speaker said, grinning. He had a sandy beard and big ears that seemed to spring straight out from the sides of his head. "The del Grazars are sellin' cattle, not buyin'." He grinned.

But the massive man with the heavy black mustache was not grinning. He had stepped back so that he could see Mike better, and Mike thought, as he met the direct gaze stabbing from under bushy black brows, that he had never seen eyes so hard and coldly piercing. Except perhaps his father's eyes in anger. . . .

II

"Pride of the Dons"

The man called Dave spoke, and men fell silent, so that his deep voice struck hard on the sudden silence.

"How come a stranger like you is so interested in the old Grazars an' what they're doing?"

Again it seemed to Mike that tension grew on the room while everyone waited for his answer. He stood straight. Something in him struck fire against the steady gaze of the older man.

"I'm headed toward the Circle Half Moon Ranch, and I wonder why you're so interested," Mike said. "Who are you?"

"Dave Schaal. An' you, stranger?"

Schaal was staring levelly. He seemed to be watching for any impression his name made. It had no effect. When Mike answered coolly—"I'm Mike O'Grady."—that name struck no response from Schaal.

"I take it," Schaal said deliberately, and he seemed to pick his words "you're riding toward the Circle Half Moon to see the del Grazars. Are you intendin', maybe, to stop there?"

Several men close to Schaal were edging back out of the way. The tension in the room had tightened. Puzzled, Mike could not account for it, but his answer was quick and biting. "Is there any reason why I shouldn't stop there? For I aim to, Schaal, if that's what you're leadin' up to."

The lean man with the drooping blond mustache had stayed at the bar beside Mike. Now his hand dropped suddenly to his gun. "You've showed your hand, I guess!" he exploded.

He was on Mike's left side. He had the odds, for Mike had to make a half turn while his gun came out. But as Mike's right hand flashed for his gun, his other hand flicked the knife from its leather sheath. The blade seemed a flowing line of steel that slashed across Blondy's gun knuckles before he was half through his draw.

Blondy yelled with pain. His gun clattered to the floor. He thrust his bleeding hand and its mate into the air as the knife point jabbed against his stomach.

Mike's gun was covering the room, covering Dave Schaal who stood without moving while other men jumped back out of the line of fire.

"You wanted trouble . . . an' you've got it!" Mike snapped. His voice was hard, brittle, and behind it temper was blazing.

He noted half a dozen men standing tautly, elbows crooked, and knew they were ready to draw. Strangely enough in that moment he was not afraid, although this was the first time he had looked so closely at death.

Dave Schaal's nod was almost approving. "That was quick work, O'Grady," he said. "Put up your gun. You can walk out of here safely."

Such was the power of the man's personality that Mike believed him, and holstered his gun, and stepped back with the knife in his hand.

Blondy had whipped a bandanna around his bleeding knuckles. He spoke violently. "Are you lettin' this skunk walk out after he cut me this way?"

"You butted in when you wasn't asked," Schaal told him curtly. "He took you cold, an', if he'd been as gun hungry as you are, he'd have slit your belly and emptied lead in it. Ain't you satisfied?"

Blondy swore. "He used that knife like a Mex! That ain't no way to fight! I'll get him for that!"

Blondy crowded back against the bar as Mike made a sudden movement with the knife.

"My mother was a del Grazar," Mike said thinly. "Has anybody here got anything to say about it?"

They were stunned by that statement.

"I'll be damned!" one of the men exclaimed. "He . . . he said his name was O'Grady!"

Men looked at each other, at Mike, but mostly at Dave Schaal whose bushy black eyebrows had raised in silent surprise.

"O'Grady . . . del Grazar," Schaal said, as if weighing a problem. He nodded to himself, spoke without visible emotion. "Are they expectin' you at the Circle Half Moon?"

"That's my business, mister."

"There ain't any reason why you can't go," said Schaal. He looked about the room. "You hear that, boys? He can go." And then to Mike, Schaal said: "But if you're lookin' for old man Tony del Grazar, you'll find him in the big house just south of the courthouse. He's in town right now."

"You mean *Don* Antonio del Grazar?" Mike asked.

"He's Tony del Grazar to me," Schaal said indifferently. "You can see him here in San Saba, or at the Circle Half Moon, or anywhere between, for all I care. But you'd better clear out of here now. My men ain't exactly friendly to a del Grazar man."

Mike slipped the knife in its sheath, turned his back to them, and walked out. Although he did not know it, his back was straight, his head was high, and he looked lean, pantherish, and as threatening as a fine steel blade.

Dave Schaal noticed it. His eyes seldom missed anything. He was frowning thoughtfully as he turned to the bar and called for a whiskey.

The moon was just rising when Mike came to the house beyond the courthouse. An oil lantern threw yellow light over a closed door in the high adobe yard wall. Antonita del Grazar had spoken of the free-handed hospitality in this never-closed town house of the del Grazars. But now the place looked subdued, deserted, withdrawn from the new excitement in the plaza. This mansion of a grandee's empire had become an old house, drowsing in the backwater of a life new and strange to San Saba and the country about. But Mike's pulses were racing as he tried the gate and found it locked. Through this gate his mother had often walked. This was home.

No one answered the knock. He tried again, and wondered what they would say. His throat tightened, and he swallowed pain as he thought of her who should be here with him.

He knocked a third time, and, as he stood there, a two-horse buggy came racing along the moon-touched, dusty street, and drew up beside him, the horses breathing hard, moving restlessly.

Mike's hat came into his hands as a girl spoke from the buggy. "You wish someone?"

"I'm looking for *Don* Antonio del Grazar, ma'am," Mike said.

"He should be in there. Is the gate locked? Here, I'm coming in."

19

Mike stepped to help her down.

Her hand was small, firm, cool on his, and her weight was light, and she was small and slender and smiling as she stepped into the yellow halo of the lantern. She was pretty in the way Antonita del Grazar had been pretty, different from the blonde girls of the Oregon country.

A white lace *mantilla* over her hair and shoulders might have been protection against the cool night air, but it seemed to Mike the *mantilla* was only a frame for her oval, smiling face.

"Isn't it kind of risky, riding alone at night this way, the way things are around here now?" he asked.

"Perhaps," she replied cheerfully, with the faintest breath of an accent back of her words.

She reached behind the lantern to a rawhide string that Mike had not noticed, and pulled it. A bell rang inside the gate. At the same moment two riders turned the next corner and galloped toward them. The gate was still closed as they swung down from their saddles.

Mike's hand hovered near his gun until one of the men spoke in Spanish irritably: "Why did you drive off alone, María?"

She answered in Spanish, with an undertone of amusement: "I told you I would drive alone. I like it, at night, to drive alone."

The second man had stepped over by Mike. "Who is this man?" he asked.

"He was here at the gate. He wishes to see *Don* Antonio."

All that in Spanish, and then in English the first speaker addressed Mike. "I am Gregorio del Grazar. You wish to see my father?"

"Yes," Mike said.

"Your name, please, and your business?" was the suspicious demand.

20

"My name is O'Grady," Mike said. He waited an instant, and, when the name apparently had no meaning, added: "The business is important to me, if your father is here."

An elderly manservant opened the gate. Gregorio del Grazar hesitated, said: "Come in, Mister O'Grady. I'll tell my father you wish to see him."

Gregorio del Grazar looked to be almost thirty. His skin was darker than the girl's skin. He was not quite as tall as Mike, but heavier, with a pudginess that suggested a love for good food. His lips were full under his black mustache, and he did not try to disguise the scowl that backed his unfriendly and hostile manner.

The second man was younger, slimmer, more wiry. He was unfriendly, too. He walked through the gate first with the girl, saying curtly in Spanish: "I will tell *Don* Antonio."

Behind the wall, beyond gnarled old trees, the house windows glowed softly. Through an open passage leading into a central patio Mike heard voices. He was not taken back there after the girl and her escort. Instead, Gregorio del Grazar conducted him into a square room at the left of the patio, entered through an outside door. Log beams, brown with age, held up the low ceiling, deer heads hung on the walls, and bearskins and mountain-lion skins lay on the floor. The furniture was handmade and massive, with the dignity of simplicity, the soft patina of age.

They remained standing, eyeing one another.

"I have not seen you before," Gregorio del Grazar said stiffly.

Mike smiled faintly. "I guess not," he said. "I just got to San Saba."

Gregorio frowned. "A stranger . . . and you have business with my father?" he persisted.

"That's right."

21

Gregorio continued to frown. "The name of O'Grady is familiar."

"Is it?" said Mike.

The man wore a black suit. The coat was open, revealing a silver-mounted revolver underneath. His hand remained near the revolver and he remained suspicious.

A door in the back of the room opened and a tall old man stepped in. He was taller than Gregorio, taller than Mike. He was thin and gaunt, so that the skin was tight over his cheek bones and around his eyes. Hair and mustache were white, and his mouth was thin-lipped and bloodless, and his black suit hung slackly from square, erect shoulders as he stopped and looked at Mike.

"I am *Don* Antonio del Grazar," he said coldly. "What do you want?"

Mike had lived twenty years for this moment. Now his chief thought was the antagonism these two men had for him. They did not know him, yet they disliked him, had barriers up against him. But, of course, it was because they did not know who he was.

In Spanish Mike spoke to the tall, gaunt old man: "*Don* Antonio, I am Miguel O'Grady."

Don Antonio stared without expression. "I know of no one by the name of O'Grady," he said—in English.

Mike tried again, in Spanish.

"Your sister, Antonita, was my mother. She . . . she died last week in Santa Fé."

A muscle twitched in *Don* Antonio's face. That was all. A single muscle under his eye twitched. "I have no sister by the name of Antonita," he said.

The room was very still. Mike felt the hot blood rushing into his cheeks. He heard his voice rasping with a sudden surge of bitter anger. "You lie, damn you! You know you lie!"

22

Gregorio's hand made a sudden movement toward the revolver under his coat. Mike's own gun was out before the pudgy hand had drawn the silver-mounted weapon.

"You," Mike flung out harshly, "keep out of this!"

The tall old man stood there. Like Dave Schaal he stood unmoved in the face of violence. Only Dave Schaal had been stolid, intent. This old man, eldest of four brothers, head of the del Grazar clan now, stood there coldly, bitterly, disdainfully. His brittle words fell on the silence of the room.

"My young sister, Antonita, died twenty-two years ago."

Mike's mind groped to understand it. Here was something twenty years of the Oregon country had never taught him. Here was a new kind of pride, bitter, unyielding pride that lasted without end, beyond the grave. Unjust pride that made him lash out: "I'm damned ashamed I'm related to you! She never hurt you . . . any of you! She went off and lived her life the way she had a right to, and always was proud of her folks, and taught me to be proud of them! And all this time you've stayed here, stiff-necked an' damning her!"

Don Antonio stood unmoved before that angry torrent. He was old, like the house, gaunt like the old trees outside, hard and unyielding in a way Mike had never met.

"You are not related to us," *Don* Antonio said coldly. "Your name is O'Grady, you say. Why do you come here to the del Grazars?"

"My mother wanted me to come."

"You have come," *Don* Antonio said bleakly. "Now you can go."

The door behind the old man was ajar. Mike thought he saw a wisp of movement there, passing, vanishing. In the silences, voices in that patio beyond the door were no longer audible. Even they had gone coolly and silently when an O'Grady came under the roof.

23

Pride and anger flared against that implacable wall. "I'll go when I'm ready . . . an' be damned glad to go!" Mike said hotly. "But first, while I'm here, what about my mother's share of the estate? You asked for it, an' by God you'll get it now, sir!"

For the first time *Don* Antonio displayed emotion. A flush crept into his gaunt face. His voice shook as he answered.

"I thought so. Only that could have brought you here. You have wasted your time. There is nothing for you."

"I guess," said Mike, "we'll see about that. I'm beginning to see why you never forgave her. Who got the lands she was supposed to get?"

Gregorio said then softly: "Have you any papers to back up such a claim?"

Don Antonio waved a gaunt hand toward the younger man. "My son is a lawyer. Doubtless he can give you good advice."

Caution checked the hot retort Mike was about to make, admitting he had brought no papers. His mind hadn't been on papers and land when he came. Gregorio's plump face was bland and slightly amused now. He knew, Mike saw, that Antonita del Grazar had taken no papers when she vanished with her husband. This Gregorio had studied law. He knew the tricks. And he was waiting with tricks when he should have been thinking of fairness, justice, right.

Mike let the muzzle of his gun drop down by his leg, and grinned at them, father and son. His grin was bitter, cold, bleak. "I didn't come for the law, an' I won't talk law," he said in English. "But I'm here in San Saba, an' I'll stay. Think it over, you two buzzards, an' don't forget I'm half del Grazar, although I'm ashamed to say it now. You . . . never mind about showing me out. I'll find the way."

Gregorio paused in his advance toward the door, and stood motionlessly while Mike backed to the door, watching them. Perhaps Gregorio did not catch the meaning. But *Don* Antonio did. His thin, bloodless lips pressed into a tight line as he stood tall and erect and watched his visitor leave without exposing his back. The del Grazar pride writhed bitterly at that lack of trust.

Outside, under the gnarled old trees, Mike holstered his gun and drew a deep breath. He was cold inside with the dead enthusiasm of a lifetime. Behind the thick door he had just closed the del Grazars were now remote and strange. Beyond the old adobe wall was the San Saba plaza and the future.

The aged manservant was not at the gate. Mike found the wooden bar that locked the gate, lifted it, and stepped outside. As the gate closed behind him and the wooden bar thudded softly into place, a voice at his elbow said: "I heard what happened . . . and I am sorry, Mister O'Grady."

III

"The Law of Gunsmoke"

She stood there in the moonlight with the white lace *mantilla* across her arm. She was earnest, regretful, sincere. The saddle horses and the buggy had been taken away. They were alone as Mike whipped off his broad-brimmed hat and looked down at her.

"Thanks," he said, unable to keep the bitterness out of his voice. "I'm glad there's someone in this family like . . . like I thought I'd find."

"But I," she said, "am not a del Grazar. I am María Guadalupe Sedillo, and it is none of my business. I should not be out here. But I do not want you to go away without understanding."

Mike's laugh was short and hard, perhaps to hide the

25

dull, dead feeling inside. "I understand well enough. They made it plain."

She shook her head. "No. *Don* Antonio only said what he could say. He is an old, bitter man. He cannot change. I think sometimes he is a little desperate because he cannot change, and too proud to be anything but bitter about it."

"You're talkin' riddles to me, ma'am," Mike said. "I heard what he told me, an' it was plain enough. He wouldn't even admit my mother was his sister. He was afraid I wanted something he had . . . an' all I wanted at first was to be friends."

"To him you are a *gringo*, and he hates all *gringos*."

"My mother was his sister," Mike insisted doggedly.

"But that was a long time ago. I have heard about it. She went against the custom, and in those days the custom was everything."

"Ma'am," said Mike coldly, "what has custom got to do with a girl who's in love . . . or with family ties? She was his sister. She was one of the family. An' they've hated her memory for twenty-two years because she had the nerve to go against their selfish ideas. Her brothers, I guess, kept on hating her because they grabbed her share of the land and wanted to keep it."

María Guadalupe Sedillo was troubled as she stood there in the moonlight, looking up at him.

"The custom," she said, "was everything. How can I make you see? The *conquistadores*, hundreds of years ago, were few, and the country was big, and they were proud, for one man against a thousand they had conquered. They were wise, too. They knew if they did not keep their blood pure, their grandchildren and those who followed their grandchildren would be no better than the Indians from whom they had taken the land. They must not marry out of their people. For two hundred years the del Grazars kept the custom, and held their own, and were proud and strong."

Mike shifted restlessly. "My father was as good as any of them, ma'am."

She smiled sadly. "But he was not of the blood. He was a stranger, no different to these del Grazars than the Indians, and the *peónes* whose blood was thick with Indian blood. He laughed at the custom, and your mother broke the custom, and from then on she was dead to them." María Sedillo put her hand on Mike's arm earnestly. "*Señor* O'Grady, you do not know what the custom of two hundred years can be. When she married outside the blood, she struck at every member of the family who was proud of his name."

Mike said nothing. He was looking down at her, thinking he had never seen a girl so lovely. Her touch was light, her voice was soft; in her native Spanish it would ripple softer, and her earnest sympathy was like balm to raw wounds.

She took his silence for bitter disagreement, and sighed. "It was not only that," she said sadly. "Your father was the first American to defeat the del Grazars. It was almost a sign. Since then many more Americans have come. We could hold back the Indians . . . but the Americans are worse than the grasshoppers. The grasshoppers go and there is plenty again . . . but the Americans stay, and devour, and take. *Don* Antonio is old and wise. I have heard him talk. We can't hold the country against them. They get the land by trickery and force, and take the trade. Our young men are not strong. They drink, gamble, and grow wild and helpless when they try to be like the Americans, as many of them do. More Americans are coming in all the time. They say the railroad is coming, too, so that thousands more will come. There is nothing for the old people but bitterness and hate for all Americans. Your father was

27

the first, *Señor* O'Grady. The del Grazars have lost much since then. You will always be a *gringo* to *Don* Antonio . . . and he can do nothing but hate you."

"How about you, ma'am?" Mike asked awkwardly.

She shrugged. "I do not matter. I am only a woman . . . and too young to hate. But I can be a little sad at what is happening. And I am sorry for you, for you would not have come here if you were not *simpático*. But you see now you must go back where you came from. They will never have you."

Mike laughed shortly. "I'm here," he said. "I'll stay. If I'm a *gringo*, I'll be a *gringo*, an' take what's mine. *I* wasn't raised to follow the custom."

She smiled sadly. "You see, you are American . . . like your father. You are alone. There are many of them. Forget this San Saba country, *Señor* O'Grady."

"Forget it?" Mike said. He wasn't feeling dead inside now. Far from it. "I am just starting to know it," he said. "And if anything happens to me, here's my thanks for your sweetness . . . an' something to remember me by."

Mike bent quickly and kissed her on the cheek.

"I'll be back," he promised.

María Guadalupe Sedillo gasped and stepped away. She was standing against the wall in the moonlight, poised for flight as Mike left.

But she did not cry out. Mike remembered that as he made for the plaza.

The San Saba plaza was vastly different from the shadowy old yard with its ancient trees. That was the past. This was the present, the future, boiling with *gringo* energy.

The barkeep in the saloon told Mike that Dave Schaal had gone to the Boston House. Newly built of adobe bricks, the hotel lobby was filled with the same strange mixture of men that flowed through the plaza.

The clerk said: "Dave Schaal? I think he's in the dining room."

Mike remembered then that he was hungry and walked into the dining room. He saw Dave Schaal sitting with a young woman. The other tables were filled. Mike noticed the young woman eyeing him, saw her speak to Schaal, and Schaal beckoned to him.

"Sit down, if you're waiting to eat," was Schaal's invitation. Everything the man did was surprising. He stood up and said: "Miss Hartman, this is Mister O'Grady."

She smiled. "How do you do, Mister O'Grady? Won't you sit down?"

Young, blonde, dainty, petite, she was like no other young woman Mike had ever seen. He had heard an Englishman talk as she did, and knew she was from England. Near to being tongue-tied, he managed to say—"Thank you, ma'am."—and sat down without quite knowing why he did so.

"Not eating at the del Grazars'?" Schaal asked calmly.

"No," Mike replied woodenly. "I was looking for you."

Schaal regarded him thoughtfully. "You can talk in front of Miss Hartman," he said. "Her father's one of the owners of the TVO Ranch, which I manage . . . if you don't know it already."

"I don't," Mike said. "I was wondering if you had a job for me."

It was Schaal's turn to be startled. "Why?" he demanded bluntly.

"I think you're the one to fit in with my plans," Mike told him coolly.

"Do you?" said Schaal with irony. "What are your plans?"

"Do they matter?"

"You're hired," Schaal said.

Miss Hartman laughed. "I should take that as a compliment, Mister O'Grady. I've never seen Dave hire a man so carelessly."

"I've met O'Grady before," Schaal said wryly. "I'm gambling he can savvy Spanish. How about it, O'Grady?"

"You win."

"I'm going to send you out alone," Schaal said promptly. "To Ojo Grande. Ever hear of the place?"

"No."

"It ain't a nice place for a *gringo* to be caught alone," Schaal stated calmly. "It's over in the del Grazar grant. Apaches are thick and the Mexicans hate *gringos*. Last time I was through there, I had nine men along and didn't feel I had too many. They sure hate us back in there."

"So you're sending me there alone?" Mike said, and his was the irony this time.

Schaal spoke across the table readily: "Twenty men couldn't get the information I want. One man passing for a Mexican could. Can you handle it?"

"Go out and spy for you?" Mike said curtly.

Schaal's eyes were hard, cold under his black brows. "Call it anything you want, O'Grady. Our interests are clashing with the del Grazars'. They've had the odds on their side from the first. We've suffered from them. I need to know what they're doing. Yesterday I got a tip that Juan Sarrero, the Mexican bandit, had been seen heading toward Ojo Grande from the border. I'm wondering who's going to hear from him if he breaks loose . . . and if the del Grazars will have anything to do with it. A Mexican riding through Ojo Grande will hear things a *gringo* won't." The ghost of a smile appeared under Schaal's mustache. "It won't be so good if they find out you're a *gringo*."

"I'll go," Mike decided.

That was all there was to it. Yet Mike had the feeling these two had been talking about him before he entered the dining room, and that Miss Hartman knew everything about that brush in the saloon and was curious about him. They spoke casually of other things—the new mines, chances of the railroad's coming, of the Oregon country. Miss Hartman was witty, interesting, and Mike thought her chuckle one of the nicest he had ever heard.

Schaal said: "I'll see you before you leave tomorrow. If you need any money, ask for it."

"I'll draw my wages when I've worked for them," Mike said.

All the beds in San Saba were taken. In the end Mike had to sleep in the haymow of the livery stable. Up early, he washed in a bucket back of the livery, ate breakfast in a little restaurant run by a Chinaman, and stopped in a barbershop for a shave.

Then he bought a rifle, scabbard, a soft leather suit with silver buttons on the coat, and a high-crowned sombrero in the Mexican style. As an afterthought he added a pair of big-roweled Mexican spurs.

Leaving the purchases at the livery stable, he drifted about the plaza until noon, asking casual questions whenever he had the opportunity. By noon he had a good idea of what it was all about.

The TVO was a new, big spread, formed of a chunk of former del Grazar land, some small purchases from natives, some leased land, and a lot of free range that the del Grazars claimed by right of usage and that the TVO was taking up as it saw fit.

The TVO was backed by English capital, which also was interested in two of the new mines. The Lazy N Ranch, also

English, and the Circle Tin Cup, owned by an American named Griffin, were all crowding the del Grazars.

After eating at noon, Mike went to a Spanish lawyer by the name of Gonzales.

"My mother was a sister of *Don* Antonio del Grazar," he told the man in Spanish. "She got none of the estate. What can you tell me about it?"

Gonzales was a short man, almost diminutive, quick in his movements, soft-voiced, polite to his caller. But his smile vanished at Mike's statement. He looked startled.

"What was your mother's name?" he asked.

"Antonita del Grazar."

"Ah, yes. I remember her. It was a long time ago. And she is . . . ?"

"She's gone."

Gonzales looked uneasy. "You will have trouble in the matter at this late time."

"I'm only asking you about it."

"By law, perhaps, the claim might be established," Gonzales said vaguely. "Who knows? Getting it would be a different matter. I remember it was said long ago she would get nothing."

"Was there a will?"

Gonzales shrugged. "*¿Quién sabe?* Such matters were often vague . . . by word of mouth before witnesses."

"Then, if there wasn't a will, the law would give her a share, wouldn't it?"

"Ah, I am not the court," said Gonzales.

It was plain that the mention of an action against the del Grazars left this lawyer with very little enthusiasm. On the other hand, there must be ground for action or Gonzales would deny it point-blank. Mike had what he wanted. He had gone to Gonzales because he had heard the man was one of the oldest lawyers in town.

He left and went to a newer lawyer—an American by the name of Johnson. Bluff, hearty, red-faced, aggressive, Johnson heard his story.

"You've got a damned good case," he said flatly. "It'll be a tough one, but I can get you action on it. The del Grazars ain't had too much luck lawin' in the courts the last few years. We got American law here now. It backfires in their faces."

"I'll leave some money with you," Mike said. "Get to work on it. If I've got to sign any papers, make 'em out quick because I'm leavin' town."

Mike rode west out of San Saba that afternoon, toward the mountains. He was in the foothills at dark, broiling a rabbit he had shot from the saddle. Later he sprawled on the blankets by the small fire, smoking, musing on the events of the past twenty-four hours.

He was thinking of María Sedillo and the pale-cheeked Miss Hartman when his hobbled horse snorted uneasily in the darkness. Mike rolled over, peering in that direction, and at the same instant a rifle cracked sharply nearby. The fire geysered sparks as a bullet struck the embers.

IV

"Bushwhack Bullets"

Mike lunged off the blankets toward his saddle and rifle. That probably saved his life, for a second shot lashed an instant after the first, striking the blankets where he had been.

Snatching the rifle from its scabbard, Mike dived half a dozen feet to the bank of a small, dry arroyo by which he had camped. Two more bullets sought him as he went down the bank in a cascade of gravel. He landed on the arroyo sand and lay still.

The camp was in a small draw bisected by the arroyo. The ridges siding the draw were covered with a sparse growth of cane cactus and prickly pear, and an occasional stunted tree. The moon was not yet up, and the wavering little fire made small impression against the darkness.

Revolver in hand, rifle in the other, Mike lay on the sand, listening. No one approached. After a little he wriggled up the arroyo a short distance and waited again.

Sheltered by a four-foot bank, he waited for a full hour before he heard a branch crack over toward the fire. Some minutes later something struck the ground near the dying fire.

Mike guessed it was a stick, tossed to draw him out if he was alive. Crouching behind the arroyo bank, he waited.

The moon was rising, but not yet over the ridge when his continued silence was taken as proof that one of the bullets had found him as he fell into the arroyo. But at that he was almost caught off guard.

A faint slither of sound up the arroyo drew his attention that way. Revolver cocked, Mike waited. Twice he thought he saw a darker blot moving on him. Each time he was mistaken. In the end the man was not ten feet away when he discovered Mike, and gasped audibly, and opened fire.

Mike shot at the same instant—twice—three times—and then the man was down in the sand, motionless, and Mike felt the smart of a bullet scratch on his left arm.

Near the fire a voice called sharply in Spanish: "¡Santiago!"

A bullet toward that spot sent the man running away. There had been only two of them. A few minutes later Mike cupped a match over the dead man's head. It was a brown-skinned Mexican, stone dead.

Mike rode west again, wondering about the ambush. He must have been followed out of San Saba. The men might have picked him for an easy victim—or have had orders to bushwhack him.

Near midnight he made a second camp far from the road in the mouth of a small cañon. There, without a fire, he slept in his blankets until the sun came up.

Before starting on, he changed into the soft leather trousers and coat, strapped on the big Spanish spurs. His skin was already well tanned by the Oregon sun. He had worn the high-crowned sombrero out of San Saba. He had no mirror, but he thought he looked the part.

For two days he vanished in the mountains. When he came out of them, far to the west, he rode half a day before he met a wagon with two escorting riders. All were Mexicans.

"Buenas tardes," Mike greeted them. "When will I get to Ojo Grande?"

They told him he had a day's ride yet. They were polite, friendly. Cigarettes were smoked while they chatted in Spanish. One of the men said they had met seven Apaches that morning who had seemed peaceful—but who could tell about the Apaches?

Mike rode on, satisfied with his appearance. The men had removed their hats and given him the politeness due a superior.

That night he slept in the adobe hut of a sheepherder beside the road. Five houses were clustered at the spot. From his host Mike learned that six years before the Apaches had killed a man and three women here. But the Apaches were quiet now, and the *señor* knew it was a will of God that poor men had to live somewhere. The del Grazars had sheep that must be tended, and someone had to live near the sheep.

The next morning Mike left with chili, boiled beans, and fried mutton under his belt, and they saw him on his way as if he were himself a del Grazar.

He had ridden through mountains and across broad plains spotted with stands of trees. There had been tall pine forests and great stretches covered with scattered piñon trees and short grass. The land here to the west was different from the desert-like stretches along the Río Grande. Now the mountains to the south were higher, more rugged. The valleys widened out. During the day's ride small huts appeared with increasing frequency.

Mike found it hard to believe that most of the time he had been riding across del Grazar land, that the Mexicans he saw had probably never known anything but del Grazar authority. All were armed. To him they were polite—but it was easy to believe a lone *yanqui* would find them dangerous.

In the afternoon the road followed a shallow mountain stream. Small, irrigated fields appeared. An hour before sunset the road skirted a wooded ridge, and then dropped down an easy grade into Ojo Grande.

Different from any settlement he had known in the Oregon country, Ojo Grande was half a hundred houses or more clustered without plan beside the river. Some were of adobe brick, others were of small tree trunks set vertically and chinked with mud. In any direction the mountain slopes were close. The setting was isolated, wild, lonely.

Dogs barked, children cried shrill warning of a stranger's coming, women stared from doorways, men lifted hats in greeting as Mike rode in among the houses.

Dave Schaal had told him he would find a combination store and saloon run by one of the minor satellites of the old Grazar clan and it would be the only trading point in a great distance. Not that there was much trade.

Mike found a tiny, bare plaza. Among the houses on one side was a small church, on the other the store, with several saddled horses at a pole hitch rack. Eyeing the horses as he dismounted, Mike decided no Mexican bandit had ridden any of them in. No self-respecting bandit would own such sorry animals, or dilapidated riding gear.

Big-roweled spurs jingling, Mike entered the dim interior of the store. Half a dozen Mexicans, lounging about inside, stared at him.

"Buenas tardes, señores," Mike greeted them with a lift of his hand.

They stared, hesitated. One man removed his hat; the others followed suit in respectful, friendly greeting.

Mike stopped a faint smile. They had accepted him as one of the *gente fina* who expected a bared head and subservient greeting as a matter of course.

A plank bar ran along one side of the room. Mike waved a hand graciously toward it. *"Señores,"* he said politely, "you will drink with me?"

They would enthusiastically. A one-eyed Mexican, lighter-skinned than the others, served them. Other men drifted in, and, when Mike carelessly tossed a gold piece on the boards and called for a second round, there was no doubt among the company that Ojo Grande was honored by a *caballero* of distinction.

"I have come a long way," Mike said. "I am tired. Is there a place I can stay a little?"

A dozen men offered their beds so insistently it was plain acceptance would confer an honor.

Mike chose the one-eyed man, who lived in an L-shaped wing behind the store. No one was offended. They accepted it as natural that the *señor* would choose the best.

The one-eyed man's name, Mike was not surprised to find, was Ricardo del Grazar. Somewhere back through two centuries this branch of the family had slipped down to humble status. But he was still a del Grazar, above the still more humble natives.

Mike gave his name as *Señor* Miguel Lucero. Everybody seemed satisfied, none more so than his flattered host. Ricardo del Grazar personally sat his guest at table an hour later, served Mike's plate with his own hands, and gave sharp orders to his wife and daughters who served silently, and remained outside the room while the men ate.

"*Señor* Lucero," this del Grazar said with emotion as he smoothed his greasy black mustache with the back of his hand, "your kindness has made me most happy. Not often does a *caballero* so honor us. My kinsmen, the del Grazars of the valley, do not often come so far from the river. *Don* Antonio del Grazar, as you doubtless know, is a cousin. Yes, *señor,* a cousin."

"Ah . . . *Don* Antonio," Mike said politely. "I was in his *casa* the other day, in San Saba. And Gregorio . . . but you know Gregorio, eh?"

"We are the same family, *señor,*" Mike was assured hastily, and taken to his host's bosom from that moment. It was proof, if any were needed, of the standing of *Don* Antonio del Grazar's branch of the family.

After the food, Mike lighted a cigarette and dallied with a glass of wine.

"There are many *gringos* in San Saba," he suggested.

The empty eye socket gave a malevolent cast to the scowl the remark evoked. Ricardo cursed the *gringos* heartily. "They are taking the country like wolves! But not near us, *señor. Dios,* but we have a way of dealing with those coyotes when they appear."

"I have heard." Mike smiled thinly. He drew a forefinger across his throat.

His host showed bad teeth in an answering grin. "Gregorio, my dear cousin, says a dead *gringo* is better than a live one. Ah, that Gregorio, he is a great man, *señor*. He has studied the law."

"But the American sheriff at San Saba," Mike suggested. "Is he not curious when one of his countrymen disappears?"

"Ojo Grande is not San Saba, *Señor* Lucero. What is the law in San Saba to us? We del Grazars have always made our own law . . . and here in Ojo Grande we follow the old ways."

"*Bueno, compadre,* the old ways," Mike mused.

At being called *compadre* his host was almost overcome with pride and affection. His hand trembled with emotion as he filled Mike's glass and slopped more wine into his own.

"*Sí, compadre . . . sí, sí,*" he assented thickly.

Mike spoke carefully, casually. "I was told strangers from across the border might come here to Ojo Grande."

"*Dios,* what manner of strangers, *compadre?*" Ricardo asked with interest. He hiccoughed, gulped at his wine, swiped the back of his hand across his mouth again, and sprawled his elbows on the table. The wine was having its effect.

Mike shrugged. "*¿Quién sabe?*" he said.

Ricardo hiccoughed again. "If they are friends of my dear cousin, Gregorio, they are friends of mine, *por Dios!*" he swore enthusiastically. "I, Ricardo del Grazar, will welcome them like brothers. When will they come?"

"*¿Quién sabe?*" Mike said, using that vague term applicable to almost anything. He finished his wine and ended the meal before the other was too drunk to stand.

The store that evening was a focus for all the men of Ojo Grande, and a good many of the women who suddenly found things they needed to buy. To stay out of sight would have made talk. Mike kept near the bar and bought drinks generously.

By the time two fights had started and a good time was being had by everyone, Mike asked his one-eyed host where he was to sleep. Staggering noticeably, Ricardo guided him to a smelly little room at the back of the house.

When he was alone, Mike decided the *Señora* del Grazar and her daughters had been unceremoniously evicted from this room for the night. But that was a family matter. Pulling off his boots, he lay down in his clothes as a matter of precaution. The last sounds he heard were guitars and singing in the store.

The next thing Mike knew, he was being yanked out of bed and slammed onto the floor.

V

"The Firing Squad"

The little room was dark. Swearing violently, Mike tried to free himself. A fist hammered at his face. Hands now gripped his arms and legs and held him, helpless.

Above his head a voice panted: *"¡Esta bueno, señor!"*

Across the room another voice snapped in Spanish: "Hold him! Pedro, the light, *quick!*"

Mike knew that voice. A match was scratched in the next room. A man sidled through the doorway holding a candle.

Gregorio del Grazar stood inside the doorway with a revolver in his hand. The pudgy son of *Don* Antonio del Grazar was now wearing leather trousers, a cowhide jacket, silk neckerchief, fancy sombrero, and a gun belt. Leather gloves were tucked under the belt. Gregorio had a braided leather quirt in his left hand as he stepped forward and smiled down at Mike.

"Buenas noches, cousin. Who would have thought to look

for you here in Ojo Grande?"

"Go to hell," Mike said shortly. "Did you follow me here with these men?"

The three men who held him on the floor, and the fourth with the candle, were strangers. Mexicans, wearing guns and knives, they were dirty and dusty, as if they had been riding hard a long distance.

Gregorio shrugged. He looked tired but satisfied.

"Why should I follow you? I have men to do that for me. I rode this way on business, and along the road we heard of the young *caballero* ahead of us. So polite, so *simpático*. So we rode hard to give you the welcome of the del Grazars."

"Well, you got here," Mike said. "Is this the welcome?"

Gregorio holstered his gun. He looked cheerful and full of good will.

"Of course not, cousin," he chuckled. "This is not the welcome you deserve, is it? But this is, eh?"

Mike turned his head quickly, but the whistling quirt cut a hot furrow across the side of his face.

One of the men laughed—and then it took all three of them to hold their prisoner down.

"If I ever get my hands free, I'll kill you for that!" Mike gasped wildly.

"*Dios,* I wanted to give you that in San Saba." Gregorio sighed. "Now I will sleep better. It is good you were not killed outside of San Saba."

"So you sent those skunks after me?"

"Oh, *sí,* cousin," Gregorio agreed very amiably. "Did you think I would forget you? Gonzales was not the man to tell of your plan. He has taken too much of our money in his life." Gregorio pulled at his lower lip. "You didn't come here about that," he decided. "What brought you here?"

"Wouldn't you like to know, you scut?" Mike leered.

The quirt slashed him across the face again. But only Gregorio's smoldering eyes betrayed a savage anger. The pudgy face continued to smile.

"You went to Schaal," Gregorio said. "I can guess the rest. Well, you can have the night to think it over. But be careful, cousin. The fellow at your left arm is a brother of the man you killed. He is only waiting for an excuse to slit your throat."

Gregorio chuckled at the thought, motioned to the men, and stood with his gun out while they turned Mike over on his face and lashed his arms behind him with a leather reata.

They jerked him to his feet and hustled him into the next room, where other candles had been lighted. The one-eyed man was standing, pallid and frightened, beside the table, nervously puffing at a cigarette. An instant later he dropped the cigarette and squealed as the quirt slashed him.

Gregorio's plump face showed fury as he quirted the howling man into a corner of the room.

"¡Cabrón! ¡Castrado! ¡Perro!" Gregorio howled at him. "Is it for this we have you here at Ojo Grande? To give up your bed to gringos? To make a fool of yourself! To let him get you drunk so all the gringos laugh at us when they hear of it!"

"For the love of God, patrón! I did not know! Mother of Mercy, you are killing me! He said he was the caballero Lucero! How could a poor pelón like me tell he was a gringo? ¡Aie, patrón!"

The victim was on his knees by then, cringing as he tried to shield his head.

In the next room the women and girls began to wail. Gregorio kicked his cowering relative down on the floor, and then stepped back, panting.

42

"Tell your women to get food for us!" he ordered viciously. "Where is the key to the store cellar?"

Mike was dragged into the back of the store, where tobacco smoke still showed blue against the burning lamps. He caught a glimpse of faces pressed against the front windows as he was dragged into a back storeroom. He was tripped up and thrown to the floor again. His legs were hogtied behind him. A trap door lifted in the floor. They slid him, bumping from step to step, down into a damp, dark cellar that reeked of wine and whiskey and stored supplies.

Gregorio then called down: "A pleasant night, cousin! In the morning we will see."

The trap door dropped into place. Mike heard the lock snap and the men walk away.

By morning Mike was haggard and seething with black fury. His arms, strained back too tightly, had been numb for hours. The pain had been pretty bad until the numbness replaced it. Footsteps above told him it was morning, but some time passed before men came down to get him.

They unfastened his legs and ordered him up. In the end they had to drag him up and carry him out behind of the store, and hold him on his feet while he got back the use of his legs.

Gregorio strolled out into the early morning sunshine, picking his teeth.

"*Buenos días,* cousin," he said cheerfully. "Did you rest well last night?"

"Tell these fools to unloosen my arms for a little or I'll get gangrene in 'em," Mike said curtly.

"A nice idea, if we could wait," Gregorio said cheerfully.

He gave the man the order and watched warily with his gun out while they held Mike's free arms and walked him in a circle. Gradually blood crept back into starved tissues.

Then with rawhide strings they tied his arms in front of him, and led him over to a pole corral where horses, Mike's horse included, were saddled. The men were ready to ride.

"Where are we going?" Mike now demanded.

For a reply he was ordered to get in the saddle.

"How about some water and breakfast?" Mike asked.

"Why waste good food, cousin?" Gregorio answered amiably. "Get on your horse."

The man whose brother Mike had shot jabbed him with a knife point. There was nothing to do but climb awkwardly into the saddle, let them tie his feet, and hold to the saddle horn as his horse was led away.

Ricardo bowed to them obsequiously, his one good eye glaring hate at Mike. In the background the entire population of Ojo Grande clustered to watch the departure. Taunts, oaths, and threats were called to the prisoner by men who had been flattered when the *caballero* noticed them the evening before.

They rode south out of Ojo Grande, skirting the mountains. Mystified, Mike wondered what they were up to. One thing seemed certain—the chances were slim he'd ever see San Saba again.

They rode all morning into the south—and Gregorio was in such high humor he broke into song now and then. The sun was high and hot when they turned off the trace of a road they had been following and cut east into the hills.

Here was lonely country again. Hours back they had passed the last of the outlying Mexican huts. They rode up a rocky cañon sided by bleak cliffs, and Mike would have sworn he was the first American to come this way. His escort seemed to know where they were going.

The cañon pinched out. They rode up over a steep,

thousand-foot arm of the mountain, and plunged down through the thick growth on the other side to a narrow, grassy valley bisected by a small stream.

In the valley just ahead of them were a long picket line of horses and the compact trail camp of at least twenty men. One look at the hard-faced men in tight trousers, huge, high-crowned sombreros, many of woven straw, who waited with guns ready told Mike the story.

Juan Sarrero, the bandit, had avoided Ojo Grande. But Gregorio had known where to find him.

Sarrero was not hard to recognize. He stepped out from his men as Gregorio dismounted. They shook hands. Sarrero was a chunky, heavy-set man, solid, muscular, and middle-aged. Gold buttons were sewn up the side of his tight trousers and liberally over his snug coat. His felt sombrero was banded with silver braid, and his huge spurs were silver. But the two big revolvers he wore looked business-like, and his dark-skinned face had a hard, cold cast.

"*¡Diablo!*" he exclaimed as he shook hands. "I thought you were not coming. We have been here three days."

"Yesterday was the day agreed on, Sarrero."

"*Señor* Sarrero, if you will, *Don* del Grazar."

Gregorio hesitated. "*Sí, Señor* Sarrero," he said sulkily. He had tried to be haughty, had been covertly insulted by having the *don* hooked up to his last name, and been forced into politeness. That put Sarrero in good humor.

"Did you bring the first payment?" he asked.

"*Sí.* Gold . . . in my saddlebags."

"*Bueno,*" said Sarrero, staring at Mike. "We will talk about it while we eat. Who is this man?"

"A *gringo* for you . . . to deal with as you wish."

"What shall I do with him?"

Gregorio shrugged. "I don't want to see him again."

Sarrero smiled, and touched the end of his mustache. "That will be easy," he said. "Let him eat with us now while I hear about him."

"Food will not help him."

Sarrero grinned again. "My guests do not stay hungry. Bring him to the fire."

Portions of a deer were roasting over a long bed of coals. A squatting man was making tortillas on a large flat rock nestled in the glowing coals. Coffee was boiling in a big pot.

Sarrero snapped an order. His men hustled Mike off the horse, led him to the fire, and sat him down with his hands still tied in front of him.

A tin plate holding small chunks of hot venison and two tortillas, and a cup of black coffee, were put on the ground beside him. Sarrero and Gregorio were served the same way. The other men grabbed plates and cups and helped themselves, laughing and talking as they began to wolf the food.

Sarrero's men looked as hardcased as their leader. All were heavily armed with the latest type weapons and belts and *bandoliers* of cartridges. Their clothes were fancy, their riding gear the best. Banditry had evidently treated them well south of the border.

They had brought along pack horses and spare horses and seemed prepared to live off the country as long as they cared to. They were in high spirits as they ate. Mike heard some of them questioning Gregorio's men about himself.

But as he made clumsy shift of the food with his bound hands, he listened to Sarrero and Gregorio talking beside him. Their conversation indicated that Gregorio had sent a man south of the border to suggest what was wanted and to arrange this meeting with the bandit where the plans would be completed. Back here in the Ojo Grande country no one would know a Mexican bandit band was within striking distance of the river settlements.

Speaking emphatically in Spanish, Gregorio said: "These *gringos* are robbing the grass from above ground and the silver from under the ground. They treat us like dogs . . . we who have been here two hundred years. They forced their *yanqui* law on us, and now they win in the courts and kill when we try to protect our rights. Before God, it is not right! I will do something about it."

Sarrero clapped his guest on the shoulder. "*Don* Gregorio, you are a man after my own heart!" he cried heartily. "What is it you are paying me to do?"

"The *gringo* ranches near us are taking our land, and *gringo* mines are unjustly on our land," Gregorio said, scowling over the injuries he was listing. "And there is one ranch and one man who leads all the rest. The TVO brand and the man named Schaal who has charge of it. If his buildings are burned down, himself and his men killed off, and their cattle run off, it would be easier for us."

"And what of the fighting I will have to do?"

"I am paying you well. You will have cattle to sell if you can get them over the border. There are mines you can raid for silver and gold. But if you wipe out these ranches next to our land, no mine raid will pay you better than will the del Grazars."

Sarrero pulled the cork from a bottle of wine with his teeth and tilted the bottle up. Smacking his lips, he jammed the cork back in and asked: "Why not hire *gringo* gunmen and do this yourself?"

Gregorio spat and scowled at Mike. "Who can trust a *gringo*? We del Grazars have nothing to do with them."

"*Sí, sí.* " Sarrero chuckled. "They are *muy malo*, eh? Now about the mine called La Angelita . . . and the mine called La Gloria?"

"Those are our mines!" Gregorio snapped. "They must not be touched!"

"But they are rich mines, eh? I have heard so. Your *mejicano* workmen take out much rich ore, and you take the silver from the ore at your *hacienda*."

"Not much," Gregorio denied with sudden caution.

"I have heard differently," Sarrero blandly declared. "I have heard there is a cellar in the rock under the *casa* of *Don* Antonio del Grazar filled with silver bars and sacks of gold. Some of it's been there since his grandfather was little."

"You heard lies," Gregorio insisted.

"*Amigo*"—Sarrero chuckled—"you are a man after my own heart. Oh, *sí*. I love you like a brother. But I have heard differently about the rock cellar . . . and God has not been generous with us lately."

Gregorio suddenly was uneasy as Sarrero put his empty plate aside and wiped his hands on his trousers. The uneasiness changed to fear as Sarrero drew one of his guns carelessly.

"I have been thinking, *amigo*"—the bandit chuckled again—"that these *gringos* are *muy malo hombres*. Ah, *Dios*, we have met them on the border. They are bad fighters. Perhaps they won't be killed so easily. But if we go to that little rock cellar under the *casa*, it will be so easy. No? So very easy. You have no *gringos* on your land. Only these soft *nuevo mejicanos*, like yourself, who we laugh at across the border. It will be easy getting into that rock cellar. And if we shoot everyone we find, we will be beyond the border before there is trouble. Perhaps these *gringos* at San Saba would not even ride after us."

Gregorio gulped. His pudgy face had suddenly paled. He cast a wild look around. Mike had already noticed that, when Juan Sarrero put his plate aside, his men had unobtrusively left their food and gathered about the four del

Grazar riders. Two of them had strolled up behind Gregorio.

Sarrero nodded at them. They caught Gregorio's arms, hauled him to his feet. At the same moment the four men were made prisoners, also.

Mike laughed harshly at the look on Gregorio's face.

"Cousin," he said, "your pet snake has bit you. If ever I saw a dirty skunk stink himself up, this is it. What you put me through is worth it."

The del Grazar pride was still there. When Sarrero said—"Now we will talk about that silver, and how to get to it, and how many men we will find."—Gregorio said defiantly: "I will tell you nothing!"

"Like a burro, he needs the whip." Sarrero sighed.

At his orders, Gregorio was thrown down on the ground. His boots were yanked off. Grinning men held him down while the bottoms of his feet were beaten with a stick.

A little of that was enough. Sobbing, groaning, Gregorio babbled ready answers to the questions.

Grim-faced now, a little sick, Mike had leaned forward when Gregorio named María Sedillo as one of those at the old del Grazar ranch.

He would have stopped the thing, if possible; he would have interfered, if there was a chance when Gregorio, limping on his lacerated feet, was led off with his men toward the heavy brush through which they had recently ridden.

Sarrero picked up the wine bottle and drank again.

"*¿Sabe español?*" he asked Mike, who had not spoken as yet.

"*Sí.*"

"He is a fool," Sarrero said contemptuously, nodding

after the little party. "And fools were made to be plucked. His kind play the grandee and shout for our necks until there is trouble, and then they come down in the dust to us for help. *Dios*, never have I seen a *gringo* look such a *caballero*," Sarrero said, grinning as he looked over the wine bottle at Mike. "Why did he want you dead, *amigo?* And his quirt has been across your face, eh? Why?"

Grinning thinly, Mike said: "He doesn't like *americanos*."

Sarrero grinned back and drank some more wine. "That is no reason," he said, drawing a deep breath. "He does not count now. We will forget him, eh?" A ragged volley of shots came from the brush. Sarrero chuckled. "*Sí*, we will forget him," he repeated. "I like you, *amigo*. I would like to be your friend."

Awkwardly Mike got to his feet and stared, narrow-eyed, as the other drank leisurely once more from the bottle.

"I would like to be your friend," Sarrero repeated sadly, lowering the bottle. "It desolates me, *Señor Gringo*, that you must die, too. I will not sleep well for thinking of it."

Mike grinned coldly. "You almost had me fooled then . . . but not quite. I thought you had something like this on your mind. So you're going to have me marched over there in the brush and made buzzard bait, too?"

"My young friend, you will never feel it," Sarrero assured him generously. "I have killed many men. It is over in a breath. I call the good God to witness."

More than half of the men had gone off with the firing squad. They were still in the brush. The other men had returned to their food, taking the whole thing as a matter of course. The saddle horses were still standing nearby.

"*Call someone to witness this!*" Mike snarled, and jammed his bound wrists forward.

VI

"The Road to Freedom"

Sarrero was not looking for anything like that from such a helpless prisoner. The cupped hands caught him under the chin with the full weight of Mike's powerful body behind them. Sarrero's head snapped back at an angle. He flopped over to the ground with only a startled gasp issuing from his lips.

Mike bolted past him toward the saddled horses. Gregorio's big bay horse was nearest. Startled, it turned away. Lunging forward, Mike got the saddle horn between his palms, and clung on as the horse reared. The men about the fire were on their feet, shouting, when Mike vaulted for the saddle.

The bolting horse snapped him hard into the leather. He hung onto the saddle horn and kicked his feet into the stirrups as the bay roared past the long string of picketed horses. Gunshots blasted behind him. He set his feet firmly in the stirrups, swung forward, grabbed one rein, brought it back to his teeth, and did the same on the other side and got the second rein.

He almost went out of the saddle when the bolting horse plunged down into the bed of the little stream and raced up the opposite bank. Bullets were whistling close as Mike spurred hard and crouched low. A glance over his shoulder showed the firing party running from the brush. The men at the cook fire were scattering out and shooting with rifles and revolvers.

That picket line of horses had been a godsend. They had served as a shield for the first few moments. Now the excited Mexicans were firing wildly at a phantom target fleeing at an angle away from them.

The little valley was not wide; the nearest brush was not far away. Mike set his teeth, fought down a desire to duck and dodge from the whiplash of bullets, and spurred the big bay into a frenzied gallop.

Something struck his hip. A numb feeling spread from the spot. Looking down, Mike saw where a bullet had sliced through the leather of his trousers and gouged deeply into the muscles of his leg. Blood was already welling up into sight.

But that was a small matter, that was only a hole in his leg, no worse than the whip weals across his face. The brush came nearer—nearer. The bullets were not so frequent. Looking back again, Mike saw several men riding after him. But most of the horses back there had been unsaddled, and Sarrero's men did not seem to have much taste for riding bareback with hackamores.

The bay plunged into the first brush and took the rise of the slope as if his bunching muscles were catapults hurling him up the mountain. Crouching low, Mike burred to the saddle while branches whipped and slashed at his head and body. He had no hat, no chaps or gloves, but the roughing he was taking now was nothing to what he rode away from.

The bay was a fine horse. The morning's ride seemed not to have tired it by the way it fought up the mountain ridge, higher, higher—until the brush thinned to cleaner tree growth, and pines began to space about. They reached a mountain meadow on the high slope, and another slope beyond pitched down into a small rocky cañon.

Across the meadow Mike pulled up, looked back, listened while the bay caught its wind through flaring nostrils. It seemed to him he heard far back the sounds of men shouting and branches snapping. But perhaps he was mistaken. A wind was sloughing in the pines nearby. With that wind Mike sent the bay fleeing down into the cañon.

He had to ride carefully the last few hundred feet, where bare rock sloped steeply, and sheer rock had to be skirted. In the cañon bottom there was no sun, so high and steep were the sides. Another little thread of water brawled easily into the north along the rock-studded cañon floor.

This time, as Mike paused briefly, he heard men and horses far up above. But they were high up; they could not see down into the cañon yet. Mike turned the bay north with the current of water.

North was the rutted road and mountain passes toward San Saba and the Río Grande. North, too, with the water, the cañon would not pinch in unexpectedly and trap him.

Blood was soaking his leg now. Pain from the wound was stabbing, twitching nerves and muscles. But that was only pain, and the blood was not too much, and he could still ride strongly.

Mike grinned, drew a deep breath, and shouted with the relief of it. *Don* Mike O'Grady, fire and steel, young and hanging hard to life, laughed, and the faint echo came back to him above the clashing of the bay's shod hoofs against the cañon rocks. He rode north quite cheerfully although he was being doggedly followed.

With that rock treasure chamber at the del Grazar ranch already within his grasp, Juan Sarrero would move heaven and earth to get the one man who might carry warning ahead of him. Mike looked down at his wrists. They were chafed raw beneath the tight reata strands. He had no way to free them now. Gregorio had taken his gun, knife, rifle. Gregorio had thought of everything—but the workings of Juan Sarrero's mind.

All hatred for Gregorio was passing now. It was hard to believe Gregorio was still not somewhere in the background nursing his *gringo* hate, so casually had it happened. A short, limping walk—a few shots—and the man was gone. What a twist of irony it was that, after a lifetime of *gringo* hate, the bullets that had killed Gregorio had not been fired by a *gringo*.

No, there was no hate for Gregorio now. Hate had killed him. Although Mike laughed at the relief of being alive, something had happened inside. Perhaps María Guadalupe Sedillo had been right, he considered. Perhaps 200 years on the land they had won by sheer courage and daring did give these sons of the *dons* the right to resent newcomers whose ways were not their ways, and who wanted by any means the things they had.

All the del Grazars could not be like Gregorio, or the old and bitter *Don* Antonio. Antonita del Grazar had not been. Understanding began to come to Mike as he rode for his life down that rocky, winding cañon.

Gradually the cañon widened out and began to swing to the west. The rocky sides grew less steep. The going became better. Presently there was a steep terrace of rock leading up to brush and earth slopes above.

He put the bay to the rocks, giving it its head, and the horse made it without slipping and pushed into the brush, and kept on up. In a little while, some hundreds of feet up, Mike sat motionless in the saddle and heard shod hoofs passing over the cañon stones far below, passing—and galloping on. He grinned again, and turned the bay's head on up the mountain, and rode leisurely, resting the horse.

Three hours later Mike knelt beside a third little trickle of water miles away and soaked his wrists patiently. Gradually the rawhide began to stretch. Then, with both arms through the crudely knotted reins, to hold the horse, he looked for a sharp rock edge, and squatted and patiently sawed the stretched rawhide back and forth on the rock. He was perspiring when the last strand parted.

The saddlebags were still on the horse. He found them heavy with gold coins. Old coins for the most part—that might have rested for generations in the darkness of a rock cellar. There was also a box of cartridges for the rifle, and a small package of jerky. Mike gnawed the sun-dried meat, rolled a cigarette, and felt like a new man.

The bay was tiring. A lesser horse would have been deadbeat long before from those grueling slopes. But there was more ground to be covered yet. Mike limped over, climbed painfully into the saddle, and rode on, bearing north.

Darkness found him still riding. The distant howl of a wolf was echoing from the sky when the moon came up. Still Mike rode on into the north. Suddenly he was at the twin ruts of the road, far east of Ojo Grande, and the way lay open to the San Saba.

It was mid-morning when he reached the five Mexican huts where he had slept on the way west. The people greeted him without animosity. Gregorio had evidently not imparted to them his suspicions of the lone rider ahead of his party.

There Mike ate, got a package of food, fed his horse, and bought with gold a second horse, the best they had. No strangers had come along this road from the west yet. Mike headed east again.

Through the day he rode hard, changing horses every few hours, eating in the saddle. Well after dark, in the moonlight, he staked the tired horses out with ropes he had also bought from the Mexicans, and slept again for five or six hours on the ground.

Before starting in the morning, he drew his belt in two extra notches. He was losing weight fast. The sleep had not rested him. His eyes felt bloodshot and heavy in his dust-caked face. The horses were stiff and reluctant to start in the before-dawn chill. His wounded leg was stiff, too, and feverish.

But he was on his way again, back past the pine forests, the long open stretches of grass, with the mountains high to the south and dropping away into the north in wooded ridges. He passed two wagons, driven by Mexicans, and warned them that Sarrero, the bandit, was to the west, and rode on, slowing a little. The land was starting the long slope to the distant Río Grande, and there would be a cañon several hours ahead marked by a bald-topped mesa where he would turn north to the TVO, the nearest ranch.

The road was clear behind. Mike had no warning of trouble when a burst of gunfire came from a clump of trees a hundred yards or so off to the left of the road. Mike heard the sodden slap of a bullet striking flesh. The horse he had bought from the sheepherders reared, tried to run, and pitched down on its knees.

VII

"No Help for Greasers"

Turning back, Mike grabbed for the rifle, and just got it out as the horse rolled over on the scabbard. He had let go of the lead rope. The bay horse had run off a few yards with the rope trailing, and now stood uncertainly as three riders burst out of the trees and galloped toward him, firing as they came.

The high-crowned hats, narrow trousers, bandoliers sluing from shoulders stopped Mike from trying to catch the nervous bay. These men of Sarrero's must have ridden night and day to ambush the one man who carried warning of their presence toward the Río Grande.

The dying horse was the only cover available. In a few moments it would be no cover at all. Mike stood in the open, exposed, and sighted his rifle at the first rider. He was deliberate about it, careful, very careful, for he dared not miss. Then he gently squeezed the trigger.

The man wilted, drooped in the saddle, toppled over, and plunged to the ground.

The other two men opened fire with their revolvers. They had spread out, and were coming in from two angles at full gallop. Mike was calmer than he would have thought possible. He had to be cool as he squeezed the trigger again. This time a bandit reeled and caught at the saddle horn.

Consternation showed on the dark face of the third man. He yanked his horse at a tangent to the road, and slipped over, Indian-style, half concealed behind the horse. His intent seemed to be a widening gallop about the spot, shooting over his horse. Mike got him with the next shot. Down on the horse's neck, hanging on with both arms, the Mexican barely made the shelter of the trees, and vanished.

Trembling, the bay horse had stood through it all. Nervously it backed away as Mike limped toward it, speaking soothingly. He managed to get the trailing rope, and led the bay back and set about getting the saddle off the dead horse. He accomplished that after unbuckling one of the stirrups.

Mike pushed on hurriedly. Sarrero and his men could not be far behind now. Before many hours they would be at the Circle Half Moon.

The steady pound of the bay's shod hoofs echoed back

from the bald-topped mesa as Mike turned north toward the TVO. San Saba was on into the east, where the land, now growing arid and brown, dropped down to the dry stretches by the Río Grande.

But San Saba was still distant. Any help there might be slow, long-delayed. Juan Sarrero would not waste any time. Dave Schaal and his TVO men were the only certain help.

So Mike drove the flagging bay unmercifully through the late afternoon. Nostrils flaring, alkali dust coating its sweating sides, the bay responded gamely.

The sun was still well above the horizon when he came through broken country to a little valley opening into the east and found at its head the windmills, corrals, and adobe buildings of Schaal's TVO Ranch. The bay was staggering from exhaustion when it reached the corrals where two hands were saddling a horse.

"Where's Schaal?" Mike called to them.

One of the men was the raw-boned Blondy whose knuckles Mike had slashed. A dirty bandage was still around the hand as Blondy jerked a thumb toward the house and growled: "Schaal's in there. What the hell do you want here?"

Mike rode around to the front of the house without answering. He was limping to the front door when it opened and Miss Hartman stepped out.

She looked at his gaunt, haggard face, cut with the raw whip furrows, and at his blood-caked leg, and spoke with swift concern. "Schaal's in the house. I'll get him. No . . . come in yourself."

But as she turned back to the door, Dave Schaal came out. His stabbing gaze under bushy black brows showed no surprise. "What happened?" he asked impassively.

"Plenty," Mike said. "Sarrero and his men are riding this way."

"How many men?" he asked.

"About seventeen or eighteen. I killed one, and wounded a couple more."

A flicker of admiration showed in Schaal's eyes. "Have to fight the whole bunch?" he asked.

"Only the three. They followed me, and jumped me about noon today. Gregorio del Grazar rode over to Ojo Grande to meet Sarrero. Gregorio was planning to have you and your neighbors cleaned."

Schaal scowled. "I see where we're going to have to clean out that whole Mex tribe before we get along here."

Mike was rolling a cigarette. He was so tired his hands shook.

"Gregorio is dead," he said. "Sarrero killed him and the four men with him. Sarrero decided to pass you folks up and raid the del Grazar place. He's heard they've got plenty of wealth hidden."

Dave Schaal laughed then, loudly, harshly—as Mike had laughed at Gregorio.

"I don't know how you found all that out," Schaal gasped. "But it's the funniest thing I've heard since I left Texas. He hired Sarrero to raid us, did he, and Sarrero up and killed him, and is going to raid his place, instead? I never heard the beat of it!"

Even Miss Hartman was smiling uncertainly.

"There aren't any Americans at the del Grazar place," Mike said. "Their Mexicans won't put up much of a fight. Sarrero would skin his brother alive if he thought it would pay him to do it. He'll do worse to the del Grazars. And . . . women are there, and probably kids, who won't have a chance."

Schaal had stopped chuckling. He was smiling grimly. Miss Hartman's face had sobered.

"What's all that to us?" Schaal asked. "Anything that happens to them now is on their own heads, isn't it?"

"No," said Mike. "Not those women and children. They didn't have anything to do with this."

"He's right, Dave," Miss Hartman said.

Schaal went impassive and stolid. "Why tell me about it?" he asked Mike.

"You and your men and your neighbors are the nearest to them. You're the only ones who can help them."

Schaal shook his head. "No," he said.

VIII

"Son of Perfidy"

Mike stared doggedly at the man. "Don't you understand what's going to happen?" he burst out. "I got away from Sarrero . . . and he sent men after me. He couldn't have been far behind them."

"Dave, you've got to help them," Miss Hartman said.

Schaal's face was flushing with gathering anger. "I won't meddle in this," he said harshly. "You know what all has happened, Miss Hartman. I'll tell you, O'Grady. Four days ago a bunch of cows I was bringing over from the Pecos were jumped east of the Río Grande at a dry bed ground. They were stampeded back into the dry country they had just come over . . . and we won't get a lot of them out alive. Two of my men were shot up at the same time, too. That was del Grazar work. Last week we found one of my line riders out to the west of here shot through the back and dead almost ten days. That was more del Grazar work, although we can't prove it. Burro Mesa spring, the only water in twelve miles over that way, was poisoned . . . and we lost almost two hundred head before we found it. More del Grazar work. I've been in range wars before where it was give and take, and hell waitin' for the slow man. But I never seen such a bundle of dirty tricks used before. I've almost got to the point of shooting the whole damn' del Grazar tribe out of the country anyway. If this Mex bandit is going to do it for me, I wish him luck. Their women and kids aren't any of my concern. I'm trying to build up a ranch here."

"Maybe," Mike said tonelessly, "the del Grazars have their side of it, too, trying to hold the land they've always had."

Schaal shrugged contemptuously. "If they can't hold it fair, that's their hard luck."

"Dave," Miss Hartman said, greatly troubled, "I think you're wrong. We've got to do something."

"Now, miss, you keep out of this," Schaal told her with growing irritation. "Your father pays me to handle this ranch like I see fit. I know what I'm doing now. I'd be a fool to take men off our land, when we may need 'em before this Sarrero gets out of the county. No telling but what he'll change his mind and head for us, after all."

"He won't," Mike said. "He's after that cache of silver and gold under the del Grazar house."

"I've said my say," Schaal stated heavily.

Mike dropped the unlighted cigarette and touched the red whip weals on his face. "Gregorio del Grazar did this with his quirt," he said tonelessly. "He tied me up and told Sarrero to kill me. I got a bullet through my leg getting away. That was a lot to take from the del Grazars. A damned sight more than you'll ever have to take yourself. And yet I mighty near killed that horse and myself getting here to help them. Two wrongs don't make a right. There's a sweet, pretty girl at that house who ain't even a del Grazar. No finer woman ever lived than my mother, and she was a del Grazar. There may be more like her there. If you wipe your hands of it this way, Schaal, I wipe my hands of you. You ain't the white man I thought you were. There isn't time for me to ride into San Saba and ask for help. I'm heading on to the Circle Half Moon to do what I can. I'll thank you for a fresh horse, and, if there's any white man in you at all, you'll start someone to San Saba with the news."

Schaal's face crimsoned. "You take a horse and get the hell out of here!" he flared. "I've had my say and I know what I'm doing!"

Pale, determined, Miss Hartman burst out: "Dave, you're terribly wrong . . . the first time I've ever heard of your being so. You're too bitter over all that's happened lately. If you won't go, *I'll* go!"

"You won't leave the place!" Schaal snapped. "I'm responsible for you."

Mike was already limping out to the horse. They could do their arguing alone. Time was flying. He had a long way to go yet. They were still talking when he galloped back to the corrals.

"Schaal says to give me a fresh horse," he told the two men. "I'm riding on."

Blondy cursed under his breath and walked away while his short, bowlegged companion entered the next corral, roped a horse, and helped Mike transfer the heavy, silver-studded saddle.

"Fancy leather you got," the shorter man commented enviously.

"It ain't mine."

"You've got damn' good friends then, mister. None of my friends would lend a tricky saddle like this."

Mike smiled grimly. "The owner went on a trip and he won't be back for a long time. What's the best way to

62

get to the Circle Half Moon?"

"Hell! You ridin' to the del Grazars?"

"Yes."

"Watch yourself. They're snakes. You head northwest. . . ."

Dave Schaal and Miss Hartman had not appeared when Mike climbed stiffly into the saddle again and headed toward the distant butte that marked the way to the Circle Half Moon. The sun was setting. He had long miles to cover—and with him he took the knowledge that even now he might be too late.

The sun vanished; darkness closed down. He rode by the stars, cutting across the open country toward the Cañon de la Muerte—the Cañon of Death. Dave Schaal had said in San Saba that the cañon had been named because long ago a war party of Indians had been trapped in it and slaughtered.

Mike reached it, after crossing a long, flat mesa. There suddenly before him in the pale starlight was the deep, shadow-filled gash, silent, yawning in the night. Its volcanic rock sides were steep, treacherous. But there was a way down, and up the other side. Then, a little farther to the north and he was at the headquarters of all the del Grazars.

In the moonlight the big house, the corrals, and the outbuildings perched on the high ground above the cañon like the sprawling nest of an eagle. A rock cliff rose starkly and darkly behind, and the cañon bounded on the east. Only to the south and west was the country level.

A hundred times Antonita del Grazar had talked to him of this spot. It was even more impressive now under the pale, cold moon. No boiling town plaza, no pushing *gringos* were here to dim the record of two centuries. Close as the world and its new ways had pushed, not yet had it reached here, nor did it seem tonight as if it ever would.

Dogs rushed out barking as Mike rode past corrals where horses stamped and nickered, past small adobe houses where doors opened on dimly lighted interiors and men and women peered out to see who came. He had been right. Women and children were in these little huts clustering closely around the foot of the big house.

The big house itself was built back against the cliff, a mansion of many rooms, and wings and patios, two stories high against the cliff in the central part, old and massive like a fort, built of lava rock, adobe, and logs.

When Santa Fé, in the north, had been the only capital in a million square miles of wilderness, the del Grazars had faced the frontier from this spot, with their back against that rocky cliff and their eyes looking out over their empire. But tonight, as servants came out with lanterns to take the horse, only a few lighted windows showed against the night, and inside an old man nursed a futile, helpless bitterness.

Stiffly Mike got down and tossed the reins to a peering figure with a lantern. "I will see *Don* Antonio," he said in Spanish.

"He is in the house, *señor*. If you will knock on the door. . . ."

Mike used the heavy, hand-wrought iron door knocker on a solid wooden door, and the door was opened by a meek-faced woman servant whose eyes grew wide at the tall, haggard figure she saw.

"Tell *Don* Antonio that Mike O'Grady is here with news of importance," Mike said in Spanish. As the woman hesitated, Mike stepped into the low, long, dimly lighted hall.

With an uneasy look at him the woman left him there. People were in the house; he could hear them talking in some distant room. A woman laughed, and fingers struck a few chords from a guitar. Then through the doorway where the woman servant had vanished, María Guadalupe Sedillo slipped into the hall.

"I thought from what Trinidad said that it was you," she said hurriedly. "Why did you come here? Your face . . . what has happened?"

"I met Gregorio," Mike told her stolidly. But he wasn't stolid inside. Tonight she wore black that billowed out from her slender waist and made her troubled face by contrast pale and delicate.

Startled, she said—"Gregorio?"—and looked at the marks on his face again, and turned one small hand palm up in a gesture of helplessness. "I was afraid it would happen," she said miserably.

"It doesn't matter now," Mike told her. "You're not angry with me?"

"Angry? For why . . . ?" She saw his faint smile. Color crept into her cheeks. "Your manners at times, *Señor Gringo,*" she said severely, "are not of the best." And then she was troubled again. "Did you come here to fight *Don* Antonio? He is old, and my godfather. I don't want that."

"I came here to help him, ma'am."

"He will be here. Come with me."

The room into which she took him was big, high-ceilinged, lighted by several lamps. Bearskins and buffalo rugs were on the floor, hand-carved wooden *santos* stood in little niches in the wall, and the corners held decorated pottery of Indian make. It was an old, gracious room, much lived in, mellowed by the ghosts of the past. But the tall, gaunt figure that entered brought a chill into the mellowness.

"You again," *Don* Antonio said coldly. "What now do you want?"

Mike touched his cheek. "I met Gregorio," he said. "You'd better know it first."

The thin, bloodless lips did not move. Sunken eyes stared at the whip marks. "If Gregorio did that on his way to El Paso, the trip was worthwhile," *Don* Antonio said bleakly.

"He didn't go to El Paso."

"Eh? Where is Gregorio, then?"

"He's dead," Mike said.

María Sedillo uttered the exclamation of distress. *Don* Antonio stood there as if he did not comprehend, but his face seemed to grow thinner, and his erect shoulders drooped a little. At that moment the slim young man who had ridden up with Gregorio in San Saba hurried into the room. His face was disturbed. He spoke in Spanish, but Mike understood.

"This man rode in on Gregorio's saddle. Your men recognized it."

"Then," said *Don* Antonio with a sudden bitterness that shook his whole frame, "I will kill this *gringo* myself! Get my gun!"

"Listen, you fool," Mike flung at him harshly, "I didn't kill your son, although I should have! He caught me in Ojo Grande, where he went to meet Juan Sarrero. You with your damned pride, lying to me about El Paso, while you're thinking Sarrero is going to raid your neighbors! You're as bad as your Gregorio, poisoning water holes, shooting your neighbor's men in the back, stampeding their cattle, skulking to have them killed off by a dirty bandit from south of the border. It wasn't because of you that I came here. It was the women and kids. Your damned Gregorio was killed by Sarrero because Sarrero has decided it's easier to raid you and get at the rock cellar under the house here. I've damn' near killed myself to get here and warn you. Now the rest is up to you. Schaal, at the TVO, won't help you, after all he's suffered from your dirty tricks. The nearest help is San Saba. You'd better get ready for trouble. Sarrero may be here any minute. And when he comes, it won't be your old bones that will suffer. It'll be the people around the place, like María Guadalupe here."

No one noticed that he had used her first name. *Don* Antonio had shrunk a little before that torrent of words, had withered before the blast. Fear that was not physical fear came into his face.

"I don't know these things of which you speak," he said. "I have had nothing to do with a bandit. I have poisoned no water holes or had men shot in the back."

"Then who's been giving orders around here?" Mike snapped.

Old bony hands spread helplessly. The old man looked at the younger man. "José," he said, "what of this?"

The younger man looked uncomfortable. "*Don* Antonio, I am only a friend of the family. Not even as close as my sister here."

"It is so, then?"

"It was not up to me to talk to you of Gregorio's doing, *señor*."

"There should have been no tales about my son to bring," *Don* Antonio muttered. He stood a moment in silence with his chin down, aloof from them, far away, and then his shoulders straightened and he lifted his head, and his voice was calm. "When are these bandits coming?" he asked Mike.

"They weren't far behind me. You won't have time to send for help."

"Will you be going now, *Señor* O'Grady?"

Here was pride to the last, refusing to ask for help after what had passed between them.

"I'm staying," Mike said. "And I'll need more than the rifle I brought."

"We have guns," *Don* Antonio told him—and before Mike's

eyes the gaunt, tired old man dropped off the weary years and became young again as he turned to the door, shouting orders, sending the slim young man running, and María Sedillo slipping hurriedly out of the room to the women.

Before leaving the room himself, *Don* Antonio spoke swiftly to Mike with a hard, grim ring in his voice. "Better men than miserable Mexican bandits have come for the gold under this house. We will see."

Mike could only nod. He was beginning to see why del Grazars had held this place for two centuries.

IX

"Gringo Savior"

The house was in an uproar, outside and in. Poorly dressed women and children were crowding in from the small houses outside, scurrying to the back rooms. Chests holding rifles, revolvers, and belts of cartridges were carried into the big front room to be distributed among the men.

Of the del Grazar family and friends, there were only three men Mike had not seen before, and two of them were old, like *Don* Antonio. But those old men were calm as they took up weapons.

Women, too, came for guns, María Sedillo among them, and Mike thought it strange to see her small hands holding a rifle. She smiled wanly at him and vanished to the back of the house.

Don Antonio issued sharp orders—two men up on the flat roof, others at the upper windows, two at the front door. The rest—with *Don* Antonio and Mike outside. When they were outside, the massive front door was barred against them, and there were no lights in the front of the house. The big building loomed darkly there against the cliff like a fort.

Mike had heard orders given to empty the corrals. There would be no horses to run away—or none to escape on. Out in the moonlight, among the little adobe huts, with the cañon protecting them on the east and the rock behind, they waited for what might come out of the night from the south and west.

An hour—two hours they waited, with *Don* Antonio moving from man to man to see that all was ready. They were not many, twelve men, and some of the ranch hands looked pretty poor to Mike. Not much to guard a rock cellar full with gold and silver and a house full of women and children. They were waiting for men who lived by fighting and loot. But perhaps a miracle would happen and they would not come.

Mike saw a crouching shadow coming past the corrals a moment later—and then another, and another—men on foot coming up to the house. He sighted at the nearest one and fired.

Then they knew Sarrero and his men were there, for the night erupted gunfire in front of them, and a yelling line of crouching, dodging men swept in toward the first buildings. If it had been daylight, they might have had a chance, but moonlight and shadows were mixed, men were hard to see. That first rush brought Sarrero's men to the outer huts where they had shelter.

Mike saw one man drop, thought he hit another. Toward the house a man cried out. From the corner of his eye Mike saw another stagger out into the moonlight and fall.

From the doorway of one hut Mike fired at the corner of another hut fifty yards away where a gun had flashed—and didn't hit the man, for the gun flashed again and a bullet smashed into the door frame at his shoulder. This was better shooting than Sarrero's men had done in the day-time, but they were closer now, and not surprised. If they got between the house and these outer huts, they would have little more trouble. Already the gunfire of *Don* Antonio's men was slackening off, as if several of the hands had run away or been shot.

Then *Don* Antonio shouted for them all to get back into the house. A flicker of fire came from the spot where he called. As Mike ran toward the house, he saw the tall old figure trotting, also. Flame was visible in the hut that *Don* Antonio had just quitted.

The front door opened to receive them. Mike stood outside the doorway and shot at the gun flashes of Sarrero's men who were following them.

"Get in!" *Don* Antonio ordered Mike harshly, and followed him in, the last one.

As the door was slammed and barred, bullets thudded against the thick wood. But none got through, so thick was the door.

Don Antonio's orders sent men to guard the windows. Someone was groaning. A lamp was lighted in the hall. One of the *peónes* lay on the floor holding his stomach and rolling his eyes as he groaned. Blood was dripping off *Don* Antonio's wrist.

"How bad is it?" Mike asked.

"It is nothing," he was told. "Will you watch the door, *señor?* I can trust you. The windows are high and small. I think they will try to break in a door. We will have light out there quickly." *Don* Antonio trotted out of the hall, calling orders.

Three of the native women ran into the hall and dragged out the wounded men. Mike found himself alone with one of the poorly dressed servants.

"Mother of Mercy, if the other men were only here!" the

man stammered. "They are out on the range. They will not be back for days. And our throats will be cut by then!"

"Shut up!" Mike said savagely.

The next instant the massive door shivered as a heavy weight crashed against it. Bits of the adobe wall fell to the floor. Again and again the door was struck. Mike guessed that a long, heavy corral pole was being rammed against it. Overhead on the roof he could hear guns crashing. Outside men were shooting rapidly and shouting threats.

Then the fastenings that held the bar at one end pulled out. Mike skidded a chair behind it and smashed the lamp chimney against the wall with a gun barrel as the door flew open and the end of a long, heavy pole rammed in against the wall. A wave of yelling men charged the doorway.

Mike's blazing guns met them. He could see them, for the hut *Don* Antonio had fired was burning inside, throwing lurid light out into the night. The first man pitched through the doorway as Mike's roaring guns cut him down. Mike was conscious that his companion had vanished. He didn't have time to think of that. Too many men were outside trying to get in. Too many guns were throwing lead through the partially opened door.

He stood in the shelter of the door as best he could and dropped another man, and a third. A bullet clipped his hair, another his wrist. Hands were shoving guns around the edge of the door and firing blindly into the hall.

Mike cursed the men who had run. When his guns were empty, he'd have no time to reload. Then his right hand and forearm went numb as a bullet knocked the revolver out of it.

From the next room one of *Don* Antonio's elderly guests ran into the hall, and a bullet hit him and he sprawled across the floor. Mike's last revolver snapped uselessly. He smashed the empty gun at the first head that appeared inside the doorway. The man dropped. Hands outside dragged him out before Mike could get his gun. Swearing, Mike jumped back and groped on the floor for the gun the wounded man had dropped. But the hall was dark. He couldn't find it.

This was the end, Mike knew. They'd be inside in a minute, if they hadn't forced some other entrance. If only he had a gun. What could a few *peónes* and old men do against a bunch of gold-starved outlaws, anyway? Why didn't they come in that open doorway?

His ringing ears suddenly picked out a new burst of yells outside. The night seemed full of shots now, and the doorway was empty, deserted.

Mike found the gun he was groping for and ran back to the doorway, and then stepped outside, for there was no one at the door. The shooting was back among the huts now, retreating fast. Mike ran that way.

A quarter of an hour later he came back with Dave Schaal and some of the TVO men. The rest were scattered out, looking for bandits that were afoot.

"We heard the shooting when we came up out of the cañon, and rode like hell," Schaal explained. "Found their horses back a little and scattered 'em. They won't get far afoot. We'll pick 'em up in the morning. Did they get into the house? Hurt any . . . uh . . . kids?"

"I don't think so," Mike said.

Schaal said nothing. Just ahead of them the roof of the burning hut fell in. Sparks and flames shot up. But all the other roofs were of dirt, so it did not matter much. Men had run out of the house and were watching. *Don* Antonio was out there, holding a bloody cloth about his wrist and giving orders. He walked to meet Mike and Dave Schaal.

His English was stilted, formal.

"So it was your help that saved us, *Señor* Schaal? I am in your debt."

"Never mind," Dave Schaal said impassively. "I got to thinking about your womenfolks and kids. Miss Hartman was anxious, too."

An uncomfortable silence followed.

"Hell!" Mike said disgustedly. "I've told Schaal you didn't know about a lot of things that have happened, *Don* Antonio. Maybe he won't admit it, but I reckon he understands."

Don Antonio cleared his throat. "After tonight, *Señor* Schaal, I don't think there is anything we can't settle by talking."

It was still there, that pride that would not unbend and ask for what an old man's gaunt face was pleading. Dave Schaal was man enough to see it. "Hell, yes," he said. "I guess we can talk things over . . . neighbor. O'Grady here has sort of made me see things different."

Don Antonio took the hand Dave Schaal extended. He was gaunt and old, but his thin face was softer and his voice no longer bitter as he smiled. "We are proud of my sister's son, my friend," he said. "I hope he will stay with us. I am not too old not to . . . to need another son."

It was *Don* Mike O'Grady then, as quick to tears as to laughter or anger, who looked into the gaunt old face and grinned, and blew his nose on his bandanna. "Thank you, sir," he said. "While you two talk around here, I'll go into the house. I've got business in there."

It was *Don* Antonio del Grazar, wise from a long lifetime, who chuckled and said: "I think María Guadalupe is upstairs."

But Mike was already hurrying toward the house.

Bandit of the Brindlebar

T.T. Flynn completed this short novel on August 18, 1935. It was bought at once for *Star Western*, a magazine to which Flynn had been a regular contributor since his story, "Hell's Half-Acre", had appeared in the first issue, published in October, 1933. Flynn's original title for the earlier story had been "Conquistador's Gold" and under this title it has been collected in *Rawhide: A Western Quintet* (Five Star Westerns, 1996), now also available in a paperback edition from Leisure Books. The present story appeared in *Star Western* (1/36) under the title "Last of the Wild Shotwells". The author was paid $400. For its appearance here the author's title and text have been restored.

I

"Orphaned"

Bill Shotwell brought the news home that evening. He came in more quietly than usual, stood about uneasily, ignoring the hot coffee and plate of food old Sam Lee, the Chinese cook, had put out on the table. His younger brother Les was studying his school lessons at the time. He had a ten-mile ride each way to school every day and, with chores and studying nights, there wasn't any spare time from daybreak to bedtime.

"Where's Pop?" Les asked without much interest. "Didn't he come back with you?"

Bill rolled a brown paper cigarette, more clumsily than usual. Bill was only twenty, six years older than the kid, but he had been a man for several years. He'd had to be since old Pete Shotwell had started hanging around Brindlebar, bucking the games.

Lighting the cigarette, Bill scowled at the bearskin nailed up on the opposite wall, and answered in a hard, brittle voice: "The old man's dead. Yance King, the sheriff, shot him."

Even if you were only fourteen and, as far back as you can remember, the old man had been half drunk most of the time, brooding, morose, hardly conscious that you were around, the fact remained that he was your father. Sometimes, when he was feeling good enough to take notice, he was pretty nice.

Les's throat choked up. His eyes began to glisten, so that the flame of the oil lamp blurred on the table. "What'd the sheriff kill him for, Bill?" he asked unsteadily. "You want we should saddle up an' go after Yance King?"

"Don't you get any damn' bad ideas," Bill answered. "Maybe the old man got what was comin' to him . . . I dunno. I wasn't in the Diamond Hitch Saloon when it happened. But he killed Jake King, the sheriff's oldest boy, so I guess we're even." Bill stood there with the lamplight on his face, an older, harder face now, and spoke on: "The old man accused Jake of slick work in a card game, an' Jake went for his gun, an' the old man killed him. Yance King was standin' at the bar. He dropped the old man. It's over. Nothin' we can do about it. They're goin' to bury 'em both at Brindlebar tomorrow. The old man didn't give a damn for the ranch anyway, these last few years. No use bringin' him out here. Go on with your lessons."

But Les was through studying for the night. He went

outside under the bright stars, where it was quiet and he could think. He liked to do that—get off alone.

Old Sam Lee presently shuffled softly out and found him.

"Whatsa malla, you don' come in klichen an' eat pie?" Sam asked severely, which was his way of being sympathetic.

Les went in and tried to eat the pie, but he couldn't make it, and went back outside.

The night was soothing, restful. He always had liked the night in this Brindlebar country where he had been raised. Under a bright moon you could see the mountains looming in the far distance, see the nearer mesas, dark and lonely on the plain. Les thought the Brindlebar country was about as fine as anyone could want.

Because he was young, and life had to go on, and the Brindlebar country was still there, the memory of his father soon began to dim, and he could think of the dead man without a lump in his throat.

School went on through early spring. Sometimes it was fun. There was also Lucy Morrow. Fourteen was pretty young, but you could like a girl just the same—and Lucy liked to be liked.

Lucy rode to school, too, in good weather, from the Bridle Cross ranch house, some seven miles from the schoolhouse. Often she and Les rode the last two miles along the road together, going and coming. That was pretty nice. Lucy always had something good in her lunch pail, which she was willing to share if she was teased enough.

"Someday," Les said once, as he finished some of Lucy's dried apple pie dusted with brown sugar, "I'm gonna grow up an' marry you, Lucy."

Lucy giggled, tossed her yellow braids, and said: "You'll

have to be better-looking than you are now, Les Shotwell. Anyhow, I don't think I'll ever get married. It's too much trouble."

But that was girl's talk. Les thought he'd really marry her when he grew up. Most people did get married.

Then school was out and there was work to do around the ranch, helping Bill and Shorty Cox, the single ranch hand.

Dimly Les could remember when there had been eight or ten ranch hands, before his father had shot a man, gone to prison for two years, and his mother had died. The old man had started drinking and gambling after he had come back.

He had gambled away most of the big ranch, sold off the cattle and a lot of the land. There wasn't much left now, hardly enough to pay taxes and keep going. Bill was having a hard time. Cattle prices were away down. They didn't get much out of the roundup.

First Bill had tried to fire Sam Lee, who had been on the ranch since before Bill was born. Sam chased Bill out of the kitchen with a meat knife, locked the door, and refused to come out. So Bill fired Shorty Cox. Shorty went.

"I hate to go, Bill," Shorty apologized. "I know how you're fixed here. But tailin' a few cows up all winter for my grub ain't gettin' either of us much."

"Sure, I know," Bill agreed in a hard voice. "Every man's got to look out for himself. I aim to do that, too."

Les didn't make much sense out of that until Yance King rode up to the ranch house one Sunday, early in the winter. Several riders were with him. Bill was not any too friendly when he stepped out to meet them.

"Lookin' for something?" he called.

Yance King was a tall man, sloping in the shoulders, with a drooping brown mustache that was always stained with tobacco juice. Now he twisted sideways in the saddle, spat a thin brown stream to the dusting of snow on the ground, and answered Bill with a growl. "We're just lookin' around. Seen any stray cattle lately?"

"Any reason why I should?" Bill answered curtly.

"None . . . right now," Yance King snapped. "But maybe. . . ."

He left the remark unfinished, but even Les, standing beside the doorway, sensed that the sheriff was looking for trouble. So were the other four men with him. So, even, was the boy who had come along with them.

Les knew that boy, young Jack King, about sixteen now, tall, lanky like his father. Les had never liked him; he stood now with a blank face while young Jack scowled at him.

Bill's face was blank, also, as he eyed the mounted men. He spoke to Yance King. "Meanin' anything by that remark?"

"Suit yourself!" King rasped. "I don't like you, Shotwell! I'm tellin' you now I'm keepin' an eye on you!"

Bill suddenly grinned—nastily. "You mean you're tryin' to pin somethin' on me," he said. "All right, go ahead. But as long as you ain't got nothin' now, get the hell off the place. I don't like you, either."

Yance King yanked his horse's head up. "I won't forget you," he promised savagely, and led his men away.

"Someday I'm gonna lick the hide off that Jack King," Les promised. "He's made talk to the boys in Brindlebar about the old man bein' a card slick."

Bill had been staring after the sheriff's party. He whirled angrily.

"All you got to do is get through school quick as you can . . . an' keep your mind off the Kings! They mean bad luck . . . you hear? Yance King rawhided the old man into the pen an' busted his heart, when he could 'a' kept him out, an' then put a bullet in him in the end. He's got it in for us because his boy got killed at the same time. He's scratchin' for somethin' to hang on us."

"What'd he want to send the old man to the pen for?" Les mumbled.

"Because," said Bill harshly, "your mother took a Shotwell when she could 'a' had Yance King. He never got over it. He's hated everything called Shotwell ever since." Bill stepped over, grabbed Les's arm, and shook it. He was all stirred up. "The night Maw died she told me about it," Bill said through his teeth. "She told me to always steer clear of Yance King, an' keep you clear of him. I guess she knew he'd get the old man in the end, an' she was thinkin' about us. I promised, an' by God," said Bill harshly, shaking Les's arm again, "I'm gonna keep that promise! We don't want no truck with the Kings, man or boy!"

Les jerked his arm free, mad now himself. "Maybe you're scared of 'em! I . . . I ain't!" he said furiously.

"Scared?" said Bill. He laughed shortly. "I could take a rifle an' get Yance King tomorrow. But I'm steerin' clear of him like I promised. All I want is to get you through school an' started out right. I . . . I promised Maw that, too." Bill was a man, but he swallowed. "God, she was a sweet maw, Les," he said huskily. "I wisht you'd been old enough to re-member her better. She worried a heap about us . . . about you mostly." Then Bill's voice broke and abruptly he stalked into the house.

Les stood there with another lump in his throat. But it didn't last long. He'd been too young to remember much about his mother. . . .

The weather was open and mild that winter. But there was a heap of work around the ranch. Despite that, Bill rode away now and then for days at a time. Each trip he left orders for Les not to tell anyone he was gone. When Les asked questions, all he got was a cussing out.

Bill took one of those trips early in March, and came back the third night, just after midnight. The weather was raw, blustery; the wind was whining and slamming in gusts outside when Bill burst noisily into the house. He knocked over a chair, careened into a table, and made such a racket that Les rolled out of his bed wide-awake.

Bill was just turning up the flame in the living room lamp when Les stepped through the doorway, and stopped, gaping. Breathing heavily, with great effort, Bill stood there, supporting himself by holding onto the table edge. His hat was gone, his clothes were wet and covered with mud, as if he had been crawling on the ground. Bill's face was streaked with blood that had run down out of his hair. Big dark splotches of blood showed on the front of his shirt, too.

Bill reached out a bloody hand and grabbed Les's shoulder for support. "Help me into bed! Get Sam to help fix me up. I . . . I can't stop the bleedin'!" he gasped.

Sam Lee shuffled in just then, and lent a hand to get Bill into the bedroom. Bill collapsed on the bed heavily, lay there struggling to get breath while Sam darted to the lamp and struck a match.

Ranch life taught you what to do in matters like this. Les started to get Bill's clothes off those bullet wounds. Bill had a bad one in his chest, another in his side, and a third one in his leg. The blood on his face came from a great gash in the scalp, which looked as if Bill's head had hit hard against a sharp rock. The wounds in his chest and stomach had almost stopped bleeding. The leg wound was still oozing a red trickle.

Bill lay there with his eyes closed, breathing through his mouth. Under the dried blood on his face the stubble-darkened stain looked pallid, pale, damp with cold sweat.

"Wh . . . what happened, Bill?"

Bill did not answer—but a few moments later, when Sam Lee slip-slapped in with a basin of hot water and clean white rags and went to work on the wounds, Bill opened his eyes, turned his head, saw Les standing beside the bed, and began to speak in a thin, harsh voice.

"They'll be here after me, Les, if they can follow out the trail. Guess I shouldn't've come here . . . but I knew I couldn't last if I didn't."

Les licked his dry lips. "Who'll be here, Bill?"

"Yance King an' a posse."

"H . . . how come, Bill?"

"I been rustlin' cows all fall an' winter," Bill muttered. "Guess you might as well know it now. You'll hear plenty about it soon enough. I couldn't keep the place goin' without some cash . . . an that was the only way to get it. I knew some fellows who was makin' a pretty good thing out of wet cattle . . . an' I threw in with 'em. I . . . I wanted to keep you in school an' get you started, Les."

Les wanted to sniffle, even if he was getting pretty old now. Something in Bill's voice made him feel that way, something protective, fierce—and still a little tender.

"I don't care what you did, Bill!" Les gulped. "You'll be all right here."

Bill rolled his head weakly on the pillow in a negative gesture. "Don't go getting any fool ideas, Les. If Yancy King an' his men come here, keep outta their way. They was layin' for us tonight. Penned us in a corner an' we had to shoot our way out. I reckon King has been watchin' me close, like he said he would. It was too dark to get a good

81

look at any of us. Maybe . . . maybe King didn't figure I was in on it. I oughta ride away from here anyways."

"Fool talk!" said Sam Lee angrily. "You don' go!"

But even Les knew Bill could not leave that bed if he tried to. Bill would be down on his back for a long time.

"I oughta get a doctor," Les said.

"You can't," Bill whispered. That was all he could do now—whisper. "You got to keep it hid that I'm shot up."

II

"A Brother Dies"

All that Bill had previously said about Yance King came back now. When Bill's eyes closed again, Les picked up the gun belts and guns he'd taken from Bill. Never before had he seen Bill armed like this with two guns. Many of the shells were gone from the belt loops.

Bill did not notice him leave the room. Sam Lee was too busy to care. Les stepped out the front door, carrying the guns.

Bill's horse was still standing there, rein-tied to the ground. Les had never seen that dun horse before. It stood with its head drooping low, sweat-streaked, deadbeat. The dim light coming out of the door showed a raw, red furrow on the horse's flank, and dried blood on down below it.

Bill's rifle was in the leather saddle scabbard. Les took it out, led the horse back to the nearest corral, jerked off the saddle and bridle, and ran the animal off. It went slowly, limping painfully, and vanished into the windy night.

Leaving the saddle there on the ground, Les went back to the house with the guns. He was not certain what to do with them, but he didn't want them to get out of his hands.

Just feeling them brought a measure of comfort. Les always had liked guns. He'd been shooting ever since he could remember, and was getting better all the time.

Through the bedroom window he saw Sam Lee straighten up beside the bed. Bill said something. Sam shook his head. The deeply wrinkled face of the old Chinaman looked sad, grave. When Sam Lee raised the back of a claw-like hand and dug it into his eyes hurriedly, Les knew Bill must be pretty bad. He had never before seen Sam show emotion like that.

Before Les reached the front door, the gusty wind lulled for a moment. He heard horses galloping not far away, coming toward the house.

That must be the posse—and Yance King. Les ran into the house, bolted the door, blew out the lamp, and called to Sam to do the same thing in the bedroom.

"The posse's comin'!" Les called.

The bedroom doorway went dark as Les opened one of the two front windows. He slid the rifle across the sill and waited. He felt hot, shaky—but hard inside, queerly hard.

Les knew that he was pretty young yet, but, as he waited at the window, he felt fiercely protective toward Bill, like Bill had sounded toward him. It was dark outside, no moon, only an occasional star. Inside the house the blackness was absolute. The riders out there came on, until they were a hundred or so yards away. Then they slowed to a walk as they drew near the house. Les called: "Who is it?"

They stopped.

Yance King's harsh voice answered. "Who's that?"

"Les Shotwell."

"Where's your brother?"

"He . . . he ain't here," Les lied, and hated to do it. He never had gotten into the habit of lying.

"What're you doin' up this time of night in a dark house?" Yance King demanded.

"I heard you comin'."

"He's lyin'!" another voice said. "Let's go in and see!"

"I heard that!" Les called. "I ain't clear who you are, but keep ridin'! You ain't wanted around here!"

Yance King's rasping voice rang out: "Bill Shotwell's in there an' we aim to see him! Tell him to speak up! There's men behind the house! He won't get away that way!"

"He . . . he's asleep," Les lied again.

His hands were shaking as they gripped the rifle. He knew hell was gathering to break loose—and there wasn't anything he could do now but keep on until it broke.

"Men, that pup is lyin'! Bill Shotwell's in there wounded bad, or gettin' ready to make a run for it!" Yance King said loudly. "I think he's wounded. One of them jaspers was leakin' blood heavy when he rode away!"

"By God, if he's in there with his hide so much as scratched, I'm all fer hangin' him quick an' gettin' it over with!" one of the men said violently. "If he's wounded, we know he's the one we want! We better make a good cow thief outta him. Let's go in and see."

Les knew that only the gun in his hand stood now between Bill and a noose. Yance King had another Shotwell cold, where he wanted him. Raising his voice, Les called: "I'm warnin' you all away! First man rides close gets shot!"

"This is a sheriff's posse, you little fool!" Yance King shouted. "If you've got a gun, put it down before you get hurt! We ain't here to shoot brats . . . although you wouldn't be much loss! You're probably as bad as your brother an' old man!"

"None of us could get as bad as a King!" Les yelled. "If you want a bullet, come an' get it!"

The sheriff's reply out of the dark was almost a snarl. "There's somethin' funny in there, boys! Let's get in there an' see! Pour it to 'em!"

Les ducked over to one side of the window as a fusillade of shots ripped the raw, gusty night to shreds of hammering sound. Glass crashed out of the window. Splinters flew out of the door. The adobe wall of the house got the rest of the lead.

The posse rode in close, still shooting. Guns blasted just outside the front door, smashing bullets through the planks at anyone who might be standing inside.

A foot kicked the door open.

Les had dropped the rifle. He was hugging the wall with Bill's two large .45s in his hands. His mouth was dry, his throat tight, his heart hammering madly. He was frightened so badly his legs felt weak and wobbly, but he knew now with desperate certainty he could only do two things. Run— and let them have Bill—or hold them back as long as possible. Maybe Bill would get out some way.

As the door flew open, Les pumped shots into the opening.

Outside the door a man yelled with pain. The shots through the doorway stopped. The other guns slackened off. Les heard someone groaning and cursing in retreat from the front door.

Yance King bawled a furious order: "Scatter out an' each man try an' get in a different way! I believe that damn' kid's doin' it all!"

Les jumped and almost cut loose with his guns as Sam Lee's cautious voice spoke close to him: "Les? Wheah you?"

"Here," Les said thickly, under his breath. "How's Bill? Could he get out?"

"Bill no moah. Die," said Sam Lee woodenly.

Les heard him, knew it was so, and wasted no time in emotion. "Get back in your room an' lock the door, Sam. I guess they won't hurt you."

"Wha' you do, Les?"

"Me? I'm leavin'!" Les said.

He had to raise his voice to say it. Gunfire was crashing again outside; window glass was breaking as men attacked the windows. Brushing past Sam, Les ran across that familiar room that he had known all his life. He took with him the sensation of leaving the room for the last time—the house, too, if he was lucky. He ran back toward the kitchen, made for the back door, ran out into the night.

A man standing there in the darkness called: "Who's that?"

Les jumped, ducked, bolted off to the left. Behind him a gun cut loose.

A second gun followed—then a third over at the corner of the house. Lead hummed and droned as it ripped blindly through the darkness.

A bullet clipped Les's ear. Another struck his left arm, high up. It felt like a cold iron pressed hard to the skin. Then the warm blood came pouring out—and all the time Les was running hard, into the night, carrying the belt guns and rifle.

In a few minutes the shooting stopped. Riders came galloping after him. But they couldn't see in the blackness. They searched blindly, and Les kept on, away from the house, the corrals, the bunkhouse, kept on until he was gasping for breath and strength had drained out of his body.

He stopped, looked back, swearing, heart hammering wildly. Dim lights showed in the house windows. The riders were still searching for him. One man was coming fairly close.

Les dropped flat on the ground, gripping a .45 so hard his hand ached. But the man rode away again. Les stood up and walked on rapidly.

Warm blood was still creeping down his arm. He felt the wound. A jagged hole had been torn in the outer muscle. With his bandanna handkerchief he bound the wound as best he could and went on.

III

"Friends from the Owlhoot"

All that night Les walked north toward Wolf Creek. He had no reason for heading that way except that Wolf Creek Cañon and Crazy Horse Mesa were the most desolate parts of the Brindlebar country. You could hide out in the Wolf Creek district if you knew where the water was. Jack rabbits would give you food. A man could live for a long while around Wolf Creek Cañon if he had to.

Les never doubted Yance King would be looking for him. Yance King had gotten the old man and Bill. Les was the last of the Shotwells—and now Yance King had a shooting to hang on him. Yance King wouldn't overlook that bet. Young as he was, Les was sure of that.

Toward morning he began to get light-headed. His arm had been hurting more every hour. The bleeding didn't seem to stop like it should. The wound felt feverish, swollen.

Wolf Creek seemed a lot farther when you had to make it on foot. Les's mouth was dry and thick inside. He wanted water worse than he ever had in his life before. He stubbed against a small rock and went down before he knew what was happening. A little later he stumbled and fell again.

This time Les had to force himself to stand, and then lift the heavy guns and belts. He was dogged about that. They were Bill's. Somehow he wanted to hang onto these mementoes of Bill's. They were all he had left of Bill. Hours back, against the skyline, a lurid, reddish glow had marked the end of the ranch house. Yance King and his men had fired the place. Yance King was wiping out the Shotwells with a vengeance.

The gray, cold dawn was in the eastern sky when Les staggered through a thicket of willows, lurched down the sandy bank of Wolf Creek, and threw himself flat on the sand beside the narrow, shallow thread of water. After drinking, Les slopped water up over his face and sat there for a while. Presently he drank again, and forced himself to stand up.

But he staggered. The bleak, sandy bed of Wolf Creek was wavering queerly. Les dragged up the guns and turned back toward a thicket of willows. At their edge his knees gave way. He sank down on the dry, cool sand. It felt soft, luxurious, comforting. Les rolled over on his back and stared dully at the sky. That was the last he knew for a while.

A hand shaking his shoulder brought him out of it. Les struggled to a sitting position with wild thoughts flaming in his brain. The sun was glaring down. Two men were standing over him.

For a moment he couldn't remember—then he grabbed for a gun. He had a hold on one of the belt guns when the nearest man jerked it away. Les couldn't get any strength in his grip.

The stranger said gruffly: "We ain't gonna hurt you! What's the matter? How'd your arm get hurt thataway?"

Les tried to stand up. He was rolling like a drunk when

the second stranger reached out a hand and supported him. This man was tall, wide-shouldered, and most of his face was hidden by a brown beard, bushy and untrimmed, so that it had a wild, untamed look.

The second man was tall, too, but thinner and younger. His face was long, lean, solemn. One of his ears bent queerly out. He looked so sad it was almost funny.

Both men were heavily armed, even to knives at their belts. Both looked tired. Dark circles lay under their red-rimmed, bloodshot eyes. They were smeared with dried mud, as if they had been crawling on the wet ground the night before.

Les shook off the stupor with a great effort and glared at them. His left arm felt twice as big as it ever had before. It was hot, feverish, shot with throbbing pain. The dizziness came back. He had to concentrate hard to keep the two men from wobbling there in front of him.

"Never mind my arm," Les croaked—and even to his own ears his voice sounded strange. But it was the best he could do. "Gimme my gun! I ain't hurtin' you two. Go on an' let me alone!"

The younger man was clean-shaven, except for a thick, reddish stubble. He spat on the dry sand. "You're talkin' bigger'n you look, youngster," he said. "That's a mighty bad arm you got. Where'd you git it, an' these guns? Look at this one, Tom." He handed over the gun he had taken from Les. "Ain't this the iron you gave Bill last night? The one you got at Magdalena last month!"

"By God! So 'tis!" the other man rumbled. His voice seemed to come up from cavernous depths behind the wild, bushy beard. "Where'd you get this, boy?" he demanded.

"It's mine," Les said defiantly.

"Who're you?"

"Les Shotwell's my name."

"Bill Shotwell's brother?" the bearded man exclaimed. Then he asked: "What happened to your arm?"

"Got a bullet hole in it," Les said fiercely. "Damn you, gimme that gun!"

Before they could answer him, they began to dance and whirl. Les knew he was falling. Desperately he tried to pull himself together. He went to sleep again before he hit the sand.

After that life was pretty mixed for a while. Les came out of the stupor now and then, and realized that he was on horseback. His left side seemed on fire and in pain. His head hurt. He was sick.

Later on he knew he was lying on something, and there wasn't any sun, any sky. All was dim, quiet. Men moved about and their talk sounded far away. Hands worked on his arm. Now and then hot liquid was put to his lips and he drank mechanically. But most of the time he slept and hurt and had wild visions.

Finally he woke up. His head was clear. His left arm was sore. But he could see clearly enough, and he could think. He was in a tiny cabin that held a handmade table, a box to sit on, and two wall bunks.

Les was lying on one of the bunks. A man stood in the doorway, smoking. Out of the vague, distant past, out of that nightmarish period of vision, of pain, Les remembered him. This was the tall, skinny young man with the reddish stubble on his face. Only now the stubble was a short, bristly beard.

"Hey," Les called weakly.

The stranger wheeled in the doorway, saw Les sitting up.

"How you feelin'?" he said gruffly.

"Hungry, I guess."

The other grinned. "You'll be all right," he said. "Kinda touch an' go there for a while. Your arm feel all right?"

"Hurts a little."

"Uhn-huh. It'll be that way for a while yet."

"Where am I?" Les asked.

"Up on High Lonesome Mountain."

"That's a long ways off," Les said slowly. He'd never been to High Lonesome Mountain, but he knew where it was.

"About two hundred miles from Brindlebar," the other said. "Crazy Tom figgered we'd better lie low. We've been up here a week."

"How'd I get here?"

"We carried you. Crazy Tom got word your brother Bill is dead. You might as well know it. Yance King, the sheriff, kilt him."

"I knew it before I left the house." Les nodded. "Bill was dead before Yance King could get to him an' put a rope around his neck. Bill come in that night all shot up. I . . . I been here a week?"

"Uhn-huh. Your arm was mighty bad. We figured for a while we'd have to dig a hole an' leave you. But you're tough. You must be rawhide an' leather clean through."

"I don't feel so good," Les muttered, and then he remembered Bill, the family, the burning house—and he felt worse. "Yance King burned us out," he said dully. "An' I shot one of his posse. I reckon I better keep goin' an' get me a job."

They both looked at the doorway as the older man stepped in, carrying a rifle. His beard looked bushier and wilder than ever. He had a kind of crazy look.

"I'm a warty, ole toad!" he declared loudly, parting his cavernous whiskers in what evidently was a grin. "Ain't we

91

got a party now? Shaw! So you're feelin' uppity again, son?"

"He's rarin' to get out an get him a job," the younger man said. "With Bill dead an' the ranch burnt out, he's got to rustle his own chuck now."

"Yance King's lookin' for me, too," Les reminded gloomily.

"Yep. I heered that from a Mex I talked to the other day," the older man said. "You shot one of the posse."

"I'd do it again!" Les flared. "Yance King was eggin' 'em on to get in an' hang Bill!"

The two men looked at each other. The younger man spoke to Les. "I reckon you know Bill was rustlin'?"

"He told me."

"He was with us. We got lost from Bill in all the shootin' that night. Didn't know he'd been hit, or where he was goin'. I reckon you'd better string along with us for a while, youngster. We ain't so good an' we ain't so bad. But Yance King won't git you while we kin handle guns. I'm Sleepy Steve Edwards, an' this is Crazy Tom Jensen. That suit you?"

Les drew an uncomfortable breath. "I wouldn't make much of an outlaw. Bill wouldn't want me to. I better get me a job."

"Maybe you're right, son," Crazy Tom agreed. "But we'll see you in a job before we leave you."

IV

"Ghosts on the Trail"

About 150 miles north of the Brindlebar country, beyond the Four Sisters Mountains, lay the Fox River range. Slocum, the dour foreman of the Fox River Cattle Company's Diamond S Ranch, was a curt and business-like man.

"Les Smith's your name, eh?" Slocum said, giving half his attention to a horse fighting a snub rope in a nearby corral. "And you want a job punchin' cows? Huh?" Slocum stared at the young, eager face. "Ran away from home, didn't you?"

"No, sir," Les denied.

"Where's your folks?"

"Dead."

"I've heard talk like that before. You're too young to punch cows for us. The cook needs a helper. Fifteen a month."

"Your cook's got a new helper, mister," Les said.

Endless buckets of spuds to peel, dirty pans and dishes, greasy dishwater, a hot, smelly kitchen, a sour-tempered cook who cursed loudly at the slightest displeasure, all that was a far cry from school and life on the home ranch. But it was a start, and there was a chance that Slocum would relent about the cowpunching job.

Les knew he'd finally get a riding job. He wasn't cut out for a cook's daily grind. In the meantime, he was earning his own living. Bill would have been proud of that.

Weeks, months—three months and a half—slipped by. Memories of the Brindlebar were fading—until one evening after supper Slocum stepped out of the gathering darkness into the cookhouse doorway.

"Ever been around the Brindlebar country, Smith?" the foreman asked.

Les was swishing a cake of soap in a rag through a pan of scalding dishwater. His hand faltered, his heart began to pound as he lied. "Never been over that way."

"Anyone ever call you Les Shotwell?" Slocum rasped.

Les shook his head and lied again. "Who's Les Shotwell?' he asked.

"By God, Slocum, I told you he was a sneakin', lyin', thievin', all-around bad one!" a voice snarled just outside the door. Yance King stepped over beside the Diamond A foreman.

"My mistake," Slocum said curtly. "If he can lie that cool, I guess he's as bad as you say. You're fired, kid. We don't want your kind around here. I should have had an idea from those guns you brought in with you."

"I'll take him back with me," Yance King snapped, crowding into the doorway. "I've spent three months lookin' for him. We knew how to gentle his kind back at Brindlebar. Come on, you young pup!"

Les had been standing helplessly, heart pounding, a sick feeling growing in the pit of his stomach. His guns were over in the bunkhouse. His horse was out on the grass. Everything had been right—and in a moment Yance King had overturned his life again.

But not quite. Les jerked up the pan and hurled the scalding dishwater fully into Yance King's face. The sheriff's scream of pain was echoed by the foreman's agonized yell as part of the water drenched his face. The pan clattered to the floor as Les dashed for the other door.

Luckily the cook was out for a few minutes. Yance King and the foreman were still blinded and cursing with pain as Les slammed the other door and dashed toward the bunkhouse.

Some of the men had heard the cries and were running from the bunkhouse through the new darkness.

"Slocum wants you!" Les called—and dashed on into the bunkhouse, grabbed up his guns—Bill's old guns—bolted out, and made for the nearest corral where two saddled horses were tied.

Taking the nearest horse, he was in the saddle and riding hard away before he was noticed. Shouted orders to stop were followed by shots. But Les was gone before any pursuit could get under way.

Four days later, outside the sun-baked cow town of Morganville, Les met Sleepy Steve and Crazy Tom Jensen, riding out.

"So you wouldn't stay put." Sleepy Steve grinned. "We been wonderin' about you, kid. You look peaked. They work you too hard on the Diamond A?"

"Yance King hunted me down there."

Crazy Tom cursed the Brindlebar sheriff. "Come along with us, son. You should've done it in the first place. Yance King won't worry you then."

It was as easy as that to jump to the owlhoot trail.

Les didn't think much about it at the time. Sleepy Steve and Crazy Tom were friends, safety, companionship. The next few months were a strange jumble of moving on, stopping now and then for a few days, absences of Crazy Tom and Sleepy Steve. Occasionally they met other men who talked a new jargon: wet cattle, blotted brands, safe buyers. Gunfights were spoken of; reward notices for different men were discussed. When they rode into strange settlements, they kept to themselves. Finally it was natural to help drive a few cattle at night.

Les was a member of the outlaw brotherhood before he realized it. The old ranch days, school, all belonged to a past that was rapidly fading. But Yance King did not fade, or Lucy Morrow. Now and then Les thought of Lucy with an empty feeling in his middle. He remembered her as the prettiest girl he had ever seen; he could see her yellow braids, and he'd always remember her laugh.

Perhaps it was memories of Lucy, or of Bill, that gradually made Les restless, uncertain about his way of life, that finally drove him out once more alone, to work again and earn his living.

"It don't seem right not to work for it," he told Crazy Tom and Sleepy Steve.

Again Crazy Tom nodded slowly. "It ain't for us to say, son. But if ary thing goes wrong . . . you know where to find us."

In months Les had grown years. Good horses, guns, the reckless confidence of the owlhoot did things to one inside that were marked outside. This time old Nat Fargo, a week's hard ride from the Brindlebar range, stroked his short gray bead and said: "I'll give you a try. If you can do a man's work, I'll give you a man's pay, young as you are."

Four times in four months a man's pay was handed to the young fellow who called himself Les Brown. Les worked harder than he ever had before. He liked it. But in all that time he was unable to banish a haunted feeling.

A Saturday night came. Les watched a card game in a saloon in Paloma, the nearest town to the Fargo Ranch, and suddenly looked up to see old Nat Fargo coming through the doorway with Yance King. The same old, sick feeling hit him in the pit of the stomach again.

Nat Fargo pointed.

The bitter, horse-like face of Yance King followed the gesture, and Yance King's harsh voice cut through the room. "By God, I thought so! It's the Shotwell brat! Shuck them guns and stand still!"

Yance King was reaching for his own gun, deliberately, calmly, sure of himself. His gun was out of the holster before Les drew one of Bill's old .45s faster than he ever had before. Men dodged out of the way as the roaring shot smashed the gun out of Yance King's hand.

King staggered over against the bar, bellowing an oath. Confusedly he stared at his bleeding hand, from which one finger was missing. In that moment Les could have killed him. He thought instead of what Bill had told him.

"I don't want no truck with you!" he flung out. "Stand still! You, too, Fargo! I'm leavin'!"

Guns out, Les circled warily around them to the door, whirled on the sidewalk, ran for his horse, and galloped out of town. He kept going, far toward the west and southwest, toward Sleepy Steve and Crazy Tom Jensen. There was a grim, fateful quality about Yance King's hatred of the Shotwells. It promised to be unending.

Days later Crazy Tom heard the story and spoke his mind bluntly. "You should've kilt him, Les. He'll get you sooner or later if you don't."

"All I want is for him to leave me alone," Les said gloomily. "I ain't a killer."

"You're gettin' smart enough to know that's askin' too much," Crazy Tom said bluntly. "But I've told you. Go on an' be a fool an' see how much I care."

But Crazy Tom didn't mean that. Wily, wise, philosophic, he was almost a father by now—the only real father Les had ever known. And in the months and years that followed he taught Les every trick of the outlaw trails. Les found himself liking the life more and more. Here today, somewhere else tomorrow, money in your pocket, new scenes, new faces, friends, excitement, high living. It was a heady life for a youngster. He could laugh at stories that Yance King had threatened to hang him. When an outlaw who Sleepy Steve knew slightly broached a plan for raiding the SR Ranch, some miles south of Brindlebar, Les thought nothing of it.

97

They met the man at Phantom Springs, which was a log store holding a scanty stock of merchandise and a lot of whiskey. One-Eyed Jones, who ran the place, kept a few cattle on the range behind and a bunch of horses near his corral. He had a pockmarked Indian wife who did not speak English, or at least never gave any sign that she understood.

You could get drunk at One-Eyed Jones's Phantom Springs store, hole up there for a day or a month, outfit with fresh horses and grub, leave messages for friends, and get the latest news of the owlhoot trail. So when the bowlegged, little outlaw called Jeff Pitts broached his proposition in an undertone at One-Eyed Jones's dirty little bar, everything seemed natural enough.

"This SR Ranch is loaded with fat cows an' short on riders," Jeff Pitts told Crazy Tom and Sleepy Steve in the gray twilight creeping in from outside. "I was past there the other day an' wishin' to hell I had a couple of good rannies to help me. We can ease down there, cut out a bunch of cattle, an' get cash for 'em before anyone on the SR knows what happened."

One-Eyed Jones had walked out back when he saw heads come together by the bar. It was an old story to him.

Les was drinking water. Crazy Tom had told him not to start on liquor until he was a man full grown, another year yet, anyway. Crazy Tom poured himself another drink, tossed it off, ran his hand through the wild stubble of beard, and mused: "Don't sound so bad, at that! We're runnin' short on money, too."

Pitts tossed off his drink and smacked his lips. His nose was stubby, turned up a little on the end, and his black mustache seemed too big for his narrow, thin mouth. "You'll get plenty of cash outta it." He spoke in a nervous, jerky manner. "The easiest pickin's you've had in a long time. All you got to do is to ride in an' get 'em."

The four of them rode south toward the Brindlebar range that night. They were three days on the way, riding away from the roads, keeping clear of ranch houses, doing most of their moving by night, holing up during the day.

Les did not like the snub-nosed, bowlegged Pitts. On the other hand, it didn't matter. Crazy Tom was running things now. Whatever he did was all right.

They scouted around for a day at the south end of the SR range. The cattle were there right enough, bunches of them: sleek, fat, almost ready for the fall roundup. The four outlaws saw no SR men.

The country through here was broken, rolling, studded with low, stunted trees, dotted with willows and brush along the occasional waterways. Crazy Tom was jubilant as they met beside a small creek and cooked a sketchy meal over a tiny, smokeless fire of dead sticks.

"You got it about right, Pitts," he said. "This'll be easy. Get your food down quick, boys. There's a hundred head of good stuff we can get down that big draw an' out through the wire in no time. We'll boost 'em along all night an' make Skunk Crick by mornin' to bed 'em down."

Crazy Tom knew what he was talking about. He always did in matters like this. They had brought a spare horse apiece from One-Eyed Jones's corral, horses whose brands were strange to this part of the country.

Saddling the fresh horses at the head of the big draw, staking out the old ones up on a slope, they scattered, rounded up the cattle they wanted, and headed them down the draw toward the break in the SR wire, already waiting.

Midnight found them miles from SR land, trailing the cattle under a half moon, with Les following behind with the spare horses. Half an hour before dawn they made

Skunk Creek and threw the cattle into a small grassy draw.

The draw was a quarter of a mile long, a few hundred yards wide. The sides were steep and it came to a head at the upper end. Along the top of the side slopes low trees grew thickly. After watering, the cattle were too tired to think of leaving the draw.

Crazy Tom was satisfied. "If no nosey cowpoke comes ridin' that SR wire where it's been fresh cut, an' finds the trail out, they won't have no idea they been bothered," he said. "Pitts didn't have such a bad idea after all."

Pitts was tired. His thin face was drawn and he was nervous.

"I told you it'd be easy," he said. "Me, I'm gonna get my clothes off, splash in that Skunk Creek water, an' then sleep heavy for a little."

"You must be a mud turtle. I never heard of nobody wallowin' in a creek before they could sleep," Crazy Tom snorted sarcastically.

Jeff Pitts walked down to the creek, out of sight. Les started a pot of coffee halfway up on the side of the draw, by the trees. Sleepy Steve and Crazy Tom were watching the cattle. Without warning a fringe of riders burst in from all sides, shooting.

Les sprang to his feet and jumped across the fire, overturning the pot of coffee. One of the first men he recognized was Yance King. The Brindlebar sheriff had followed them.

V

"Trap for Rustlers"

The cattle were bawling and crowding in the draw below. Through the cold, gray dawn the bitter bark of gunfire rose, high and sharp. Yance King's men were thundering down into the draw. Five of them to every rustler. Their purpose was plain. Lead law—and an end to Crazy Tom's bunch of riders.

Les still wore his belt guns. He had unsaddled and hobbled his horse. Saddle and rifle lay near the fire. Two strides took him to the rifle. Pumping in a shell, he whirled to face two riders who had burst out of the trees not fifty yards away.

They had turned sharply toward him, were riding him down, throwing lead as they came. Les heard the snapping, angry whine of a bullet close to his head as he jerked the rifle to his shoulder and set his finger on the trigger.

The sights settled on the first man, who ducked and tried to swerve his horse. He must have known it was too late. His face twisted into a comical mask of fright. Under his scraggly black mustache his mouth opened soundlessly.

Then the bullet hit him. He swayed far out in the saddle, pitched over toward the ground. The foot on that side hung in the stirrup. The horse dragged him.

The second man, a dozen yards behind, hauled his horse, rearing to a stop. Slickly he slid from the saddle and landed in a crouch, the reins hooked on one arm. Using his six-gun, he fired carefully, taking time to aim.

Les fired as the man hurtled down—and missed the flying target. A bullet fanned his side. Another flicked through the brim of his sombrero. He aimed more carefully, squeezed the trigger. The man tumbled backward and writhed on the ground.

In a span of seconds all that had occurred. Les threw a quick look around. He saw Sleepy Steve's horse running with an empty saddle, saw the cattle stampeding over Sleepy Steve's body.

Crazy Tom Jensen with smoking guns was trying to ride

through the cattle to the slope where Les stood afoot. Crazy Tom was coming to help. All that Les got in one flashing, clear-etched picture.

He saw the man he had shot out of the saddle being dragged along the slope after the bolting horse. He saw Crazy Tom break through the last of the cows and rake hard with big-roweled spurs as he put his horse to the slope. Les saw Yance King, across the draw, jerk his horse to a stop while his other men galloped on. Yance King stood up in the stirrups, lifted a rifle.

Les jerked his own rifle up. But Yance King shot first. Crazy Tom dropped his guns, fell forward across his horse's neck. The animal started to buck. Crazy Tom's limp body went flying through the air. It landed hard, rolled over and over, lay still.

Les fired as Crazy Tom was bucked from the saddle. He saw Yance King go out of the leather, land on a shoulder, and slide to a stop.

Les didn't wait to see if he had killed Yance King. He sprinted along the slope toward the second man he had shot down. That man was still squirming feebly on the ground. His horse, a long-legged black, was backing away, nostrils red and wide with fright. The reins were still locked in the crook of the man's elbow.

As Les raced to the spot, lead kicked spurts of dust near his feet, cut small twigs from the trees at his side, snapped and screamed all about him. He reached the man, tore the reins from the flexed arm, made a flying mount to the saddle as the horse bolted for the trees.

Sleepy Steve was down, trampled, done for. Crazy Tom had gone out of the saddle like a dead man. Jeff Pitts would have to take care of himself.

Plastering himself close down on the black's neck, Les

shut his eyes as the horse crashed into the tangle of growth along the top of the ridge. Branches slashed and raked him. Bullets zipped and slashed through the growth on all sides. The shouts, the crash of guns, the drumming thunder of the pursuit rolled up the slope after him.

Yance King had kept his word. Yance King finally had brought to the last Shotwell the death he had promised. Getting away from that raging pursuit of armed men was a forlorn hope.

A second draw lay on the other side of the ridge. Les burst out on the slope leading down toward it with clothes torn, hands and face scratched, bleeding, but the horse was running strong, the pursuit was still back in the trees.

He cut across the slope, and down, toward the mouth of the draw and Skunk Creek. Willows and cottonwoods grew down there, but on the other side of Skunk Creek the land was more broken. If a man could get across there, and keep going, he might stand a chance.

Bullets again began to snap and lash closely as the first of Yance King's men reached the open. Not forty yards away a small, lean figure plunged on foot out of the willows with a six-gun in each hand. It was Jeff Pitts.

The little outlaw recognized Les. He couldn't have been mistaken as he cut loose with both guns. The first bullet smashed Les's leg near the hip. The shock was like the blow of a club. A quick grab at the saddle horn was the only thing that kept Les from reeling over.

He steadied an instant later. His belt guns were still loaded. Without slackening the black's mad gallop, he drew the right-hand gun and emptied it at Jeff Pitts. The little outlaw wilted where he stood, falling back into the willows, and Les sent the black racing across Skunk Creek, through the brush on the other side, on into the more broken country where cover was better every mile.

Everything was plain now. Jeff Pitts had never met them by chance at Phantom Springs. Jeff Pitts had been looking for them. Yance King had failed to get the last of the Shotwells by fair means, so he had tried foul. He had sent Jeff Pitts to bait the three of them on where he could trap them, cold.

Never had Les been on a horse that could run like the black beneath him. He had sensed it in the first few hundred yards; he found it out in the next half hour. The pursuit dropped back. The pain of the wounded leg increased. It was like that first flight from Yance King after Bill's death. Now, as then, Les kept going doggedly, heading south this time, hour after hour.

Yance King might have kept his men at it, but Yance King was back there in the draw. The weather was hot. Water grew scarcer toward the south. Two of the rustlers had been killed. They didn't have Yance King's smoldering enmity to drive them on a chase that might last for days.

Toward noon, while Les waited in the brushy cover on a high ridge, watching his back trail, no one came after him. He waited two hours, and then crawled painfully back into the saddle and rode on some miles to the next water. There he bathed the raw, open wound. The bullet had torn a jagged hole up toward the hip bone. Les could hardly move the leg. The pain was growing into agony as Les bound it with strips off his shirt, and rode on.

An hour before sunset he sighted the smoke of a homesteader's cabin. Gaunt, hollow-eyed, he rode toward it. Dogs barked as he rode up. A stoop-shouldered, bearded man stepped out to meet him. Behind in the doorway a woman and three children stared curiously.

"I'm shot up," Les told the man bluntly. "I've got

money to pay for my keep. Will you take me in until I can ride on?"

"How'd you get shot up?" the man asked uncertainly.

It was then that the woman came out of the doorway. Her face was broad, kindly, and compassionate. "Never mind what happened, Paw," she said firmly. "Look at the blood on his leg. He's only a boy, too. Help him in. We ain't turnin' anybody away, good or bad, when they're in the fix this boy is."

Her husband seemed ashamed of himself. "That's right, Maw. Light, son. We'll take care o' you," he said heartily, and stepped forward to help Les out of the saddle.

They were nesters named Fitch, poor, hard-working, isolated, and half-wild. Les needed them. He was in a bad shape for days. Several weeks passed before he could ride.

When, once more, he could sit in the saddle, he knew that he would limp a little the rest of his life. The bone had healed wrong. By practicing Jeff found he could disguise most of the limp, and in the saddle he was as good as ever.

The day he left the cabin, Les laid all his money but a twenty-dollar gold piece on the bare wooden table.

"We don't want it," Mrs. Fitch said, tears glistening in her eyes. "We been glad to do what we could, Les."

They called him Les now; they knew he was a rustler, but they had become friends.

"Take it," Les insisted gruffly. "I can get more. Money ain't any pay for what you've done, but it's all I can give you now."

He forced her to take the money. It was more wealth than the Fitches had possessed in years. It would mean a lot to them. They stood in the cabin doorway, mother, father, and kids, and watched him out of sight.

Feeling lonely, Les rode south out of the Brindlebar

country, south toward the dry lands along the border, away from the memory of Yance King and his lasting hate. Crazy Tom and Sleepy Steve were gone. He was on his own now—Les Shotwell, barely eighteen—and life waited, rich and full, beyond the far, hazy horizons.

VI

"Guns for Hire"

New, different, alluring was that border country into which Les Shotwell rode. It was a dry country, a brown-hued land, where the sky was forever blue and the sun warm and bright. Desert and plain rolled across incredible distances. Low mountains swelled against the horizons. Cactus, tarbush, and sharp-spiked Spanish bayonet replaced the willow and greener brush of the Brindlebar range.

Here on the border soft Spanish sounded as often as English, and one quickly grew used to smiling brown faces, to the flat-roofed adobe houses in little *plazas* and on lonely ranches. If the flashing brown eyes and ready laughter of the *señoritas* were different from the girls back home, Les found nothing to dislike about them.

Here along the border the owlhoot trail was broad and wide. Along that invisible line where Yankee law stopped, in the saloons and *cantinas* of a score of towns from the Mexican Gulf to the California sea, roved outlaw faces that graced many a Reward poster. Les met men whose trail he had crossed with Crazy Tom and Sleepy Steve, and others whose names he had heard. A young fellow who could handle his gun with sure, uncanny speed, who could ride tirelessly day and night, who knew every trick of the outlaw trail, always sober, smiling, and without fear did not have to

106

ride alone. A slender, wiry young fellow, with teeth flashing in a dark face, with blond hair slightly curling, who could sit in a poker game all night and day, and then go out to sing gaily of love and life and laughter, could not lack friends.

It seemed to Les in the years he rode the border, and often deeply into old Mexico, that he was finding all that was worthwhile in life. The Brindlebar, the old man and Bill, Sleepy Steve and Crazy Tom, Yance King and his hatred of the Shotwells—all that had been a crazy-quilt picture leading up to this life. Along the furtive trails had come word of that last meeting with Yance King. Crazy Tom and Sleepy Steve had died—and so had Jeff Pitts. But Yance King had recovered and sworn to get Les Shotwell someday. Then four years later came word that Yance King was crippled and sheriff no more. After that all the disquieting memories of the Brindlebar were wiped away. The bitter hate, the lasting enmity of Yance King, which had subtly colored Brindlebar memories, ceased to be a threat.

Out of those early years the memory of Lucy Morrow persisted, fresh and undimmed. Her yellow hair, her ready smile, her warm friendliness clung in Les's mind. He watched constantly for—and never found—a girl who measured up to those memories of Lucy Morrow. Sometimes Les called himself a fool for thinking about Lucy so much, for itching to go back and see her once more. Now and then he heard of Lucy from men who had drifted by the Bridle Cross Ranch. Lucy had not married; Lucy was prettier now than she ever had been as a kid.

But Les did not go back. He was busy. The name, the fame of Les Shotwell had grown with the years. Men of the owlhoot were eager to ride with him, to call him friend, to ask his help when profit was in the air. But Les did not stay with any one bunch long. He remained Les Shotwell, who rode alone. A score of sheriffs along a thousand border miles were apt to swear when his name was mentioned. Men eager to build a reputation by killing the widely known Les Shotwell met his guns and were themselves buried and forgotten.

Les never reached a point where he liked to kill; it was something that had to be done. Without ever deliberately planning to do so, he had progressed to a pinnacle where to survive he had to be ruthless. No longer did he sit with his back to doors and windows. His eyes constantly studied strange faces. His guns—Bill's old guns—were always with him, day and night. That was Les Shotwell at twenty-five, handsome, hard, daring, dashing, with a ready smile and chill blue eyes.

The following spring, in a bar just off the plaza in El Paso, a hand on Les's arm brought him whistling on a heel so swiftly that the owner of the hand stepped hastily back. Several of the customers of the bar knew Les. They grew quiet, watchful. You never could tell what might happen in a moment like this.

Les's right hand was above his gun; he was poised like a hawk ready to swoop. His voice held an edge as he spoke to the short, bearded stranger who had touched his arm. "What's on your mind, stranger?'

"Didn't mean to startle you," the stranger apologized hastily. "Isn't your name Shotwell?"

"Happens to be. And don't put hands on me when I'm not lookin', mister."

"My mistake," said the stranger hurriedly. "Could I have a word with you? Private."

"Come in the back room," Les said briefly. He cast a searching glance about the barroom, and walked behind the stranger into the back room, where half a dozen tables were used for card games.

This morning no one was playing cards. A Mexican with a torn shirt nodded over one of the rear tables, a half-empty bottle of whiskey at his elbow. Les shook the man's shoulder.

"*Vamos,*" he ordered curtly.

"*No quiero,*" the man mumbled, rubbing bleary eyes.

The man looked up, recognized the speaker, and staggered up so hurriedly he knocked the chair over.

"*¡Sí, señor!*" he agreed with a trace of panic. "*¡Sí, sí!*" He lurched rapidly out of the room.

The black-bearded stranger showed white teeth in a smile. "You've got 'em trained, I see. They don't like Les Shotwell, eh?"

"I leave people alone if they leave me alone," Les said curtly. "What's your business, mister?"

"Maybe you've heard of me, Shotwell. Name's Brady." The man looked expectant.

Les shook his head. "I met a Brady in Guadalajara two . . . three years ago, but he wasn't you."

"Brindlebar," Brady suggested. "I was a lawyer when you were a youngster back there. I did legal work for your father."

Les frowned as he tried to remember. His face suddenly cleared. He grinned. "Sure. I remember you, Brady. You didn't have a beard then. Looked younger, too. Sit down. Have a drink."

"Thanks."

Les calmly appropriated the Mexican's bottle and poured drinks.

"Luck," said the lawyer, and drank, and smiled as he turned the empty glass in his fingers. "I was younger then," he said. "And so were you. A lot of dust has blown off the roads since those days. You've made a name for yourself."

Les grinned wryly. "It just happened. I ain't too proud of it. How's everything in Brindlebar? Ever see a girl I used to know . . . Lucy Morrow?"

"Sweet and pretty and never married yet," Brady said promptly. "Funny, too, the way she's held off. All the other girls her age have been married long ago."

"That's queer," Les said slowly. He poured himself another drink and put it down. Maybe it was the whiskey; maybe it was just past memories that made his pulse beat faster. "Might be she's waitin' for some particular fellow to come along," he suggested.

"Maybe," Brady agreed laconically. He leaned elbows on the table and spoke earnestly. "I've been looking for you a long time, Shotwell."

Les lifted his eyebrows and said nothing.

"It's this way," said Brady. "You knew the railroad came through the Brindlebar country several years ago. It brought in a lot of new settlers. They took up free land . . . and now there's a hornet's nest of hell brewing on the whole Brindlebar range."

"How come?"

"A heap of the Brindlebar range always was big ranches," Brady explained. "There were a few small ones, like the one your father had, and Ben Morrow's Bridle Cross, and some others, but most of them were big outfits. In the past ten years a lot of Eastern and English money has been put into Brindlebar land."

Les nodded, listened.

"Those big outfits have been losing cattle fast lately. Maybe not so much as they claim, but a lot. It was natural the new homesteaders would pick up a steer now and then for winter meat, or brand a few mavericks."

"I've branded a few myself," Les said, smiling faintly.

Brady was not embarrassed. "This is different," he stated earnestly. "I'll tell you before I go on, I'm representing the small fellows. Most of them are hard-working family men trying to get along. The big outfits have gotten together and decided the range is going to be rid of them. And the big outfits have money to spend." Brady pounded the table. "The big outfits are bringing in gunmen, paying fancy wages to burn a man's roof over his head, ruin his water, run him off his land, and kill him if he fights back."

Les grinned. "The Brindlebar sounds exciting," he said with irony.

Brady shook his head grimly. "The small men have decided to fight fire with fire. They've pooled their resources and are hiring men to fight as fast as they can find them. Not a man will be driven off his land if guns can keep him there. Why not ride into the Brindlebar and help, Shotwell?"

Les shrugged, said nothing.

"I'll make it pay," Brady said quickly. "That's one reason I came to El Paso. I heard you were here. We need someone to take charge of these gun hands we're hiring. Will you take the job?"

"I'm not a hired gun hand," Les replied shortly. "You turned up the wrong card there, Brady."

The lawyer was not abashed. "Look at it this way," he urged. "You came out of the Brindlebar. You know some of these small ranchers. Men like Jeb Thursday, Dike Winters, Ben Morrow. They were your father's friends once. You don't want to see them run out, do you?"

"Ben Morrow?" Les repeated. He poured himself a drink, took it, scowled at the table.

"Ben Morrow suggested I get you," Brady confessed.

111

"You're the man we need."

"I'll take the job," Les decided abruptly.

VII

"Son of a Sheriff"

Les Shotwell came back to the Brindlebar country alone, as he had left it. Even to himself Les would not admit he was riding back to a dream he had left behind long ago. The brown, dry lands of the south gave way to the greener tones of a familiar landscape. Old landmarks began to appear. Old memories rolled back.

Noon of the last day's ride found some thirty miles still to go. Les was wondering what he would find at the Bridle Cross when out of the solitude through which he rode drifted the clear, thin snapping of distant gunshots.

A piñon-studded ridge a quarter of a mile away barred the view in the direction of the gunshots. Les galloped to the ridge and drew in among the piñons along the crest. Several miles away a dark plume of smoke was climbing lazily toward the turquoise sky. The gunfire was rapidly coming closer. It sounded like men shooting as they rode hard.

Scattered clumps of piñon trees and a rolling landscape restricted the view. The first rider was close, very close, when Les saw him riding bareback, slashing with the rein ends, kicking with his heels as he urged the lathered horse to greater effort. He vanished behind more piñon trees, and, when he reappeared, the sun glinted on a revolver in his hand. Les made out a short beard, saw the man look hastily back over his shoulder as guns began to speak again behind him.

Into the open where the lone rider had first appeared, three riders followed, strung out, pouring leather, snap shooting with rifles as they rode. The chase was coming directly toward the ridge. Les spoke aloud disgustedly. "Three to one! Rifles against a six-gun! That ranny'll lose his hair in another mile!"

Already Les had drawn the rifle from the saddle scabbard. It was Bill's old rifle, as much a part of Les now as his own hand. He drew a sight on the first of the pursuers and squeezed the trigger. The bullet struck the horse at which Les had aimed. The rider pitched off, losing his rifle. He struck the ground hard, tumbled over, staggered groggily to his feet.

The two riders who followed pulled up and stopped. They could see that the fugitive had not fired the shot. Grinning slightly, Les fired again. This time a man lurched in his saddle, and grabbed a shoulder, letting his rifle slide to the ground. They heard the shot, saw where it came from, and realized that help was hidden on that ridge. The wounded man retreated at a gallop, bending low, holding the saddle horn. The other waited for the man who was on foot. Riding double they retreated toward cover.

The fugitive reached the piñons and turned across the slope and came to Les.

"You oughta have a rifle before you make a flight with three rannies like that!" Les called as the man rode near.

A short, reddish beard hid part of the stranger's face. Hatless, his hair was flying awry. Clad in overalls, he wore plain shoes instead of riding boots. He had no cartridge belt or holster for the revolver in his hand. Shoving the gun into the waistband back of his belt he spoke thickly. "Thanks, friend. They were comin' up fast on me."

Les nodded toward the dark plume of smoke in the distance. "Trouble over there?"

"My cabin and haystack," the man said bitterly. "They fired me out, shot my partner, an' tried to get me." He mopped a high, perspiring forehead with a blue bandanna handkerchief, and continued with a harsh, bitter edge to his words. "I tried to be peaceful an' keep my own land . . . but they come down on me anyway! From now on I'll fight 'em till hell freezes over!"

"Fight who?" Les asked.

"Those purse-proud, uppity son-of-bitches who think they own the whole Brindlebar range!" was the violent answer. "And every black-hearted gunman they bring in to burn the roof off a homesteader like me!" The quick glance he shot at Les contained more than a hint of suspicion. "Maybe you made a mistake," he suggested. "Maybe you shot at the wrong ones."

Les grinned. "I wasn't thinkin' about that. It just looked like you needed a little help. But as long as you brought it up, I'm headin' for the Bridle Cross Ranch."

The other's suspicions vanished. "I reckon that explains enough. I'm Angus McDermott. Pete Smith, my partner, is dead. They caught us out in a field before we knew what was happening. I'll ride on to the Bridle Cross with you. What'd you say your name was?"

"I didn't. It's Shotwell."

Angus McDermott wrinkled his forehead, shot a quick glance at Les. "I've heard folks speak of you. Les Shotwell?"

Les nodded.

"A heap of folks will be glad to see you at the Bridle Cross," McDermott declared grimly. "Let's ride on. More'n three men were at my cabin."

McDermott talked as they rode, sketching the violence

that was rising like a crimson tide over the Brindlebar range. He was bitter, hard, desperate. Disgustedly he said: "I'll stop at Brindlebar an' tell the sheriff. 'Twon't do no good, though. The big fellows put him in an' he makes no bones about bein' for 'em. He makes a bluff at bein' fair. 'No fightin' in Brindlebar,' he ordered. But that's only a cover-up for what's out on the range."

Brindlebar was on the way to the Bridle Cross. Les rode into town with McDermott. Brindlebar had not changed much. A few more houses, a little more prosperity, a railroad station, loading pens, steel rails stretching east and west to the outer world. But it was still the same Brindlebar, the same little courthouse, the same sheriff's office that Yance King had occupied in those years he had nursed his hatred of the Shotwells.

They stopped in a barroom, had a drink, then Les rode to the courthouse with Angus McDermott. He waited outside by the hitch rack while McDermott went in to report the outrage on his property.

Les was standing under the towering cottonwoods, smoking a cigarette, when a slender figure emerged from the courthouse and came down the brick walk toward him. He glanced idly, looked back, stared. His heart began to pound. It was Lucy Morrow, a Lucy grown into the bloom of young womanhood—but still the same yellow hair, the same pretty face. The sight gave Les the same tug at the heart that her memory had always brought.

She saw him standing there. Her eyes—those blue eyes Les remembered so well—looked up at him with a cool, almost unseeing glance. He was a stranger to her. Lucy reached the walk, hesitated, looking up and down the street.

"Lucy?" Les said. He couldn't keep a throbbing hoarseness out of his voice.

She glanced at him quickly, frowned slightly. She didn't recognize him; she resented his familiar use of her name. "I don't think I know you," she said, still frowning.

Les had never imagined it would be like this. He was taken aback. "I'm Les," he said. "Les Shotwell."

"Oh!"

A world of meaning was in that one word. Lucy smiled then, uncertainly. She took the hand Les extended. Her fingertips were limp. She was uneasy as she said: "You've been away a long time, haven't you?"

A lump climbed up into Les's throat. He couldn't speak for a minute—he, Les Shotwell of the border country. Misery made him feel like that. A stack of dreams to which he had clung through all these years crashed down between them. Lucy's embarrassment and uncertainty only made it worse.

"I . . . I've often heard of you," Lucy stumbled. She was standing back now, looking at him almost with aversion.

Les nodded, found his voice. "I reckon you have," he replied without visible emotion. "Too bad you had to hear the things you probably have."

"Perhaps lots of it wasn't true," Lucy said vaguely.

"Most of it was true, I guess," Les said woodenly.

Lucy couldn't think of anything to say to that. She asked in the same vague manner: "Are you going to be around here long?"

"Can't tell. I'm going on to the Bridle Cross to see your father."

"Oh!" said Lucy again. An antagonistic light leaped into her blue eyes. Aversion was plain there now. "You're one of . . . *them*," Lucy said.

With that one accented word she classed him with the riff-raff, the professional gunmen who were gathering on the Brindlebar range.

116

"Yes," Les agreed tonelessly. "I'm one of . . . *them.*"

Lucy made no effort to leave. She looked back at the courthouse as if expecting someone and wishing they would hurry so she could leave.

Miserable, awkward, Les almost heaved a sigh of relief as Angus McDermott strode out of the courthouse and came toward them. Behind McDermott came a tall, thin young man with a sheriff's star on the front of his leather vest.

Angus did not look back at the sheriff who followed him down the walk. Nor did he try to keep his angry voice from the sheriff's ears as he drew near. "I knew it wouldn't do any good to stop here! He says he'll look into it, but more'n likely he thinks Pete and I was puttin' our iron on beef that didn't belong to us!"

"Sorry to keep you waiting, Lucy," the sheriff said a moment later. "I was busy."

"That's all right, Jack. I . . . I was talking to . . . to this man. This is Les Shotwell, Jack. You remember him?"

Les had been staring with unbelief. This tall, lanky young sheriff with the bony, bold face was familiar. Only one young man in all the Brindlebar country could look like that—Jack King. Yance King's son! Yance King had been crippled and retired—but his boy wore the sheriff's star for him.

VIII

"Killer Crew"

By the ugly look that leaped into the man's face, Les saw that Yance King's hatred still rode the Brindlebar. The feud had never died; it was here with them now. Once more it was King against Shotwell.

Jack King spoke with the arrogance that had always been

in his father's manner. "What are you doing here, Shotwell?"

"You'll be hearing about it, maybe," Les said.

Jack King looked at Angus McDermott, back at Les. "It's plain!" he snapped. "You're here to make trouble!"

A buggy drove up to the hitch rack. Les saw Angus McDermott watching and did not turn. In him a smoldering anger was rising up to savage pitch. Yance King had killed Bill and the old man. Yance King had made an outlaw out of Les, had run him off the Brindlebar range. Now another King, still guarding the Brindlebar, had snatched Lucy Morrow and all that her memory had meant to Les. It renewed his hatred for the Kings. He wanted to wipe out the King men as Yance King had tried to wipe out the Shotwells.

"I'm here anyway," Les said coldly. "What about it?"

Jack King's voice was stiff with anger. "You're a notorious outlaw, Shotwell. I don't want a man like you in my district. Get going!"

"An' if I don't?"

Jack King was armed, angry. "You'd better!" he warned.

Les laughed at him. "This is as good a chance as you'll have to run me off. Get Lucy out of the way an' go to work. I'm worth a heap of reward money."

Jack King hesitated, moistened his lips. He was pale. Les knew the sheriff was thinking of all those who had died to make the reputation of Les Shotwell.

Lucy Morrow was thinking the same thing. Panic came on her face as she stepped quickly between them. "Don't try to arrest him here, Jack! He'll kill you!"

"Go away, Lucy," Jack King said half-heartedly. "I'll . . . I'll handle him."

Lucy ignored him and spoke to Les fiercely: "Why did you have to come back here? Won't you get out?"

A familiar voice behind Les bawled: "Get outta the way, Jack! I been waitin' years for the dirty son-of-a-bitch!"

Jack King dragged Lucy aside. Only Angus McDermott's quick draw saved Les.

"Hold it!" McDermott yelled.

Les knew as he spun around what he would find. On the buggy seat crouched a bony, hard-faced old man. His mustache was white, the hair under his broad-brimmed Stetson was white, but age had not dulled the hate in his eyes or weakened the hand that had drawn a gun.

But McDermott's quick move, Les's quick spin around had balked the old man. Yance King crouched there in the buggy like a coiled rattler whose prey had moved beyond striking distance.

Les leaped back so that he could see the sheriff, also. It was well he did so. Jack King had started to draw as Les's back swung to him. He snatched his hand away hastily now.

"What'll I do to this old coot in the buggy?" Angus McDermott asked harshly.

"Don't shoot him. This girl might get hurt," Les ordered. "I won't have the heart to face her old man if she's hurt. You two get in the buggy!" he told them. "Drive down the street an' don't look back!"

"Come on, Lucy," Jack King said thickly. He helped her in the buggy, followed her.

"Next time I see a King out on the Brindlebar range, I'll start shootin'," Les said to Yance King.

Yance King dropped his gun in his lap, snatched the whip from the socket, lashed the horse. The buggy careened down the street in a cloud of dust.

Ben Morrow was a big, slow-moving man whose once dark beard was now shot with gray. His welcome at the

Bridle Cross was blunt and frank. "We need you," he said to Les. "Angus McDermott and his partner aren't the first ones, and they won't be the last in this trouble." Ben Morrow and Les were out by the corrals, in the moonlight, where they could talk alone. Les was smoking, Ben vigorously chewing tobacco.

"All I see to do is raise hell twice when they raise it once," Ben Morrow said heavily. "Blood and lead seem to be the only cure. I hate it. All my life I've been a peaceful man. But I won't have a chance along with the rest unless something is done quickly. The QS, the Rafter T, the XOL, and the Lazy Anchor outfits are the main ones behind all this. Clint Breckenridge of the SI is at the bottom of it. These other outfits mostly have absent owners, and Clint Breckenridge has won them to his way of thinking. Yance King has helped it along. He's living on his ranch now, next to Clint Breckenridge. He's with the big fellows, tooth and nail against the small ones."

"What's he aim to get out of it?" Les asked abruptly.

"Power . . . and he thinks the power lies with the big fellows." Ben shrugged his shoulders. "By the looks of our hired gun hands I'd say Yance was right. Ten men I've got. More comin'." Ben hesitated. "But I don't know about them. They're drinking heavily, and they've been acting like they're willing to take over the whole Brindlebar range themselves as soon as enough of them get together here."

"Let's go over to the bunkhouse," Les said, "an' look at them."

Two big oil lanterns lighted the bunkhouse. A card game was going inside. One man lay in a bunk in a drunken slumber. Two more were drinking, talking loudly. They all looked up as Les stepped inside ahead of Ben Morrow.

One look and Les knew them for a bad lot. He had moved

among their kind for years, but there had been few times when he would willingly have mixed with a bunch like this.

"Which one of you calls himself Blizzard Bates?" Les asked slowly, looking around.

"That's me, stranger. What you want?"

The speaker rose from the other side of the card table. He was big, massive, tough. A full, black beard hid most of his face. But thick, full lips could be seen and his eyes were close-set, mean. He wore two guns, leather chaps, and his sleeves were rolled up over massive, hairy arms.

Les looked him over. "I hear you're runnin' this bunch."

Blizzard Bates turned his head and spat on the rusty iron stove behind him.

"What of it?" he challenged, turning back. "Who are you?"

"They call me Les Shotwell. I'm givin' orders now."

A bandy-legged, fox-faced little man pushed his chair back hastily and moved over by the bunks against the wall. "Are you Les Shotwell from down on the border?"

A second man, across the room, who had been drinking from a bottle, said: "He's Les Shotwell, all right. Better watch yourself, Blizzard."

Blizzard Bates threw his cards down on the table and ripped out with an oath. "I've heard of you, Shotwell! But you don't mean nothin' to me! I'm runnin' this bunch! Savvy?"

Without turning his head, Les said: "Morrow, get outta the doorway."

He heard Ben Morrow retreat into the open. The two other men at the table got out of the way quickly.

"You can't bluff me, Shotwell!" Bates warned angrily. "I've heard about you border-jumpers! You strut big over the Mexicans you've kilt! Up in the Jackson Hole country we trim your kind down quick!"

Les grinned. "I'll bet you scare 'em to death with talk. It don't look like you an' me'll get along here. Pack up an' git."

Bates grabbed for a gun without speaking. The blurring speed with which Les met the challenge ended in three shots that made one crashing roll of sound.

Blizzard Bates staggered back against the rusty stove. His gun was on the floor. His right hand was a bloody mess. A second bullet had struck his arm higher up.

"Next one who tries that gets killed," Les said tonelessly. "Get your truck an' ride out of here, Bates. Down on the border we don't even let your kind start to brag. That'll be the one rule around here from now on. I'll do the talkin'. Any objections?"

"By God, no!" the bandy-legged little fellow said hastily. "We came here to fight for pay. If you can give orders better'n Bates, it goes with me."

The other men seemed to feel the same way.

A little later Bates rode off, groaning with pain, swearing under his breath. Where he was heading for no one knew, or cared.

Ben Morrow insisted that Les sleep in the house.

"Just to be sure none of them puts a knife in you when you're asleep," Ben said.

Lucy Morrow was there when they went in. She had just driven home in a buggy.

"You remember Les, don't you, Lucy?" Ben Morrow said.

"I saw him in town today," Lucy replied coldly.

That was all. She went to her room. Ben Morrow looked troubled, but said nothing.

In the morning they met at breakfast. Lucy ignored Les. He could see that she hated him. But there was other business to fill his mind now. Les talked long with Ben Morrow. Two more gunmen rode in. Riders from other small ranches dropped by with messages. Another homesteader had been burned out late in the night.

That evening, at dusk, with a clear understanding of what he was to do, Les rode out of Bridle Cross with his gunmen.

IX

"Raid of the Nesters"

They rode north to the XOL ranch, which was owned by an English syndicate and managed by one Murray, an American cowman. Murray had been on big ranches all his life. He probably had some reason to distrust small ranchers living next to a big spread. Probably he had lost enough cattle in the past to justify his feelings. Whatever the reason, Murray and his men were taking an active part in the range war.

Les and his men swooped down on the XOL headquarters at midnight. They had a grim, cold-blooded job to do—and they did it. Before the XOL men knew what was happening, haystacks were sending spears of flame toward the night sky. As the XOL men tumbled out of the bunkhouses, they were raked by a merciless storm of gunfire. On Les's orders any man who tried to get away was left alone. Those who stayed to fight in the dancing shadows and lurid fire glow were shot down when possible.

The XOL men were out-shot. Les's men dashed in and fired two of the buildings. Whooping, lacing the night with gunfire, they galloped off. Behind them the sullen red glow against the sky served notice that the small ranchers had started to fight with the same weapons that had been used against them.

One of the outlaws had been killed; two more were wounded. But for those risks they were drawing high wages. They scattered, covered their tracks as much as possible, and straggled into the Bridle Cross around dawn.

The tired horses were turned loose, fresh horses were saddled to be ready if needed, black coffee, ham and eggs were served around, and the men tumbled in for sleep.

Angus McDermott had been in the night's raid. He stayed in the house with Ben Morrow and Les, and discussed the next moves.

Ben Morrow was worried, but defiant. "They'll track you men here," he said to Les. "All I hope is you're around when the trouble starts. Next time you'd better take the Lazy Anchor."

"Why not Clint Breckinridge?" McDermott questioned harshly. "He's at the bottom of all this!"

"Burning him out would only make him worse," Ben Morrow stated positively. "If we can sicken the absent owners of these other ranches, maybe they'll get cold feet and call this senseless persecution off. Profits are all they're interested in. If we can make them see they'll get more profit by ranching peacefully than listening to the wild talk of men like Clint Breckenridge and Yance King, the worst will be over. Then we can handle Clint Breckenridge and Yance King."

Les stood up. He was tired, sleepy. "I hope Jack King comes after us," he said grimly. "The sooner he's killed the better. Yance King, too."

Les turned as a passionate voice spoke in the doorway behind him.

"If the sheriff must be killed for doing his duty, God

help us all! Les Shotwell, you're . . . you're more vicious than any reports about you ever suggested. Dad, how can you associate with outlaws and killers like this?"

Lucy wore pink slippers and a gay-flowered dressing gown. Two thick golden braids of her hair framed her face. She was slender and beautiful, and white with anger and scorn.

"Lucy, you go back to bed," her father ordered.

"How can I sleep with a . . . a man like that under the same roof?"

"If you can put up with Jack King, you ought to stand me for a little," Les said to her.

Ben Morrow spoke sternly. "This isn't women's business, Lucy. You and Les went to school together. He's helping us now. You ought to be thankful he's here."

Tears glistened in Lucy's eyes. "He isn't the boy I knew at school. He's cruel, savage, dangerous! His . . . his kind should be killed off like rustlers. If you would keep out of this business, Dad, Jack would see that the Bridle Cross is not harmed."

Ben Morrow lost his temper then. "Damn Jack King!" he told his daughter violently. "What right has he to promise me protection while other men . . . my friends . . . are ruined and driven off their land? Does that young whelp think I'm going to hide behind my daughter's skirts? If he was a real sheriff, he'd be protecting my friends, too! He wouldn't be able to promise I'd be left alone! He damned himself with his own dirty mouth when he told you that!"

"You're headstrong and unreasonable!" Lucy threw at her father. "Jack wants to help you and you won't let him! If . . . if anything happens, it will be your fault. And . . . and nothing you say against Jack makes any difference to me! I think if this keeps up I'll . . . I'll hate you!" Lucy gulped

125

down a sob as she fled to her room.

Ben Morrow finished the black coffee in his cup at a gulp. "I wish her mother was alive," he muttered. "I can't do anything with her. Well, you two had better get to bed. No telling what'll happen today."

Not until late afternoon did much happen. Two riders drifted in from El Paso, sent by Brady. Half a dozen small ranchers rode in. Word had spread swiftly about the raid on the XOL.

Then, later in the afternoon, a cloud of dust marked the approach of many riders.

Les gave his orders calmly: "A rifle at every window in the house and bunkhouse. Hard to tell what'll happen."

At least fifteen men were in the crowd of riders that approached. When they were a quarter of a mile away, Ben Morrow picked up his rifle and sent a bullet over their heads. They stopped. Three men came forward. Jack King was among them.

Ben Morrow, Angus McDermott, and Les stepped out from the front porch to meet them.

"What do you want?" Ben Morrow demanded coldly as they rode up.

Jack King wasted no words. "The XOL was burned out last night, Morrow. The men who did it were traced here. It's my duty as sheriff to warn you that you're harboring outlaws."

"Damn you an' your duty as sheriff, King!"

Jack King ignored Les, who watched him fixedly. "What do you aim to do, Morrow? From all I hear you're the leading spirit in this."

Ben Morrow nodded. "Maybe I am."

"I don't want to see you in this," Jack King said.

126

"Your feelings don't matter a damn to me, King . . . any more than mine do to Clint Breckenridge there! Is that all you came to tell me?"

Les had been watching the short, fat, red-faced man who sat a big bay horse beside the sheriff. He hadn't liked the man from the first sight, and it wasn't on account of the costly silver-studded bridle and saddle, the care and money that had been put on the man's clothes. Breckenridge looked like a pompous little turkey cock. Perhaps it was the eyes that seemed to bulge, the red-veined cheeks, the manner that seemed to indicate the other would like to ride them down.

Now Les stiffened as Breckenridge burst out in high-pitched anger. "I told you it was wasted time to talk to him, Jack! He's thick with all the rest of these small cow thieves! There's only one way to handle them!"

"Whyn't you try it now?" Les suggested. "Ride in an' clean out the Bridle Cross."

Jack King reddened. "There's a woman here."

"That hasn't worried the yellow son-of-bitches who burned out the little fellows!" Ben Morrow snapped. "Woman an' kids didn't mean anything to them!"

Les drew a gun. "I told you to keep away from me, King," he said thinly. "You came here on a truce this time. It's over. Take that red-faced little turkey with you."

Jack King yanked his horse around. "I've done all I can for you, Morrow!" he called angrily.

The posse retreated.

Ben Morrow shook his head wearily as he watched them go. "I'll send Lucy in to town," he muttered half to himself. "I see it comin'. No one can stop it."

That night Les held his men at the Bridle Cross, and nothing happened. Next day more gunmen drifted in. Another small rancher was burned out while they waited at the Bridle Cross. Les had a sizeable bunch of fighters now. He left half of them at the Bridle Cross the next night.

Lucy Morrow had gone to town. Ben Morrow fairly had to drive her. "You're only makin' it worse here for me!" he told her violently. "Go into town where I won't have to worry about you!"

This second night he rode out, Les chose the Lazy Anchor Ranch, far over to the northwest. They rode wide of the Lazy Anchor, came in from the country beyond it. This time they left their horses some distance from the ranch buildings and approached on foot. As Les had expected, guards were out. Two of them were silenced, Indian fashion, before they knew what was happening.

The same scene was repeated, horses run off, haystacks fired. The ranchmen gave shot for shot. But this time Les's men kept to the shadows, in cover. However willing the Lazy Anchor men were to fight, they were mostly cowmen. Les's men were old hands at gun work, cool, steady, deadly. They had the advantage of knowing what they wanted to do, while the Lazy Anchor men had no idea what was coming next.

Clouds hid the moon and helped the attack. The Lazy Anchor buildings were fired, and Les's men scattered, vanished in the darkness, and reached their horses without being pursued.

After that they waited two days at the Bridle Cross. More gunmen rode in. Brady was sending them from the south as fast as he could. Small ranchers sent a hand or two. The whole Brindlebar range knew by now that the great test was quickly coming.

The train from the East brought a stranger to Brindlebar. He rented a buggy and drove out to the Bridle Cross alone. Well dressed, in his fifties, with a sober brown beard, he introduced himself to Ben Morrow as Jason T. Wickliffe, a lawyer from Chicago.

Wickliffe represented the English owners of the Rafter T Ranch. They were alarmed about their investment in the Rafter T. Wickliffe was prepared to make assurances that the Rafter T would have no further part in the range war if its holdings were let alone.

Ben Morrow accepted the proposition instantly. Wickliffe drove back to Brindlebar and came out again in the evening with word that the Scottish owners of the huge QS holdings next to the Rafter T wanted peace at any price, also, if assurance would be given them that their property was safe. The lawyer got the assurance from Ben Morrow, said he would wait in Brindlebar a few days, and left.

Afterward Ben Morrow opened a bottle of whiskey.

"This calls for celebration!" he exclaimed exuberantly. "It's like I said. Hit their pocketbooks hard an' they'll back down. Clint Breckenridge and Yance King will find themselves out on a limb in no time now."

"Maybe they'll see the light, too," Les suggested.

Ben Morrow shook his head. "Nope! They're stubborn. If they can't do anything else now, they'll try to smash me an' a few others who won't knuckle to 'em. That'll leave 'em kingpins on the Brindlebar."

Icy glints were in Les's eyes as he rotated the empty glass in his fingers. "Yance King won't be kingpin anywhere any more. Jack King, either. I'll be on the Brindlebar until I make sure of that."

Ben Morrow looked at him curiously. "You're packin' a heap of hate against Jack King."

"I can still remember my old man and my brother Bill."

Ben Morrow nodded. "Don't know as I blame you. Well, your business ain't mine."

Les moodily rolled a cigarette and walked out of the room. Deep down inside he knew he had lied. It wasn't the old man and Bill. He couldn't put it into words, but he could feel it. Lucy Morrow was the cause. The Kings had won out all along against the Shotwells—even to Lucy Morrow. When Les left the Brindlebar, he meant the score to be settled for good.

Word got around of the QS and Rafter T stand. Many men thought that would bring peace. But early the third night a spent horse galloped to the Bridle Cross buildings.

"Jeb Thursday's place!" the rider yelled. "They're there now!"

Jeb Thursday was the nearest small rancher, not more than six miles away.

"We've got a chance to catch 'em there if we ride hard!" Ben Morrow said hurriedly. "Get your men, Les!"

"You stay with your men an' watch the Bridle Cross," Les said.

"Not while Jeb Thursday needs me! He's one of my oldest friends! We'll all go!"

They left only the wounded at the Bridle Cross and rode hard toward Jeb Thursday's place. But they were still on Bridle Cross land when a rising crimson glow ahead marked the end of Jeb Thursday's buildings.

Out of the night they swept up to the desolation of a lifetime's hard and peaceful work. Roaring flames, great clouds of sparks, infernos at doorways and windows made any help impossible.

The raiders had gone. Jeb Thursday, limping from a bullet wound, was helping two wounded men. Three women and half a dozen children of assorted ages and sizes were out in the open without a home. Fortunately none of the women and children had been hurt.

Jeb Thursday was a gray-mustached man past fifty,

rough as a pine knot from a life of hard work. He stood, favoring his wounded leg, and gazed on the ruin of all he had built. His voice did not waver.

"I'll build again, Ben, after all this is over. I doubt if you can catch 'em. You might try. They rode north."

"We'll try!" Ben Morrow rasped. "I'll leave a couple of men to help you, Jeb. Bring the family over to my house."

"Thank you kindly, Ben. I'll do that soon as we steady things down here."

They rode north, but it was quickly clear that the trail was lost. The raiders had taken a leaf out of Les's book and scattered.

They rode back to the Bridle Cross. Ben Morrow was wrathful.

"They didn't have the nerve to come after me!" he rumbled. "But they picked Jeb because he was closest to me!"

"I ain't so sure about that," Les said. He was troubled. "It was a damn' fool stunt to leave the Bridle Cross alone. We'd better larrup back there in a hurry."

The Bridle Cross was dark, peaceful when they galloped in. But as they wheeled to the corrals to dismount and unsaddle, a fury of gunfire broke out close around them.

Even Les himself, used to violence, was staggered at the effectiveness of that attack. The moon made them fair targets. Horses squealed, bolted. Men pitched out of the saddles.

From windows, doors, shadows on the ground, guns crashed, roared, poured bullets. It was a perfect trap, a slaughter, a hammering, heartbreaking, irresistible sleet of lead that broke Les's men before they knew what was happening. When, out of the night, a wave of riders swarmed in with more guns blazing, the remnants of Les's men bolted. They were the kind to do that if the odds went too much against them.

Les saw that it was hopeless, wheeled his horse, spurred hard out toward the open range. He had been tricked like a tenderfoot. The burning buildings on Jeb Thursday's place had only been a bait to draw the Bridle Cross riders away while the trap was set for their return. It had worked, too. Ben Morrow's Bridle Cross was a shambles. As pursuit drove Les and his scattered riders fast and far, the Bridle Cross buildings went up in flames behind them.

X

"An Army Gathers"

That should have been an end of it. But it wasn't. By noon next day, in Wolf Creek Cañon, far out on the edge of the Brindlebar range, Les's men were still drifting in, dog-tired, hungry, thirsty, many wounded.

Foreseeing some such situation, Les had drilled into every man what must be done. Scatter first, lose pursuit, then ride wide as if leaving the Brindlebar, and meet at Wolf Creek Cañon. Food and ammunition had already been cached there.

But it was a sorry company that gathered. Half of them had been killed or left behind. Ben Morrow did not appear.

"I seen him fall off his horse," one of the men said gloomily.

They were dispirited. But coffee, hot beans, and bacon made them feel better.

Angus McDermott departed at once.

For four days Les waited there in the Wolf Creek country, resting men and horses. By that time their numbers had doubled again. Angus McDermott had spread the word. Other men had picked it up and carried it on. Over all the Brindlebar, to every small ranch and homestead, went the grim message: Now or never. If the Brindlebar was to be safe for the small men, they must come and fight.

They came, sober, hard-faced men, who had worked and wanted only peace, yet who now came loaded with ammunition and guns to fight for that peace. They brought word that Clint Breckenridge had set up drinks for every man in Brindlebar, had boasted loudly how he and Jack King had tricked the bandits who had been holed up at the Bridle Cross. He had driven them off for good, Clint Breckenridge was boasting. Their dead were buried, their wounded in jail. Any outlaw now caught on the Brindlebar without permission would be dealt with promptly—which meant that only those who Clint Breckenridge favored would be spared.

Ben Morrow, badly wounded, was in Brindlebar, being nursed by Lucy. Clint Breckenridge had retired to his SI Ranch with all the armed men he could muster and was sending riders out to scour the range for any outlaws they had missed at the Bridle Cross. Jack King, the sheriff, was swaggering about Brindlebar, backing up the whole business, and spending his evenings with Lucy Morrow.

Les heard all that with a cold, unchanging face. He said little. But on the third day, with only a promise to be back soon, he rode forth alone.

Night in Brindlebar was apt to be quiet. It was this night. If anyone had curiosity about the lone rider who rode slowly through the dark streets, that curiosity was discreetly veiled.

Ben Morrow, badly wounded, lay in a bedroom of the second floor of Doc Biglow's brick house. No guards were posted. Ben Morrow was too ill to be moved by friend or foe. The Biglow hitch bar was empty when Les wrapped the reins of his horse around the wood and walked stiffly to the front porch. Drawn window shades hid the lighted living room, but the nearest window was up, and, as Les stepped on the porch, he heard Lucy Morrow say: "I'll answer the door and save Missus Biglow a trip downstairs."

Jack King said: "Sit still, honey. Maybe it's for me."

Les silently opened the front door and slipped into the dark entrance hall. The living room door opened, light streamed into the hall, and Les plunged into the doorway with a drawn gun.

"Watch yourself, King!" he snapped. As Jack King saw the gun and instinctively raised his hands, Les prodded him back to the living room with the gun muzzle.

Lucy uttered a cry and came out of her chair. "You, again!" She stared at Les from dark-circled eyes.

"Me," Les agreed coldly.

Jack King looked at Les's face. What he saw there made him moisten his lips. "What do you want?" he asked with an effort.

"You," said Les briefly. "I rode in to settle up with you, mister. I'll give you the draw. It's more'n you deserve. Lucy, get outta the room, please."

"No!" Lucy refused in a tight voice. "I'm through running. I came into Brindlebar . . . and my father was almost killed. Now you want me to leave while you kill Jack. I can't hate you now," said Lucy wearily. "And words don't mean anything to you, Les Shotwell. Only violence and death. But if you shoot at Jack, you . . . you can shoot at me, too. I don't think I want to go on alone."

Small and defenseless, utterly tired and forlorn, Lucy looked as she stood there. Jack King was pale, desperate. Les had come hardened to his purpose—but now he repeated: "Alone?" And then: "You love him a lot, don't you?"

Lucy hesitated, then nodded.

"I can't do it then," Les said heavily. "I kind of loved you myself for a good many years, Lucy . . . while I was alone. I don't want you to suffer. Keep him away from all this until it's over. The other men won't feel this way about him."

Fleeting amazement passed over Jack King's face. He looked stunned, unbelieving, slightly ashamed. Then his face reddened. He spoke thickly. "I don't want any favors from you on account of Lucy!"

"You're gettin' 'em in spite of the fact that your old man made me an orphan and then an outlaw," Les said, backing to the door. "I wish I could do more for you, Lucy. Good bye."

"Good bye," Lucy said. It was only a breath of a sound. As Les closed the door, he saw that Lucy was stunned, wondering, also. For the first time her face was free of scorn, contempt, aversion.

That picture Les took to his horse and out into the open night, far from Brindlebar.

Darkness was two hours gone when the Wolf Creek riders reached the small valley where Clint Breckenridge had built his SI Ranch headquarters. Lighted windows warned that the SI was not asleep.

A small stream ran in front of the ranch buildings. Great cottonwoods grew there, and trees grew on the valley slope to within a hundred yards of the barn, corrals, and house. Les waited until he was surrounded by a restless ring of champing horses and silent, waiting riders.

"We're early. Nothing to do but wait for McDermott and his men," he told them.

"Hell . . . why wait? Let's go down an' clean 'em out!"

one of the men said harshly.

As others agreed with him, five rapid reports of a revolver hammered on the night over toward the ranch buildings. Lights went out in the house.

Les swore aloud. "The fat's sizzlin' now, boys! We're spotted! Try to hold 'em in the house until McDermott gets here!"

Thundering through the underbrush, down across the valley slope, the attack advanced. But before it got close, the SI buildings were studded with flaming guns. The men left their horses, crept closer on foot, surrounding the place, fighting Indian fashion. The first furious exchange of shots settled down to rapid sniping on both sides.

Steadily the ring of attacking guns drew in. Men wriggled out over the ground to the corrals, tore down poles, and stampeded the horses. Then the barns were fired.

Once more the night glowed red. Once more flames spewed smoke and red sparks high in the night sky. Breckenridge men stationed in the outbuildings retreated to the massive-walled adobe house.

Midnight came, passed. The flames died to glowing coals. McDermott and his men had not arrived. Les moved about giving orders and encouragement. He was kneeling in the shadows under the sheltering creekbank before the house when a horse galloped up behind him. In the moonlight a woman rode a winded horse through the creek water.

Les stepped out to meet her. His heart began to pound as he saw who it was. In the moonlight he could see that Lucy Morrow wore small boots, a divided skirt, an open blouse, and it seemed to Les that with the moon glow over her face she had never looked prettier. But when Lucy steadied her panting horse and spoke from the saddle, her voice was haunted.

"What are you trying to do, Les?"

"Go back to Brindlebar," Les told her. "This isn't any place for a woman tonight."

Lucy looked down at him. Her voice trembled as she pleaded: "Please stop it. Can't you see men are being murdered uselessly? It will take years for the Brindlebar to recover from this folly. And . . . Jack is in there."

"I didn't know it," Les told her. "You should have kept him in town. I can't stop this now. More men are coming. They aim to clear out this nest of snakes for good."

Lucy choked back a sob. "A man rode to Brindlebar for help! Yance King is bringing men! It will be terrible before it's over!"

"How many men are coming?" Les demanded quickly.

"I've warned you." Lucy gulped. "You'll stay here and be killed! You're blind, heedless, foolish."

Suddenly she broke off, spurred her horse up the creekbank, and raced to the house. The guns stopped firing until she was safely inside. Then Les sent word around to his men.

"Close in on the north end of the house. Get in if you can. I'll take the south end. Be careful of Ben Morrow's girl. She's in there."

The attack paused for a little—then broke in fresh, concentrated fury against the north end of the big house. Windows crashed, guns exploded, men shouted, outside and in.

Les led three men to the south end of the house. With a rifle butt one man smashed a window. Inside the black room, a lone gun blazed out at him. Les sieved the blackness inside with twin streams of lead. The one gun did not fire again. Diving through the window, Les tumbled to the floor inside, tripped over a body. The other men followed as Les reloaded, flicked a match alight, saw they were in a bedroom, and made for the door.

The fighting was still furious at the north end of the house as Les stepped into a hallway. He heard Lucy Morrow's anguished voice beyond a door.

"They're in the house, Mister Breckenridge! Stop it! Don't let any more men get killed!"

The tumult at the other end of the house drowned out all minor sounds. Les yanked the door open, leaped into the dark room beyond, and dodged over to the right in a crouch. A gun blazed at the doorway, firing until it was empty. Les waited, counting the flashes, then placed two tearing shots at the spot, and dodged on across the black room.

Jack King's hoarse voice clipped out: "That's enough! There's a woman in here!"

"Light a lamp!" Les ordered.

It was like standing by an open powder box over which a blazing brand poised. Any instant the guns might start blazing again. A match scratched; at a table against the far wall a lamp glowed.

Lucy Morrow stood beside the lamp. Clint Breckenridge sat near her, favoring a bloody leg, resting on his other knee was a cocked revolver. Beyond the table Jack King stood with a drawn gun. On the floor one of the Breckenridge men lay on his back, bulging eyes staring at the ceiling, a crimson tide covering one side of his stubbled face.

"Drop your guns!" Les told them. "Have your other men come in here an' shuck their guns, too! They'll be safe in here. Don't worry, Lucy, I'll keep your man safe now."

As Les finished, men came running in the front door. Les had been wondering why no one saw the light and rushed to the windows and door of the living room. They were coming now. The door was opening. A face peered in a window.

Lucy cried: "Look out, Les!"

Instinctively Les dodged—but not quickly enough. A gunshot shattered a windowpane. The slamming impact of a bullet in the side of his neck knocked him sprawling on the floor. Groggy with the shock, Les was able to recognize the tall, bearded figure of Yance King, charging into the room with a drawn gun. Old, dried, bitter with hate, Yance King loomed there with his gun cocked, and his snarl was an echo from those long dead years.

"Damn you, Shotwell, I knew I wouldn't die before I nailed your hide."

Men crowded in through the doorway after Yance King. Still groggy, Les realized that the fight outside was rolling back toward the sheltering trees. Jubilant shouts came from the rooms beyond the living room. Yance King's men had beaten off the attack.

That hardly mattered now. Blood was soaking Les's right shoulder. That side and arm were numb, useless. He struggled to a sitting position and met Yance King's venomous look of satisfaction.

"Looks like you got my hide," Les assented weakly. "Nail it, you old buzzard!"

Lucy cried: "No, you can't do that!" She darted in front of Les. Pale, defiant, she faced Yance King. In the lamplight her thick, soft hair had golden tints, and her voice lashed scornfully as she spoke to Yance King. "He could have killed Jack the other night . . . and he didn't! How dare you try to kill him now? Haven't you done enough to him?"

"Not half what I aim to do!"

Clint Breckenridge lunged forward, short, fat, red-faced, pompous as a little turkey cock. But now his bulging eyes flamed with hate and his high-pitched fury rang through the room. "It doesn't matter to me what he did the other night!

I'm killing him myself! Stand back from him, miss!"

"Jack!" Lucy pleaded.

The sheriff had been looking on with mixed emotions. Now he spoke half-heartedly to Breckenridge and his father. "Might as well let him go. I . . . I reckon I owe him that much."

"I don't!" Clint Breckenridge retorted viciously. "No soft-hearted, damn' foolishness is getting him off now! With him out of the way, there won't be any more trouble!"

"Let him go," Jack King urged.

"You keep outta this!" Clint Breckenridge snarled. "Get your girl away from him or I'll drag her off!"

Lucy stood her ground. "I thought there was a man in this room . . . but I was wrong!" she cried. "I've been blind! I thought you were in the right. I'd hoped you'd win! I thought that because Les Shotwell was an outlaw, he was everything bad! I know better now. Yance King, you killed his father and his brother! Last night my father told me how you hounded Les out of two jobs after his brother was killed. You wouldn't let him alone! You made him an outlaw. And yet, because of me, Les let Jack live the other night . . . and now the best you can do is kill him when he's wounded and helpless!"

Uneasy silence fell as Lucy stopped.

Breckenridge broke in with a sneer: "You make a pretty story outta it . . . but it don't mean nothing to me. Get away from him!" Breckenridge limped forward, and, when Lucy tried to push him back, Breckenridge swore, grabbed at her arm.

"Damn you!" Jack King exploded violently. "Take your dirty hands off her!"

Breckenridge whirled on him, crying a furious oath. The gun he held cocked blasted loudly in the low-ceilinged room.

As the heavy bullet drove through his middle, Jack King doubled over. Without speaking, without moving, he opened fire on Cliff Breckenridge. The big gun in his hand roared and jerked as it poured shot after shot into the fat, pompous little man whose rising fury had burst all control. Bullets were still slamming into Breckenridge as he plunged to the floor, and jerked and gasped—and lay still.

Only then did Jack King drop his empty gun and stagger as he turned to Lucy. His face was drawn, bloodless, and over his left hand, pressed against his stomach, a crimson stain was creeping. But Jack King smiled, smiled as Lucy caught his arm and Yance King jumped forward with a choked cry.

"I did the best I could for you, Lucy," Jack King said thickly. "I kinda thought Shotwell was on your mind a lot. I could see you tryin' to be the same to me . . . but you couldn't quite make it. Hang onto him if you get him. An' stop crying."

That last Jack King whispered. His knees gave as he was helped to the nearest chair. Lucy was silently sobbing. Yance King looked like a man blighted by immeasurable tragedy as he gave fierce orders for hot water, a bed, a man to ride for a doctor.

"Don't waste your time," Jack King said with an effort. "I won't last long. All I'm asking you is to do what you can for Lucy."

Just then a fresh wave of gunfire burst on the night outside. A man ran in the doorway shouting: "Put out that light! All hell's busted loose out here! They got help!"

Men ran out of the room, took posts at the windows. One of them blew out the light just as a bullet crashed through a windowpane.

Forgotten for the moment, Les staggered to his feet.

Holding a handkerchief to his neck, he called: "Hold your fire! I'm going outside and try to stop this! Give me a chance!"

A gruff voice answered out of the darkness. "Go ahead! We ain't got nothing to fight for now."

Walking unsteadily, Les passed through the doorway into the night, and shouted: "McDermott! Angus McDermott!"

Off to the left, near the creekbank, Angus McDermott replied: "That you, Shotwell?"

"Yes!"

"They said you was dead!"

"Clint Breckenridge is dead! Jack King is dying! There's been enough killing tonight! Call the men off. There'll be no more trouble!"

"Hold those men in the house quiet until everybody out here hears about it!" McDermott yelled.

Shouts passed through the night as the news traveled swiftly around the attacking circle.

Les turned back to the house—and stopped, and began to tremble as a slender figure came through the moonlight to him. "Go back, Lucy," he said huskily. "It ain't safe out here yet. An' . . . maybe Jack King'd like to have you there right now."

"He's dead," Lucy gasped. "Don't leave me, Les. I'm afraid you'll get away from me again."

Les put an arm around her. He was steady now. "Honey," said Les, "I'm going to stay . . . always."

The guns had stopped. The moonlight flooded about them, bright and peaceful once more. But Les did not know that, or Lucy, either. She had lifted her face, and Les had bent down, and they both knew it would be like this—always.

VALHALLA

T.T. Flynn married Mary C. DeRene at St. Frances deSales Church in the District of Columbia on May 10, 1923. Mary, who Flynn always called Molly, had been born in Baltimore, Maryland on February 12, 1897. Flynn went to work for the railroad, first as a brakeman, and then got a job in a roundhouse. It was at this time that he first began to write fiction. When Flynn was fired from his job in the roundhouse for writing on company time, he decided no one could write part-time. It had to be a full-time vocation, or none at all. Living in Hyattsville, Maryland, with Molly, Flynn continued to work capably and quickly at stories with a variety of different settings, but predominant at this time are railroad backgrounds in much of the fiction published under his byline in *Short Stories* and *Adventure*. Molly suffered from tuberculosis and so Flynn took her to New Mexico because the climate was reputed to be good for those afflicted with lung disorders. She suffered terribly before she died in Santa Fé on August 11, 1929. The perceptive reader might deduce that Flynn had witnessed her passing since his descriptions ever after of death in his fiction could only have been written by a man with first-hand knowledge. There are no grimaces or grins on his corpses, only the frozen vacancy, the terrible silence, the pallor as the blood vanishes from the surface of the skin. Molly Flynn's death certificate does not provide a description of her, but Walt

Coburn, who had met her, did so in his short novel, "Son of the Wild Bunch", in *10 Story Western* (10/36). In this story Pat Flynn, after the death of his wife, leaves their infant son, Jimmy, with Iron Hand and his wife to raise. Jimmy asks Iron Hand's wife what his mother was like, and she tells him: "The most beautiful woman she had ever seen, with blue-black hair and dark blue eyes. Pat Flynn had called her Molly. She had been young. The squaw had picked a wild rose, just out of bud, and had held it out to the boy. 'Like that,' she told Jim." "Valhalla" is one of those early railroad stories, completed on April 1, 1930 and sold on May 25th for $170. It first appeared in *Short Stories* (9/25/30).

The even, staccato beats of a locomotive exhaust came from the direction of the Union Station. The bright sheen of an oncoming headlight spread a strip of silver over the main-line tracks. The Christmas Kid shifted his position on the sills between two freight cars and pocketed a flat automatic. Three steps took him over the coupler to the other side. He peered cautiously out at the oncoming train. It was pulling hard, picking up speed with a long string of Pullmans and a slight upgrade to fight. Sparks flew from the stack, marking faint red streaks above the blinding eye of the headlight.

That eye drew abreast. The blast of the exhaust sounded loudly in the Christmas Kid's ears. He could see the great side rods thrusting back and forth, the red gleaming row of breather holes in the firebox side, the dim lights in the cab, broken for one lurid moment as the jaws of the firebox door opened and the fireman glanced in at the fire.

The Kid could just make out the shadowy figure of the engineer, one hand on the throttle, head and shoulders leaning out of the window. Then the big engine was past, the express car, the mail car, the baggage car, and the Pullman rumbled by. Red signal lights winked a silent farewell above the observation platform on the last car as the first section of the Sundown Limited rolled west.

The Christmas Kid drew a deep breath as he gazed after it for a moment. His throat tightened a little, and he swallowed savagely and muttered an oath as he turned back over the coupler and fished the automatic from his pocket with his left hand. The Christmas Kid was left-handed by design, not choice. His right arm was a withered, useless thing, and long years of practice had enabled him to use his other arm as well as a person who had been born left-handed.

The night was dark, moonless. A few clouds scudding overhead obscured part of the star-studded heavens and deepened the shadows. The Christmas Kid looked down the line of freight cars and listened. There were no sounds. From half a mile away the engine of the Sundown Limited whistled for a grade crossing, and the Kid took note of it instinctively.

There are such things as born railroaders. It comes in the blood and never leaves. The boy gravitates to the shining, twin lines of steel as naturally as a plant stretches toward the sun. Engines, in his eyes, are transformed from inanimate hulks of metal to living beauties with personalities. Coal smoke becomes incense, grease and overalls the accolade of greatness. And if that boy is lucky, one day he takes his place in the life that holds his love, and thenceforth curses affectionately the grind to which he has given himself.

The Christmas Kid was a born railroader. The breaks of life had given him a withered right arm. The irony of it. No cab seat for him, no right-hand seat with a hand on the throttle and the roaring steel road stretching far ahead past signal light after signal light. He couldn't be even a conductor, a brakie, or a baggage man. The men for these jobs had to be strong and tough. Even a news butcher needed two good arms to hold papers and candy and fruit and make change for the customers.

In Marty Henk's speak-easy they would have laughed at the tightening in the Kid's throat as the Sundown Limited rolled by, but they would never know. The Kid didn't think about it that much himself when he was with the gang. Marty Henk's gang. The slickest bunch of boxcar dusters that ever broke a seal and looted a shipment. The irony of it again, or perhaps a sardonic fate. For the Christmas Kid's destiny had finally brought him to the railroad. He was one of Marty Henk's best torpedoes.

Flat automatic ready for instant use, the Kid peered about and listened. The gang was down the line cutting into a juicy shipment that Marty Henk's snifters had gotten a line on. And the Christmas Kid was one of the look-outs. The railroad dicks were canny and watchful. More than once they had broken up a party and forced a gunfight. The Kid had been in several of them himself, been nicked twice with lead, and had dropped his man coolly, although the dick had lived. The Christmas Kid hadn't cared much whether he did or not. He carried a snarl on his lips and an oath in his heart; he was as hard as they come and didn't give a damn who knew it. Perhaps if he hadn't been handed a withered arm and life had given him a better break. . . .

Bells tolled in the direction of the station, faintly. One stopped; the other kept on. That would be the second section of the Sundown pulling slowly out.

A soft scuffle on the cinders nearby marked the planting

of a cautious foot. The Kid tensed and gripped his gun tightly. He peered in the direction of the sound. It was to the left, in the opposite direction from the boxcar that was being looted. But it came nearer. Someone was slipping cautiously toward the spot where Marty Henk's gang was working. No brakeman that, or railroader taking a short cut home through the yards. The fellow was trying to keep out of sight, making as little noise as possible. The Kid let him come on, a step at a time, closer, nearer. . . .

Rigid, motionless, the Kid waited. The soft, barely audible crunches came abreast. Flattened against the end of the boxcar, the Christmas Kid saw a dark form, the bare outline of a gun in an outthrust hand. The guy couldn't be one of the gang. Only one other thing he could be. A dick!

The Kid waited a moment more, then leaped, landing lightly and jamming his automatic in the man's back. "Stick 'em up, you," he snarled softly.

A half whirl of startled surprise, a muttered oath, and two arms went up. Against the lighter portion of the sky overhead a revolver showed starkly in one hand.

"Drop the gat!" husked the Kid.

It fell with a thud into the cinders.

"Who the hell 'er you?" the Kid demanded.

"Who the devil are you?" the man with upraised arms growled back, but the half-hearted utterance of the words showed that he held little doubt on that score.

"I'm de President, an' you're a dick," the Christmas Kid spat. "Who else is gumshoein' around here?"

"Give a guess," was the defiant retort.

There might not be others—and, again, there might. It was no time to make a false move. With a prisoner on his hands he was handicapped. The Kid solved the problem in his own way. A skillful swipe with the barrel of his gun, a dull thump—and his prisoner staggered and slumped to the ground.

The Kid ran for the freight car where the gang was working. Hinky Dink Barretti popped out to meet him, throwing a gat down on him.

"Lay off dat!" panted the Kid. "I jus' slugged a dick back dere. Tell de guys to watch out! Maybe dere's more around! We better lam."

"Aw, hell," growled Hinky Dink, "wrap up your guts, Kid. Don't get boilin' over one dick. He was jes' probably stallin' aroun', huntin' trouble. Go on back an' keep an eye. . . ."

Hinky Dink broke off as a shout came from the other side of the line of freight cars. *Crack!* That was one shot, loud, sharp. *Crack—crack!* The night exploded in turmoil. Shouts, shots, the thud of a dropped box on the floor of the freight car that was being looted. The smash of lead in wooden sidewalls.

"Hell!" exclaimed the Christmas Kid. "One dick! A gang of 'em has laid fer us!

The words were hardly out of his mouth before steps closed in from both sides. Angry red streaks of flame stabbed the black shadows. A bullet clanged against the sheet-steel side of an automobile freight car at the Kid's right hand, and spun up at an angle, whining viciously. Another screeched close by his head.

Hinky Dink dropped to his haunches, crying: "Let 'em have it, Kid!" His automatic spewed shots.

The Christmas Kid scorned to crouch. Flat on his feet he stood, marking the spurts of flame from the officers' guns. The automatic leaped in his fingers. Shot after shot! A dull flick struck his left ear. *Hell!* thought the Kid. *That one was close!* An inch over would have blown his head open.

Hinky Dink uttered a choking cry: "They got me, Kid!"

Shooting a glance, the Kid saw Hinky Dink sprawled in a dark huddle on the cinders, clawing feebly. His gun was silent.

Other flashes joined the ones the Kid had been shooting at. They must have half the riot squad out helping the robbery detail. His gun clicked fruitlessly. The clip was empty. It would take vital seconds to refill with the spare clip in his coat pocket. Hell was still breaking on the other side of the cars, where most of the gang was. But the Kid had a sudden hunch that the gang was getting the worst of it. There were too many men around the spot.

A dark figure came scrambling over the couplers and dropped down beside him.

"Beat it!" a hoarse voice panted. "They got Marty Henk an' Little Abe! There's coppers everywhere!"

Without stopping to say any more, the figure lunged to the right a few steps, trying to escape over the couplers of the next line of cars. One foot was off the ground when its owner spun and crashed heavily to the cinders. And stayed there.

The Christmas Kid wasn't yellow, but he knew when it was time to lam. Clutching the empty automatic, he dived forward and down. Knocking his knees and shoulders, abrading palms on the rough ballast, he scrambled under the car and leaped to his feet on the other side.

A blaze of light surrounded him. The tolling of an engine bell saluted his ears. An exhaust beat loudly around him. A hot blast of steam and oil and grease swept in his face as the big engine hauling the second section of the Sundown Limited rumbled abreast.

The Christmas Kid was trapped momentarily. As he looked swiftly to right and left, a figure scrambled out between the boxcars not many yards away, located him, and shot at him. The bullet tore through his right sleeve.

Trapped, with an empty gun, the Kid acted instinctively. The engine trailer was just rolling past. He jammed his gun in his pocket and snatched at the hand rail that followed. A mighty jerk tore him off his feet. He hung desperately in the air a moment, kicking for a foothold while the fingers of his left hand slipped. His right wasn't much good. A leg swung in past the step, kicked a tank hose. In one tense moment the Kid realized that he was slipping, and would fall under the wheels. Curtains then. Legs gone. Body mangled.

The Christmas Kid sobbed between his teeth, and with a supreme effort brought his withered right arm into use. The fingers got a bit of grip on the lower curve of the tank hand rail. He hung for an instant, one foot shoved against the tank hose, the other knee scraping the edge of the bottom cab step. Then he got the foot on the step, stood up, and climbed weakly into the cab. Marty Henk's mob, the dicks, the gunshots, and battle fell behind, and disappeared.

"For the lovva Mike!" Chris Jenson, the lanky, raw-boned fireman uttered in amazement as he stood with shovel hanging laxly in his fingers and stared at the apparition that had come up out of the night into the cab.

The Christmas Kid was dirty and disheveled from his scramble under the boxcar. One trousers' knee was torn and a trickle of blood marked the path down his jaw and neck from the wounded left ear. But his cap was pulled, low and tight, over his right eye, and he was unabashed and hard as nails.

Chris Jenson moved his shovel, and the Kid grabbed for his pocket and leveled his automatic.

"Drop dat!" he snarled, thinking Jenson was going to attack him with it.

Jenson did as he was ordered.

The engineer, who had been peering intently out at the

frequent signal blocks that studded their way out of the yards, looked over his shoulder and took in the sight.

The engineer—Old Thunder Box, as he was called the length and breadth of the division—had been railroading, boy and man, for over forty years. He was short and broad, grizzled and gruff, with a voice like a foghorn, and no respect for anybody or anything outside of the superintendent and the schedule he had to fight every run.

Now Old Thunder Box's jaw dropped and his eyes blazed as he saw the small, pinched figure of the Kid holding a gun on his fireman.

"What the hell's coming off here?" Old Thunder Box roared, twisting around on the seat box.

But the Christmas Kid, who had just been shooting to the death with a gang of earnest dicks, was not in the least abashed. He had an automatic in his hand, and, if it wasn't loaded, these two men didn't know it.

"Pipe down!" he rasped. "Both you guys be quiet, see! I don't wanna have to put a slug in your guts!"

Old Thunder Box was taken aback for a moment, and then he recovered and barked: "Where did you come from?"

"I flew in for a ride," said the Christmas Kid. "Keep right on goin', mister. I'm makin' part of the trip with you!"

"It's against the rules, see?" Old Thunder Box answered automatically.

"What is this, a hold-up?" Jenson inquired.

"Naw. Don't get all het up. I'm makin' a lam, see? The dicks was right on me heels. So I grabs the first thing that comes along. It's you guys. Let's go. Pep this baby up."

Jenson relaxed as he saw the threat of a hold-up and possible shots fade. Old Thunder Box glared at the skinny figure in the nattily tailored suit, at the pinched, white face of the Kid, with its narrowed, suspicious eyes, at the automatic clenched in taut fingers. A young old man. And then he saw the withered arm and his face softened a little. Just a little. For the harder they bluster to the world, the softer their hearts usually are.

"Step on it!" the Kid ordered. He sidled over to the fireman's seat box and dropped on the leather cushion. "Go ahead an' wrassle your coal," he told Jenson. "I ain't goin' to do nothin' but sit here. But don't make no break with dat shovel or I'll cut loose with me gat! Get me?"

"I get you," Jenson replied. "Don't worry about me. You're holding a free pass for the ride in your hand there." He nodded at the automatic.

The Kid showed his teeth in a grin of appreciation, and then furtively slipped a fresh clip in the automatic as Jenson picked up the scoop and thrust it under the coal gate. His foot felt for the air door pedal. The two steel leaves of the door opened with a hiss that made the Kid start. Jenson began to bail coal, the door opening and closing to each shovel full.

Old Thunder Box leaned out of the window again. Time enough to deal further with this matter after they were out of the city with a clear line ahead.

The Christmas Kid swayed gently on the seat box, automatic resting on his lap, his eyes watching the opening and closing of the fire door. He suddenly grinned. "Say, dat's pretty slick, ain't it?" he shouted above the extra noise.

Jenson nodded as he straightened up and mopped sweat from his face with a red bandanna handkerchief slung around his neck.

"Why don't it stay open till you get t'rough pushin' de coal in?"

"Let too much air in the firebox if the door stayed open that long," Jenson explained. "Cools off the tubes an' don't help the fire any. This way, with the door open only a few seconds each time, not much air can get in."

"Well, now, whaddya know about dat?" the Kid exclaimed admiringly.

His eyes roved about the cab. It was the first time he had ever seen one close in action, the only time he had sat on a cab seat, rocking, swaying gently as the big locomotive rushed through the miles. His pulse began to throb faster. Something was stirring his blood that had never been there before. An exhilaration, a contentment.

"Say, dis is de berries!" He chuckled to himself.

Jenson eyed the drawn automatic, and then went to the right hand gangway and leaned out for a look at the track ahead. The Kid turned his head and glanced out of the open window at his shoulder. They were riding through the suburbs now, bell tolling warningly. Past houses and dark warehouses and factory buildings, past lighted crossings where automobiles and people waited. From his seat the Kid looked down on them and at one crossing waved a tentative hand. A trio of girls standing on the sidewalk answered. The Kid grinned and sat up straighter.

"Dis is sure de real McCoy!" He chuckled again.

Jenson had been watching him out of the corner of his eye. There had been more than one moment when a lunge might have snatched the gun away from the Kid while he was looking out of the window. But—it might not. The Kid wasn't making any trouble. Jenson decided to let matters stand.

The Kid looked at the maze of pipes, valves, gauges, fittings that seemed to be on every side and overhead. He gestured with the gun.

"What's all this for?" he called to Jenson, louder. Speed was picking up, the engine was swaying and rocking more, the pound of side rods, the rumble of great driver wheels,

153

was merging into a pæan of noise that drowned out anything but a shout.

Jenson edged over. "What's what for?"

"All this stuff around! What makes us go? Open up and give me a earful about railroadin'."

Jenson looked at the hunched form of the Christmas Kid doubtfully, and then saw that the Kid was in earnest and began to explain things to him. He pointed out the injector and told how it pushed water in the boiler, the blower pipe that helped the draft, the lubricator that fed oil to valves and cylinders, the water gauge that told how much water was in the boiler and the steam gauge that gave the amount of pressure.

The Kid followed everything attentively, and then pointed to Old Thunder Box, sitting like a grizzled statue behind the throttle. "What's he do?"

Jenson moved over to the other side and the Kid slid off the seat box and followed, the gun held warily before him. He wasn't taking any chances. As he went, he thought of the gang and the dicks far behind in the freight yards. Pretty slick, making a getaway like this.

Old Thunder Box barked: "Now what the blitherin' hell is coming off?"

"He wants to know how to run it," Jenson explained.

"What for? Does he think he's going to pull off a train robbery . . . cut the engine loose and run it down the track?" Old Thunder Box scowled at the Christmas Kid darkly.

The Kid heard the words and grinned at him. "Nuttin' like dat!" he yelled. "I jes' wanna loin t'ings. I been nutty about engines all me life, but I never had a chanct to loin anyt'ing. See?"

"Expect me to believe that?" Old Thunder Box growled under his breath. But there wasn't anything he could do, in the face of that flat, dull-blue gun. He sat and looked on suspiciously as Jenson explained the mysteries of the two brake valves, one for the whole train line and the smaller, independent one for the engine only, and the air reverse, the sander valve, the throttle, the gauge cocks that showed how much water was in the boiler if the water gauge went wrong or the water got below the level of the gauge glass. Twice Jenson had to stop and bail coal in the fire, and the Kid stood back watchfully with the gun ready. He didn't forget for an instant that he was in hostile territory.

They were in the open country now. The speed indicator needle was pointing to fifty-eight. Now and then Old Thunder Box lifted a hand and pulled the whistle lever.

"I bet I could run dis!" the Kid shouted to Old Thunder Box.

That was worse than downright injury. "Well, you won't get a chance!" Old Thunder Box roared with blazing eyes. "Get over there an' stop this damn' foolishness! I got a schedule to keep!"

The Christmas Kid scowled and fingered the gun, and then retreated to the fireman's seat box. He was suddenly back in youngster days when engines were awesome, wonderful things, and an engineer a demigod. He could have forced the old man from the throttle and taken it himself. But something held him back. Him, the Christmas Kid, wanted by the cops on an old shooting rap. That reminded him that he was making a getaway from a fresh charge. If any of the dicks had been killed back there in the freight yards, the members of Marty Henk's mob would be in great demand. Center City was ninety-odd miles away. He knew Big John Vople there. Big John would give him a hide-out until they found out how things were.

The Christmas Kid drew a deep breath and his eyes returned rather wistfully to the long, shiny length of the throttle lever. *Gee, it would be swell to sit over there an' handle that! Swell to feel the urge and surge of the long heavy train, and control it with a slight pressure here and there. Le's see. You pushed that handle of the big brake valve an' the brakes went on or off, an' the dingus called the reverse had to be forward like it was now. An' the farther you pulled out on the throttle, the faster you went. Whoopee! We're sure rollin' now!*

The Sundown Limited *was* rolling. She had a fast schedule and carried an extra fare rate. On time, on time, no excuses. So Old Thunder Box, no matter how much he fumed and frothed at this incongruous situation, sat his box and drove her grimly through the night.

They might have rolled into Center City on time, and the Kid slipped down and away safely, if there had been a little more attention paid to small details at Coalgate Crossing. Coalgate was a junction, a water trough, and a coaling point for such trains as needed coal midway of their runs. The water trough began just over the junction tracks and ran for over a quarter of a mile—a long, slim, narrow, shallow steel trough filled with water. As the speeding train rushed over the trough, a curved scoop worked by air pressure was lowered beneath the tank. It scooped up the long ribbon of water by the force of momentum, throwing it through a one-way valve into the tank.

At the end of the water trough rose the gaunt, black bulk of a coal tipple, straddling the tracks. An engine could stop under it, lower a chute from above, and fill the bin from the overhead coal pockets in a few moments. There had been carelessness at the tipple. A casting had cracked until it hung by a thread of metal. The vibration of the thundering progress of the first section of the Sundown Limited had furnished the final bit of stress needed. The casting had broken at the crack. The long, heavy metal scoop tipped down and hung over the track, and no man knew it.

The Christmas Kid watched Jenson hurl coal into the firebox, two strong arms and a lithe body working in perfect rhythm. A wistfulness that he had never known crept through him. His sense of values was shifting. Gun play, smartness, the cleverness and ruthlessness that cloaked the underworld and Marty Henk's gang did not seem so clever and worthwhile as they had been.

These guys in the cab, that old fellow sitting so grimly behind the throttle peering through his goggles, the strong, active fireman fighting the fire and the steam pressure, had something the Kid never had known. Maybe, thought the Christmas Kid to himself, they were the wise guys after all. No dicks were forever after them, no worrying, planning, watchfulness and distrust all the time. Hell! They ate and slept the same as he did, probably better, and they probably saved their jack instead of gambling it away as he did. And they got to do—this. He looked on enviously.

Old Thunder Box twisted around and yelled to Jenson: "Coalgate Junction! Get ready for water!"

Jenson took a last look at the steam and water gauges and dropped his scoop. He stepped over to the right-hand bulkhead of the tank and took hold of a small control handle there. Old Thunder Box leaned out of the window. Jenson caught the cab hand rail and leaned out, also, watching for the beginning of the trough. The Christmas Kid tensed on his seat, taking it all in.

Old Thunder Box raised his arm and pulled on the whistle lever. They rushed at the small cluster of buildings that nestled about the junction, whistles shrieking. Lights flashed past. The cross tracks of the junction thundered underneath. Jenson moved the scoop valve handle. Sheets of water flew out on either side, and the tank lid clanged as the upthrust of water beat against it.

The Christmas Kid marveled.

"All right!" Old Thunder Box bellowed.

Jenson moved the scoop valve handle back and dropped the metal guard that held it there. And then they rushed under the coal tipple.

Crash!

That was the heavy coal chute striking the front of the cab! It all happened so quickly the mind could hardly grasp it: the smashing hammer of battering steel; the din of breaking glass; the winking out of the cab light; a slight lurch; a smothered, startled scream of surprise from Jenson; then the bellow of the whistle. The Christmas Kid felt a heavy blow in the side, another lighter one on the cheek. He staggered back against the hot boiler front, burning his hand on a dog as he recovered himself. The heavy train rushed on through the night.

The Christmas Kid swiped at his cheek. The fingers came away reddened with blood. Flying glass, or a splinter of wood or steel had done that. By the dim rays of the gauge light he peered dizzily across the cab. The whole side had been wrecked. The grizzled form of Old Thunder Box was slumped down at the side of the seat box, motionless. In the gangway sprawled Jenson, his legs hanging out into the night, his body working queerly with the motions of the tank apron on which he lay.

The Christmas Kid gulped, and swayed a bit as he stood there. A sudden pain in his side drew his attention. Dazedly he made out the jagged end of a piece of window frame protruding. The terrific force had torn the wooden frame loose and driven it across five feet of space into his side. Driven it deeply, breaking ribs and tearing flesh, as cleanly and ruthlessly as ever a knife or a bayonet was thrust home.

The Christmas Kid gulped again. He laid hold of the wood with both hands and gave a tug. Out of the quivering flesh came the long, ragged fragment. A gush of blood welled after it, wetting his underwear and dyeing a dark splotch on the front of his silken shirt. The Kid stared unbelievingly, and then dropped the wood.

"It . . . it cut me guts in two," he muttered dully. The words were lost in the continued blast of the whistle that had been jammed open.

The Christmas Kid stepped unsteadily to Old Thunder Box and knelt beside him. A jagged gash across the forehead, a mass of other cuts were bathing the older man's features in blood. One arm was twisted grotesquely.

From him the Christmas Kid turned to Jenson, dragging the fireman back in, so he would not slide out of the gangway. Jenson was cut up, too, his cap had been knocked off, part of his scalp torn away. But his chest was moving as he breathed.

The Christmas Kid stood upright with an effort, clutching the top of the bulkhead to steady himself against the lurches of the racing engine. He could feel the hot well of blood from the gaping wound in his side. And—inside it felt queer. In that moment a vision of the future came to the Christmas Kid, and he met it like a man.

" 'S coitains fer me," he uttered to the shattered cab, and pressed a hand to his warm, sticky side. "Hell! What'll I do?" His eyes went to Jenson, to Old Thunder Box. "It'll be coitains fer youse guys, too, if you don't get to a doc damn' quick," he whispered, and again the shrieking whistle threw the words back in his teeth.

The sound annoyed him. He went over and groped for the whistle lever. It was still there. He jerked twice, pushed up. The lever went back into place and the whistle stopped.

The Kid thought of the small cluster of buildings around the junction, far to the rear now. No help there. And of Center City, forty miles or so ahead. Doctors there, hospitals, aid, and comfort. Curtains for him—but it might save two men at his feet.

" 'S'help me," the Christmas Kid panted, "I'll drive de whole shootin' match into de station!"

He stooped over and hauled Old Thunder Box across the cab, out of the way. Then he did the same to Jenson, leaving them piled together. The effort pushed more blood out of his side. He could feel it dribbling down his leg. He pressed a hand there in an effort to stop it. When that didn't seem to do much good, he fished out a none-too-clean handkerchief, opened his shirt, and shoved the wadded cloth into the hole. But the handkerchief didn't help inside any.

Hesitating, the Kid placed a foot on the fire-door lever. The two halves of the door flew open. Just as they would for a real fireman. The Kid grinned crookedly, bent over, and looked into the leaping maëlstrom of flame. Everything seemed to be all right for the moment. He lurched over to Old Thunder Box's seat.

The side of the cab was twisted and battered, the windows torn out, the roof sagging down. But he could see out past the long, dark length of the boiler, down the tracks lying shiny and straight in the silver swath of the headlight beam.

A tiny eye of green winked out at the right of the track. A signal block moved up and flashed past. Green—that meant OK. The Kid knew that much about railroading. Green was OK, yellow meant caution, and red trouble.

He caught the smooth end of the throttle, compressed the latch, shoved in a little. The drive of swift exhausts through the stack quieted. The train coasted. He moved the big brake handle that Jenson had said controlled the train brakes. Moved it just a little, experimentally. Air hissed. The train slackened speed a bit.

"Hell!" said the Christmas Kid, vastly pleased. "I can run dis boat like she was built fer me. Watch me step on her."

He put the brake valve handle in its former position, pulled out the throttle again, grinning once more as the rush of exhaust steam bellowed through the stack and the engine surged against the drag of the heavy train. He placed an elbow experimentally on the window ledge, leaning out as he had seen Old Thunder Box do. A blast of wind swept into his bloody face. Cinders drove against it. He needed goggles. He slid from the tent, stepped across the cab, and took Old Thunder Box's goggles, which had not been broken. He slipped them over his eyes and looked through the lenses. Great!

"Ain't I de cheese!" declared the Christmas Kid. He stepped on the fire-door lever and, when the door opened, instantly looked inside again.

"Guess it needs some coal," he decided, and picked up the scoop.

Twice the shovel edge struck the side of the door and scattered coal over the deck. His withered arm handicapped him. As the engine slewed around a curve, the Kid lost his balance and almost fell on his face. The scoops of coal were heavier than he had imagined they would be. He couldn't handle them full with his bum arm. But he worked stubbornly.

He was panting and perspiring when he finally dropped the scoop and straightened up. But there was coal on the fire now. The heavy effort had done something inside. The Christmas Kid felt queer, and weaker.

"Wonder if I can make it?" he husked as he dropped on the engineer's seat.

The cool gale of wind against his face made him feel a

little better. He looked at the speed indicator. An upgrade was slowing the pace into the lower fifties.

"Got to do better'n that!" exclaimed the Kid. He tugged at the throttle. The indicator needle began to move toward sixty again.

It was fantastic, incredible, dangerous. Two unconscious men and a great trainload of people hurtling through the night, with a dying little crippled rat of the underworld at the throttle. The Christmas Kid, face pinched, arm withered, body fatally torn by the flying segment of window frame, leaning out the window like a veteran railroader, suppressed longings of boyhood driving the wine of life in triumph through his veins—and death crouching expectantly at his shoulder.

In Valhalla the souls of the heroes departed make merry and joyous, and wait for the brave coming to join them. The Christmas Kid was coming—at sixty-three miles an hour, the whistle of his great engine shrieking and wailing for a clear way as life ebbed out through the hole in his side. Coming, the Christmas Kid, guns and gangs behind, a crooked smile of contentment on tortured lips.

There never was a ride like it, this race of the Christmas Kid—and death! High, six-foot driving wheels spinning dizzily, heavy driving rods whirling in a blur, exhaust snarling a farewell. When the water got low in the gauge glass, he worked the injector as Jenson had showed him. Now and then he staggered off the seat and dumped coal in the fire.

Green, green, green—the signal blocks marched up and whisked by in a steady procession. The Sundown Limited roared through little hamlets, dark and unseeing, past lonely crossroads. Make way for the Christmas Kid, moving between fire door and throttle! Stumbling, staggering, weaving, and lurching.

Now and then he bent over Old Thunder Box and

Jenson, and did what he could to stop the flow of blood from their wounds and make them rest easier. Behind the goggles his eyes misted. He blinked desperately to keep them clear. His steps began to drag. He had to grit his teeth to make his muscles obey his will. Drowsiness clawed at him. He fought it off stubbornly. If he passed out now, these other two were goners, also.

The Christmas Kid gulped despairingly. "Kin I make it?" He shoved his fist hard into his side, trying with that puny pressure to hold back the end.

Green, green the signal blocks as the miles fled behind. And a moment came when the Kid tried to stand up to coal the fire and couldn't.

"Gawd!" wailed the Kid. "Gimme a break on dis! Gimme a break just dis onct! Dat's all I want! A break! An' den I'll take me rap!"

Even a little rat of a gangster can utter a prayer through tortured, despairing lips—even the Christmas Kid! The pinched body was crouching on the cab seat as the Sundown Limited roared into the twinkling suburbs of Center City.

Through the gathering mists his hand found the throttle and pushed it in. Lights up ahead, far ahead! The station! A last mighty effort brought the Kid's hand to the whistle lever. One mighty blast. And he slumped back and his fingers clasped the brake handle. The Sundown Limited began to slow down.

The lights rushed nearer. Switch frogs clicked. The engine swayed and lurched as it rolled over switch frogs, snaking from one track to another through the yards. A little more brake. The pace slowed further.

The Christmas Kid pushed up the goggles and dug at his eyes, trying to see clearer. More lights. A puffing switch engine. The long sheds of the station, with red-capped porters, baggage trucks, people waiting expectantly, staring curiously at the shattered side of the locomotive cab.

From his high seat the Kid looked down and saw them in a blur. Slower, slower. He gave a last yank at the valve handle. The long length of the Sundown Limited came to a jolting stop.

Word had been wired from Coalgate Junction. Men were there to see about the accident. They swarmed up into the cab. A pinched figure sat on the cab seat and grinned at them with bloody lips.

"Well, youse guys, here we are," croaked the Christmas Kid, and reeled forward into their arms. As they held him in startled wonderment, the Kid grinned weakly. "Gee, it was *great!*" he confided. "Like I always t'ought it would be. Now I'll take me rap!"

The morning papers carried a few lines about that most unusual of the Sundown Limited's runs.

The Christmas Kid, well-known gangster, brought the Sundown Limited into the Center City station last night when the engineer and fireman were knocked unconscious by a broken coal chute hanging down over the track at Coalgate Junction. The Christmas Kid, who was evidently fleeing from the scene of a robbery, was wanted on two indictments for robbery and murder and, had he lived after his unusual feat, would have been taken into custody and forced to stand trial, District Attorney Tuthill stated.

But in Valhalla, way was made for another. The Christmas Kid had found a hide-out.

THE FIGHTING BREED

T.T. Flynn completed this short novel on November 28, 1935. It was sold upon submission to *Star Western* where it appeared under the title "Fugitive Lawman" in the issue dated June, 1936. The author was paid $360. It was subsequently reprinted as "Hunted Lawman" in *.44 Western* (3/53). For its appearance here, the original title and text have been restored.

I

"Lawman"

Deputy Sheriff Larry Remington struck the Río Salado road in the early afternoon, heading for Malpaís on the Gila. Stubble roughed his good-natured face. Hard riding had gaunted him perceptibly, and gunfighting had emptied most of the cartridge loops in his belts. Disappointment rode back to Malpaís with him. But the rest of the posse, which should already be back, might have better news about the bandits who had taken all the cash in the Malpaís bank.

He swung down the Río Salado road, where it curved sharply around the prow-like point of a higher ridge, ran straight for a quarter of a mile, and then turned sharply right between the ridge and the river. He was halfway along this stretch when a rifle snapped thinly somewhere ahead, and a sledge-like blow knocked him reeling in the saddle.

The tough little claybank bronco spun half around and

went into a wild spasm of bucking. A numbness in Larry's side held him helpless. He felt himself slipping, and grabbed for the one thing most important to him at the moment—the old carbine in the saddle scabbard, and dragged it free as he was bucked off. Larry thought he heard a second and third shot, but they missed him. He landed hard, sprawling at the side of the road, shot over the edge, and slid down the steep bank in a cascade of dust and small stones.

A clump of silvery-gray *chamizo* at the bottom stopped him. For a moment he lay helplessly, mouth and nose full of dust, breath gone. The numbness in his side oozed into pain as he finally stirred. Opening his shirt, Larry found the distinct imprint of his gun in the flesh, but no blood, no wound. He had been half-twisted around in the saddle when the blow struck. What had happened was plain. A rifle bullet had smashed squarely into his gun butt, driving the weapon into the flesh, deflecting the bullet.

He grinned grimly to himself at the thought of his narrow escape. That bushwhacker had almost gotten him!

The Salado bank jogged a little here, gullying in slightly where he had slid down. The opposite side of the shallow gully hid him from the crest of the hill where the gun had barked. Quiet once more gripped the spot; only the ripple of the shallow Salado current was audible as Larry reached for the carbine and cautiously wriggled over, and up, to a point where he could see the ridge along the opposite side of the road.

A standing figure was silhouetted against the skyline on top of the ridge near the next turn. Too far away to be recognized, the man held a rifle as he searched the riverbank for some sign of his victim.

Larry carefully pushed the carbine into position,

steadied the sights, and squeezed the trigger. The gun's report seemed to push the silhouetted figure back, down, out of sight. He grinned again, and settled down to wait.

It was a full hour when he scrambled over onto the road in a sudden rush. No shots greeted him. He kept going up the steep slope of the ridge and reached the top, winded but safe.

The claybank horse was standing at the turn, looking up at him. Warily Larry walked along the ridge to the spot where the stranger had dropped. No one was there now, but cigarette smoke and scraps of food showed where the stranger had spent some time waiting. Behind the boulders that had been rolled together, three empty shells marked the spot where the man had lain. Carefully he searched the ground. The sun glinted on a small silver *concha* button almost buried in the dry dirt.

Darkness was falling when Larry reached Malpaís. When he passed Leander Castle's frame house, he called a greeting to Castle, who was watering some flowers beside the front steps. Leander turned his head, saw who it was, and made no reply

That was queer. If Larry hadn't been in such a hurry, he would have stopped and joshed Leander about it. But a little farther on when Coll Baker, the harness maker, answered Larry's greeting by turning his back, walking into the house, and slamming the door, Larry rode on with a frown deepening between his eyes. Coll Baker was a cheery soul who never did anything like that unless something was wrong.

Larry tried not to admit it, but a little knot of worry was gnawing down inside when he stopped at the livery stable to leave the claybank for the night. Sam Scoggins, who ran the livery stable, was tilted back in his chair just inside the wide stable entrance.

"Howdy, Sam." Larry grinned as he swung down out of the saddle. Sam grunted something and stood up as Larry explained: "There's a bullet scratch here to fix, an' I want him curried good an' bedded down right. He's wore out an' earned himself a party for a few days."

Sam Scroggins was comfortably fat and usually placid and cheerful. But now, in the fast falling darkness, his broad face looked unfriendly. Sam's voice was curt, too.

"I ain't got any room for your hoss tonight, Remington."

"What's eatin' you, old-timer?" Larry demanded. "You always did have room to take in my horse."

"Not tonight," Sam retorted flatly. "And don't give me no argument about it. I'm running this here livery stable."

It was strange that Sam Scoggins whose littered, dusty office, smelling of horse liniment and harness oil, had always been one of Larry's favorite loafing places, should act like that! Temper, prodded by Leander Castle and Coll Baker, flared up.

"You always had room for him before!" Larry snapped. "You're takin' him in! *¿Sabe?*"

Sam Scroggins shrugged. "I'll take your hoss," he agreed curtly, "because he's a hoss an' wore out. But it ain't because of you shootin' off your mouth. I'll unsaddle him. Get along to whatever you're gettin' along to."

Larry swallowed his temper. "What's the matter with you, Sam? You never acted like this before."

Sam Scroggins led the claybank back into the dark, pungent depths of the stable. "I ain't arguin' with you," he said over his shoulder. "I took your hoss in. That's all there is to talk about."

Larry turned, walked out the door, and strode down the street. Pete Blythe, the sheriff and Larry's boss, would know about this. Three men in a row wouldn't act as they had without something being wrong, without some reason.

Pete's little one-story frame house, which he and Larry occupied alone now, was at the other end of town. On the way, Larry turned in at the Nugget Bar. Half a dozen horses were out at the hitch rack; eight or ten men were inside. A quick, cold silence fell as Larry entered.

"Whiskey, Luke," Larry said, stopping at the front end of the bar. But the words fell flat, hollow against the unnatural silence of the room.

Larry's face was bleak as he looked along the bar at the men. For the first time since he had come to Malpaís, a ragged, hungry kid, son of a dead outlaw, he felt a wall of unfriendliness closing in around him. Down inside, something began to hurt that this should happen.

"I just got in," Larry said to Bob Langdon, who had ridden out with the posse. "How'd you fellows make out?"

Langdon took a drink of water and replied shortly: "All right, I guess."

The bartender set the bottle and glass down and turned back for water. Larry poured his drink. "Bud Taylor's back, I guess?"

"Bud Taylor's dead. He was brought in this mornin'," Bob Langdon said.

The whiskey bottle almost slipped from Larry's hand. "Who found him?" he demanded unsteadily. "Where was he? Bud was all right last trace I had of him."

Langdon did not answer.

Jess Parker, one of the three Parker brothers—Ed, Mitch, and Jess who owned the P Bar Three Ranch north of the Gila—spoke down the bar with a cold challenge. "Where's the bank's cash you went after?"

Larry gulped his drink. He needed it. "I'm askin' about Bud Taylor right now."

Jess Parker shrugged. "Jughead Taylor'll tell you about

it. He's been lookin' for you."

More customers were coming in just then. Larry nodded and spoke huskily as he turned to see who they were. "I've got to see Jughead. Anybody know where he is?"

"I'm here, damn you!" Jughead Taylor said savagely. "Now let me hear you talk fast before I kill you."

Jughead Taylor looked as ugly as a jughead horse, massive as a mountain pine, with a ragged black beard, a crooked nose, and thick, coarse eyebrows. Jughead had little regard for anyone who crossed him. He was one of the old-timers who had come into the country when the nearest railroad was a thousand miles to the east and Apache raiding parties hunted white settlers more often than they did deer. In those days you had to be tough, stubborn, and a bit savage yourself to live decently against the heavy odds. Those old-timers still had—like Jughead Taylor—a harsh, proud side given to few words and quick action.

Jughead stood half a head taller than Larry. He was armed. So were the four grim Busted Jug men who had followed him in.

Larry felt cold inside. This wasn't the time for emotion. Those Busted Jug men were primed to kill. "Taylor," Larry said, "I don't know what you're talkin' about. They've just told me Bud's dead."

"Yeah. Bud's dead." Jughead Taylor's voice had a tragic, flat emptiness. Bud had meant a lot to him.

"Who killed him?"

Bud's father—he was father of Kareen Taylor, too, the girl Larry was going to marry—stood a few steps away, head slightly forward, his big hands down at his sides. He looked poised, waiting for some action he had already decided on. He spoke again with a harsh indifference, as if not caring much what the answer was. "What kept you out so long after the rest of the posse came in?"

"Mostly tryin' to catch the men Bud an' I followed when the posse split up."

A man coughed. It sounded loudly in the silence that waited for Jughead's next words.

"Was you with Bud all the time?" Jughead demanded.

"You know I wasn't. I'd have known about his bein' dead," Larry replied curtly. "Bud an' I trailed two of the bandits south when the posse scattered. We caught up with 'em an' had a running gunfight till it began to get dark. Then the two men ahead of us split up."

"What made 'em do that?"

"How do I know? Maybe they were short of cartridges. Maybe they thought the rest of the posse was following. Maybe they just figured it was smart. But they split up. Bud took after one, an' I went after the other."

Jughead Taylor made an impatient gesture. His voice cut like the slash of a knife. "Bud knew better'n to split off after a killer who'd be apt to ambush him any minute. Bud'd stay with you, so there'd be one man left to keep fightin' if one got downed."

"Don't tell me what Bud did!" Larry objected. "I was there. He went after one man, an' I went after the other. That's the last I saw of him."

"Whose idea was it?"

"Bud's idea. He didn't want to miss any chance to get back the bank's money. He said you were a heavy stockholder an' the loss would hit you mighty hard if the bank had to close up."

Jughead made another impatient gesture. "Did you get the man you went after?"

Reluctantly Larry had to admit that he hadn't. "I couldn't track him after dark. Next morning I followed the trail half a day an' then lost it. I spent all the next day circlin' south, tryin' to cut it again, an' then landed back where I split off from Bud. Up Bud's trail, I found a dead stranger. Bud had got his man. From there Bud's tracks headed southeast, the way I had gone. It looked to me like Bud was aimin' to cut my tracks an' see what luck I'd had. But I lost Bud's tracks, too, so I headed back to Malpaís."

With that same flat emptiness in his voice, Jughead said: "An' then a couple of men cuttin' across country from Tucson found Bud. He'd been shot in the back an' left there in the open. There was powder burns in the back of his vest. Some envelopes from the bank was scattered around. He got the man with the money, all right. Had the money along with him when he was murdered by an ornery wolf he thought was a friend."

Larry felt every eye in the room on him. He had to moisten his lips and swallow before he could answer. "An' somebody's cooked up the idea I murdered Bud!"

"An' hid the bank's money away until you had need for it," Jughead Taylor added grimly.

"The man who started that is a double-damned liar!" Larry flared. "If he's a man, he'll face me with it!"

Jughead Taylor himself answered. "You're facin' him now! I started the story, Remington, an' there ain't anything in heaven or hell that'll make me believe you're innocent! Bud himself accused you!"

It didn't make sense. Jughead believed it. Everyone else in the room believed it. Larry fought down the desire to gulp another drink. He needed a steady head. "Bud wouldn't have accused me of somethin' I didn't do," he replied with a fierce, growing bitterness. "He was dead, wasn't he? He wouldn't have accused me of anything. It doesn't make sense."

"No one asked you to believe it!" Jughead said savagely. "The fact that you snuck back here to Malpaís, instead of hightailin' it on toward the border is proof you was sure your tracks'd been covered. But Bud outsmarted you, Remington. You shot him in the back, an' left him for dead, but Bud didn't die so easy. He come out of it long enough to open his tally book an' leave word in it for me. Look at this, you cow thief's maverick, before you get hung like your old man did over by Yuma!"

Larry had thought that the story of his past had died with the old man. How Jughead had discovered it didn't matter now. Nothing mattered but the dog-eared little tally book Jughead opened and was holding out.

It was Bud's tally book, all right. The edge of the leaves was stained red. Jughead's gnarled finger held it open toward the back. There was a page smudged with bloody fingerprints. A pencil had left an unsteady, labored scrawl, Bud's last words on earth—Bud's damning accusation left behind to point an accusing finger from the grave.

I'm dying.

Larry done it.

II

"Escape in the Night"

Jughead Taylor shoved the tally book back into his pocket. "Bud hung it on you, so why waste your breath?" he said violently. "Where's the bank's money?"

"Where's Pete Blythe?" Larry said.

"Pete's out lookin' for you, sick as he's been lately. Pete says, if you was his own son an' done a trick like this, he'd hunt you down an' hang you."

Jess Parker interjected sourly: "Seein' as Blythe was the one who kept Remington around these parts in the first place, an' made him deputy, he oughta talk that way. But that's only talk. This deal calls for a new sheriff, like I've been tellin' you all day. An' I ain't the only one who feels that way. . . ."

"Talk about a new sheriff can wait!" Jughead interrupted. "Right now this murderin' son-of-a-bitch here is gonna get the same kind of a send-off his old man got. We'll string him up an' save a trial. But first we got to get that money. The bank's busted without it."

"So Pete thinks I did it, too?" Larry muttered. "Pete's out lookin' for me?"

Sim Leeland, down at the other end of the bar, said: "How you gonna make Remington talk if he sets his mind ag'in' it? He's gonna get hung anyway, ain't he?"

Jess Parker stepped away from the bar, hunching up his gun belt and scowling. "Rope an' drag him out through the prickly pear," Jess suggested grimly. "A little of that an' he'll talk for the favor of a quick, easy hangin'. We all had money in the bank. I guess we can get it back now."

Larry heard that with a stony face. When a man was dragged that way, he died, slow and hard. A rope dallied to a saddle horn dragged him across the rough range, through underbrush and over stones, until life slowly left the bruised, battered body. Few more painful deaths could be devised than a drag through beds of prickly pear where thousands of needle-sharp cactus thorns would break off agonizingly in the flesh.

The four Busted Jug men had their guns out. Larry didn't have a chance to go for his gun, even though they had been careless enough to leave him armed. Jughead Taylor was frowning as he considered Jess Parker's idea.

"Are you gonna tell where you hid that money?" he demanded. "Or do we have to drag you to make you talk?"

"Nothin' I can say will change you," Larry answered bitterly. "What's the use of talkin'? Let's have another drink first." Larry turned to the bar without waiting for a reply. "Drinks are on me, Luke . . . if anyone has got the guts to drink to a trip through the prickly pear."

Luke, the paunchy bartender, looked uncomfortable. Jess Parker stepped to the bar.

"His drinks are as good as anyone's, boys. Line 'em up, Luke. We'll all need a few shots before this is over.

A hard smile came over Larry's face as he saw man after man side the bar and reach for a glass and bottle. "Not drinkin', Jughead? How about you, Mart?" Larry asked, turning to the Busted Jug man who had stayed away from the bar to watch him.

Mart Kelly was squatty and thick-shouldered; his mustache was black, his look always straight and steady. He was Jughead's foreman and had been close to Bud Taylor. Now Mart's big, single-action Colt rested on his hip, hammer back, ready to drop. Mart's reply was disgusted. "I wouldn't drink if you had the last bucket of water an' the last glass of whiskey in hell! Put your liquor down an' whip up your nerve, mister. You're gonna need it!"

Smiling thinly, Larry agreed: "I reckon I will need it, Mart. An' I'm glad there's one man here whose belly ain't bigger'n his convictions."

Larry turned back to the bar—the front end of the bar where he was standing—and pushed his hat back, and with the same motion flipped the hat at Mart and dived for the window not two steps away. Mart Kelly's gun roared.

Larry had figured on that, had known he'd probably get shot. Mart couldn't miss; his bullet got Larry in the

175

shoulder. The deputy's crooked arm crashed through the window glass, and he hurtled outside into the dark night, falling against the ground with stunning force, rolling over, scrambling up, dodging back into the darkness.

Mart Kelly's gun barked through the broken window after him. Inside the saloon, men were shooting, running. Back away from the street, the night was black. Mart Kelly's roaring Colt was shooting wildly in the darkness.

Larry ran through the moonless night, blundering over fences, past houses where dogs barked loudly. Behind him shouting men galloped away from the front of the saloon, spreading out to cut him off.

Here in Malpaís he might go a dozen places. Pete Blythe's little frame house was one place. Sam Scoggins's livery stable was another. Larry could hear riders galloping. Blood was running down his arm. With his bandanna, he plugged the hole as best he could. Then, with a hard smile, he made for the livery stable. Fortunately Sam Scoggins did not keep a dog. But as Larry came up to the back of the stable, someone galloped up to the front. The back door, by the manure pile, was unlocked. Rusty hinges squeaked slightly as Larry entered the black, cavernous interior.

Sam Scoggins and the rider were standing in the dim, yellow halo of a lantern at the front door.

"No telling which way he went. He's afoot. Ain't got a hoss yet that we know of."

"I ain't seen anything of him around here," Sam Scoggins said.

"Better get your gun, Sam. Mart hit him, but, if he gets this far, he'll be able to shoot."

"Damned foolishness lettin' him stand there with his guns," Scoggins grumbled. "If Jughead was gonna kill him, he should have disarmed him."

"The boys had him covered. It wasn't reasonable he'd make a break."

"I'll get out my old gun and cut loose if he shows up," Scoggins declared. When Sam emerged from his littered office, he was grumbling to the rider: "Whatever come over him to shoot Bud that way? He never struck me as likely to do such a trick!"

"Courtin' Kareen Taylor, wasn't he?" the rider answered. "Needed money, didn't he? Another thing nobody knowed until Jughead told it today . . . Bud knowed Remington's old man was hung for a hoss thief. The kid who come here to Malpaís was on the run from the law. His name never was Remington. Bud didn't want his sister to marry that kind of trash, but he hated to bring it out. He never told anyone but Jughead. Now it looks like he might have spoke of it while him an' Remington was out alone, an' Remington did him in for it . . . an' for the money, too. Maybe I better stay here with you, Sam."

"I don't need wet-nursin'," Sam refused grumpily. "I'll sit back there in the dark an' look sharp for him."

After the rider, who had warned Sam, had gone, horses stirred in their stalls. One horse nickered. Rats squealed and scurried in the hayloft. Sam Scoggins was humming dolefully to himself as he carried his chair back into the darker shadows.

The chair creaked as Sam sat heavily on it and tipped back against a stall front. Larry, who had edged noiselessly forward, pushed a gun muzzle against Sam's side. "It's Larry, Sam."

Sam Scoggins almost fell off his chair. "Where . . . where'd you come from?" he stuttered. "Take that damn' gun away."

Larry got Sam's gun and shoved it under his belt. "You

sounded mighty bloodthirsty, Sam. I ought to plug you."

"Was you sneakin' back here, listening?"

"It's mighty revealin' sometimes to hear what others really think about you, Sam."

Sam squirmed in the chair and recovered some of his composure. "I let you know what I thought when you brought your hoss in. I ain't changed my mind any. Take that gun out of my neck. It gives me the creeps."

"It'll give you worse'n that if I don't get my saddle on a fast horse mighty quick, Sam. Do I get it peaceable?"

"With that gun," Sam groaned, "you get the whole darn' stable if you want it. But they'll catch you damned quick."

"Maybe they will," Larry agreed. "I'm plugged pretty bad in the shoulder. But they'll have a wildcat by the tail. Tonight ain't my night to be roped an' hauled through the prickly pear like they was fixin' to do."

Startled, Sam said: "Through the prickly pear? Who aimed to do that?"

"Jess Parker brought it up. Jughead Taylor agreed with him."

Sam was silent for a moment. Then he said: "Take that gun out of my neck. It ain't needed now. Maybe you're a skunk . . . maybe you oughta be hung, but I've knowed you too long to take part in havin' you dragged through any prickly pear."

Sam knew every rusty nail in his livery stable. He moved about in the darkness, grunting, swearing softly. "All right," he said finally, leading the horse out of the stall. "Get goin'. I'll keep the claybank. Don't ever show up around Malpaís again. Understand?"

Pain made Larry wince as he climbed into the saddle. "Tell Pete Blythe I didn't kill Bud an' don't know who did. Somebody tried to dry-gulch me out on the Salado road this afternoon. Maybe there's an answer there."

"Pete's out with a bunch of men lookin' for you right now," Sam said gruffly. "You know what to expect if Pete finds you. Gimme back my gun. It ain't loaded."

"You danged old fire-eatin' hypocrite!" Larry chuckled, tossing the gun on the ground. He rode cautiously out of the entrance and turned north.

The Busted Jug ranch buildings were eight miles north of Malpaís, on Cold Creek. This evening the ranch house windows were lighted. Buckboards and buggies stood back of the house. Strange horses were in the corrals. Neighbors from miles around were inside doing what they could in the way of sympathy and help. Mostly they were women. The men were in Malpaís or out with Sheriff Pete Blythe.

The ranch dogs raised a clamor out in front. A woman visitor opened the front door and peered out. She saw a rider climbing stiffly out of the saddle in front of the porch. He stumbled slightly as he hit the ground. Holding the reins, he spoke to her. "Ma'am, will you ask Kareen to step out here a minute?"

Uncertainly she answered: "Just a minute." She closed the door quickly—too quickly—and hurried back into the parlor with news that had upset her.

"He . . . he's out there in front! Larry Remington's out there asking for Kareen!"

Several men in the crowded parlor came to their feet. One of them rasped out curtly: "All right, boys, I guess we'd better go out and see him."

Kareen was hardly twenty. Grief had hit her hard. She was pale as she turned toward the door. "Don't go out. I'll see him," she said.

They protested. She ignored them. Larry saw her

slender, black-clad figure come out the front door. She closed the door and came toward him.

"Kareen?" Larry said huskily.

A thin thread of hope had persisted in his mind. It died now before the hurt, the scorn, the bitterness in Kareen's reply. "How did you dare come here tonight with . . . with Bud in there in his coffin?"

"I was hoping you wouldn't believe it," Larry said dully. "I thought if one person'd know I didn't do it, it'd be you, Kareen. Why should I have done anything to Bud?"

"I've asked myself that all day," Kareen said unsteadily. "Why? I don't know why. I thought I knew you, but I didn't. At first I wouldn't believe it, then they showed me Bud's tally book. I had to believe it then. Hanging is too good for you, Larry."

"Bud's tally book can't be right," Larry insisted desperately. "I wasn't anywhere near him when he was killed."

The front door opened. A tall figure stepped out into the shadows at one side and closed the door. His hand was halfway under his coat.

"Mitch Parker, huh?" Larry muttered.

Kareen said nothing. The man moved toward them in the darkness. "Everything all right, Kareen?" he asked.

"Do your talkin' back a ways, Parker," Larry warned coldly. "I took enough off your family tonight, when your brother Jess made another play for Pete Blythe's sheriff's job that he's been tryin' so hard to get. Kareen, you'd better go in. There may be trouble out here."

Kareen sobbed with grief and anger. "I won't have any fighting at this house tonight! They'll take care of you soon enough, Larry. Mitch, come into the house with me!"

Mitch Parker—always hot-headed and stubborn—obeyed without argument. Gossip said that Mitch was interested in Kareen. This meek submissiveness was as good proof as any. The front door closed behind them, and the night was black and deserted once more.

Larry felt black and empty inside as he painfully climbed back into the saddle and rode away. No one tried to stop him. But that didn't mean much. Malpaís would soon know he was heading north into the outlaw country—an outlaw himself now.

Larry grinned without mirth at the thought. His old man, dead these many years, would have guffawed loudly at this strange twist of fate that changed him from sheriff's deputy to outlaw in a few hours. Larry's chin dropped on his chest, his shoulders sagging as he rode. He was weaker, but other things were bowing his shoulders—those things he was leaving at Malpaís and at the Busted Jug Ranch. Everything was gone now.

III

"Deputy Turned Outlaw"

The morning star was bright in the gray-black false dawn when Navajo Jack's dogs challenged the lone rider who came to Cow Spring. The small adobe hut, deep in the badlands, was dark and quiet as Larry dismounted, staggering from weakness. A few miles more and he'd have fallen off the horse.

"What you want?" Navajo Jack challenged behind the door.

"It's Remington, from Malpaís," Larry answered. Speech was an effort. He was hanging onto the saddle horse when Navajo Jack came out with a lantern, took one look, handed the lantern to his squaw who had followed, and half carried Larry into the cabin. Vaguely Larry was aware that they worked on his shoulder, that he gulped hot coffee and relaxed.

When he awoke, it was another day, and he was sick; in fact, he was sick for several days. Navajo Jack's squaw dressed the shoulder twice daily with herb preparations of her own. She fed him like a baby, silently, but with an attentive regard in her dark eyes.

Most of the time Navajo Jack was around, impassive, inarticulate, yet alert to every detail. He asked no questions. Larry told him nothing. The first clear-headed day he had, Larry asked for his vest. The three empty rifle shells and the silver *concha* button were still in the pocket.

"Got any idea where this *concha* button came from?" Larry asked.

Navajo Jack turned the silver button between his stubby fingers. He was chunky, muscular, and wore his hair short, American style, and dressed American, too. His dark eyes regarded Larry without expression.

"Where you get this?" Navajo Jack asked.

"Found it where some *hombres* ambushed me on the Salado road."

The squaw was staring at the button. Her husband looked at her. Nothing visible passed between them. She turned away without further interest. Navajo Jack handed the button back.

"Good Navajo silver work," he said vaguely.

"I'd like to find the fellow who dropped it."

"Why he try to shoot you?" Navajo Jack asked slowly.

"I don't know," Larry said from the pallet on the floor where he was lying. "Got any idea who he was?"

Navajo Jack shook his head. "No savvy," he stated.

But Larry thought otherwise. The squaw had had an

idea about that *concha*. Navajo Jack had warned her with a look.

The Woolly Rock district was not one particular nest of outlaws. Spreading over a lot of territory, with bleak, little-known mountains in the north, the Woolly Rock country was a no-man's land into which outlaws could ride and vanish.

They left the ranchers around Malpaís pretty much alone. Pete Blythe had raided, fast and savagely, with hard-shooting posses whenever the outlaws gave cause for such action. Pete's authority had been pretty much respected.

Every day or so riders stopped at Cow Spring to water up, now and then to camp for the night. Some of them came into Navajo Jack's house and ate. All were strangers, easily recognizable as outlaws.

On the eighth day, Larry was hunkered in the sun by the front door when four riders loped into view. Navajo Jack, cross-legged on the ground nearby repairing an old bridle, stared at the approaching men. He stood up on silent, moccasined feet.

"I think maybe you go inside," he said stolidly, and followed Larry in, buckled on a gun belt, took a shotgun from the corner, and went out again.

Larry strapped on his own gun and was waiting inside the doorway when the four rode up. One of them had been past a couple of days before. He spoke to Navajo Jack. "That deputy from Malpaís' stayin' with you, ain't he?"

"Uhn-huh," Navajo Jack grunted.

"He's off his range. We ain't havin' any deputy sheriffs back in here. Trot him out. We'll take care of him."

"This my place," Navajo Jack said. "He's my friend. What you want?"

The man who answered was squatty and powerful, with

a flat, scowling face under the wide brim of an old Stetson. "What the hell you doin' bein' so friendly with a deputy?" he demanded roughly. "You turnin' lawman yourself?"

"This my place," Navajo Jack repeated. "He's my friend."

"Well, friend or no friend, we've come for him."

"Sheriff wants him, too," Navajo Jack said. That was the first hint he had given that passing strangers had brought word of the trouble in Malpaís. "Two hundred dollars reward for him," Navajo Jack said.

The first man sneered. "You can't make an outlaw out of a deputy. Where is he? Inside?"

"You want reward, huh?"

"Hell, no! We ain't turnin' lawmen! We got our own reasons for wantin' him." The speaker dismounted, and went into Navajo Jack's house.

Larry had his six-gun out. Why they had come was a mystery, but it was plain they were primed to kill. Navajo Jack knew it, also. He took a step back toward the doorway. His shotgun muzzle came up.

"¡Vamos!" he ordered tonelessly.

What followed was so quick, so unexpected that even Navajo Jack was caught off guard. A gunshot crashed at the corner of the small hut. Navajo Jack staggered and fired the shotgun. The full charge of shot struck the dismounted man, spinning him back against his horse. He was dying as he fell.

The snorting horse bolted as Larry lunged into the doorway with his gun roaring a challenge. He winged the first man and knocked him out of the saddle with a second shot. A bullet nicked Larry's ear. Another knocked splinters from the doorway beside him. The second man sagged in the saddle, spurred off to one side. Above the crashing roll of guns, Larry heard the sharper snap of a rifle at the corner of the hut. From there a fifth man lurched into view, staggering, weaving, falling. He had approached unnoticed from another quarter and had shot Navajo Jack. In turn he had been shot by someone else. Larry's gun clicked empty. The last rider yanked his horse around and galloped away. The wounded rider followed.

Larry ran out, caught up a handgun from the nearest victim, and emptied it after the retreating pair. They raced unscathed over a rise of ground and vanished.

Navajo Jack's squaw came running from the corner of the hut with a rifle. She dropped the gun and fell on her knees by Navajo Jack. Larry learned then that Indians could be torn by emotion. The little Yaqui squaw was whispering as she cradled her husband's head and shoulders—whimpering, pleading in Indian gutturals.

"Let's have a look," Larry said, kneeling beside her.

A bullet had plowed into Navajo Jack's shoulder and shattered the collar bone; moving up, it had clipped a chunk out of the jaw bone, knocking Navajo Jack unconscious. Both places were bleeding freely.

"Help me get him inside."

She knew little English but she understood that. Calm, steady once more, she helped carry the limp figure inside. Dry-eyed, expressionless, she got clean rags, water, and opened little cloth-wrapped bundles of herbs. That was Indian savvy, better sometimes than a white doctor's efforts. Larry left her there and went outside to reconnoiter.

The two escaping riders had evidently kept going. Two of the men on the ground were dead. The third, shot by Navajo Jack's squaw was dying, with bloody froth on his lips. The rifle bullet had torn a big hole through his chest. His eyes were already closed.

Collecting guns and cartridge belts, Larry went back inside. Navajo Jack was still unconscious. Larry did what he could to help, and presently the herb dressing began to take effect. The bleeding slackened. Nearly an hour after he had been hit, Navajo Jack turned his head slightly and opened his eyes. Later, when he was washed, bandaged, and smoking a cigarette, Navajo Jack spoke weakly.

"They come back. We go."

"In a few days." Larry nodded. "When you're better."

Navajo Jack rolled his eyes at his squaw, squatting beside the fireplace with her pots and pans. "Is better we go now," he said.

If Navajo Jack thought that there was danger, there was. It was sheer madness, however, to move him. He was too weak. Nevertheless, Navajo Jack spoke to his wife. Immediately she began to load a pack horse. Larry helped her.

By dark they had eaten and were on their way. The squaw rode ahead, leading the pack horses. Navajo Jack followed, bowed over in the saddle. Larry rode at his stirrup, alert to help.

They traveled north through the badlands, through waterless country to foothills covered with shrub growth. Some time after midnight, in the faint, clear starlight, they entered a wide, shallow draw that sloped upward for a long distance, ending abruptly in a sandstone cliff a hundred feet high. The black mouth of a cave was barely visible. The squaw dismounted, led the pack horses inside. Navajo Jack had to be helped in. The squaw had lighted a pitch pine sliver that sputtered and flamed smokily, driving back the shadows in a spacious rock room. The floor was sand. The low entrance of a smaller chamber gaped at the back.

Débris on the floor, remains of several old fires against the side walls showed that the place had been used before.

Larry investigated the back room. It was much damper. The sputtering pine flame in his hand revealed a deep pool of water in one corner—cold, clear water, sweet and good. Its presence made the place a natural fortress.

Reassured, Larry took the horses out into the night and staked them close. Before coming in, he stared long at a rising red glow in the far south. He carried the news to Navajo Jack.

"Looks like your place is on fire."

Tough as he was, the ride had about finished the Indian. His reply was a guttural whisper, but at that it had a twist of dry humor. "I savvy so. I like to see them burn this."

The little squaw crooned soothing words as she fussed over her man. The torches burned low. Navajo Jack asked for a smoke. Larry rolled him a cigarette, held a match. Navajo Jack smoked in silence, finally stirred, spoke slowly.

"I don't talk much. Close mouth best. But you better know now, that *concha*. . . ."

Larry cut in: "Take it easy. Tell me *mañana*."

"*¿Quién sabe mañana?* Maybe I'm dead," Navajo Jack said.

"I reckon not. Your number ain't on the cards this deal, Jack. It'd've been up tonight already if it was."

Navajo Jack smiled faintly. In the flickering shadows, his eyes seemed to glow, shrewd eyes that had seen a lot and knew a lot that never passed his lips. But tonight he was talking. "That *concha*," his whispering voice stated, "she's like *conchas* on vest of Missouri Red."

"Who's he?"

"*Muy* bad *hombre*," said Navajo Jack.

"Never heard of him," Larry muttered. Not that it meant anything. The Woolly Rock district held many men who drifted in secretly and kept out of sight. "Why should this

Missouri Red want to kill me?"

"*¿Quién sabe?*" Navajo Jack said.

"Where's he apt to hang out when he's healthy?"

"Sunday School Wells," said Navajo Jack.

Larry whistled softly, considering. You couldn't find Sunday School Wells on the map. In fact, you couldn't find Sunday School Wells at all unless you were cutting north of the Gila through one of the dry, god-forsaken stretches that were useless to man and beast.

In the morning Navajo Jack was stronger. After breakfast Larry said: "I'll drop back in a few days, if everything goes all right. Want anything from Sunday School Wells?"

Navajo Jack grinned, which was unusual for him. "Bag sucker candy for squaw," he said. "Watch out for Missouri Red. He carry knife in shirt."

Larry left them with regret—a renegade Indian who knew how to be grateful and a little squaw who liked sugar candy and was devoted to her man. Larry had a rifle and six-gun, plenty of cartridges, and a knife Navajo Jack had insisted he take. His horse was the one Sam Scoggins had given him. He carried an old water bottle and some strips of jerky.

He was less than five miles from the cave, riding through a small cañon, when half a dozen riders appeared ahead of him, led by the tall, spare, unmistakable figure of Sheriff Pete Blythe.

IV

"Owlhoot Jail"

The man at Pete Blythe's right hand whipped up a rifle and fired a shot. Larry yanked his horse around as the bullet screamed closely. The nearest turn in the cañon was a full 100 yards behind him. Pete Blythe wasn't out here with a posse for his health. As if the gunshot were a signal, a brace of answering shots echoed back in the cañon.

Larry swore under his breath. Pete Blythe's posse evidently had split up to block their man in the cañon. Trapped, Larry hesitated, weighing his chances. The north cañon wall went up in a series of rocky ledges and steep, boulder-strewn slopes studded with scrubby pines and bushes. A horse could not get up that north slope, but a man with luck might stand a chance, if he could dodge bullets fast enough.

Leaving the horse there, Larry took rifle and water bottle and ran for the first slope, the first rocks and bushes. The hammering reports of the posse guns echoed and reëchoed between the cañon walls. Bullets screamed and whined closely as he scrambled into the doubtful shelter of the first bushes. There he stared for a moment in astonishment. Pete Blythe and three of his men were galloping away.

The rest of the posse was bursting around the cañon turn—five—six—eight riders. Larry pumped a shot at them and had the good luck to hit a horse. It stumbled and fell, and the rider went off in a sprawling fall. Four of the men dismounted and hunted cover among the rocks. Three of them retraced their way at a gallop.

Bullets began to slap and spat against the rocks as Larry worked upward, keeping out of sight as much as possible. He had to make it in short rushes, crawling, scrambling, wriggling over the ground. He was sweating and panting before he covered a quarter of the distance. A bullet ricocheted off a boulder beside his head and half blinded one eye with rock dust. Another went through his hat. A third punctured his water bottle.

Larry rolled over on his back and let the water run into his mouth and over his face. If he got out alive, he'd need that water. If he got out! Even when he made it over the cañon rim, safe from the guns below, Larry knew he didn't have much chance.

He was afoot now against a mounted posse. Pete Blythe and his men were galloping along the cañon rim toward him. They saw him, and dismounted, and started to dodge forward on foot, shooting as they came.

The scrubby pine growth was not much cover, but the ground was uneven and rocky. Larry got some cover behind a low, rocky dike that zigzagged some fifty yards or so back from the cañon rim.

A familiar voice, Jess Parker's voice, yelled: "All right, Blythe . . . there's your man! Go get him like you claimed you would."

They had scattered out, fan-shaped, and were working cautiously in toward the dike. Larry went tense as old Pete's familiar voice called to him.

"I'm comin' after you, Larry! I want you to go back, under arrest, an' let the law handle this!"

"You know I wouldn't have a chance with a Malpaís jury! Stay back! Don't make me shoot you!" Larry yelled. "Back, Pete."

Old Pete pleaded: "Larry, don't make me do this!"

Jess Parker yelled: "Go after him, damn it! You're the sheriff and you been tellin' what you'd do! There he is now!"

Pete's reply was not audible. It didn't matter. For Pete was coming like he'd come for other outlaws in the past, a grim old figure dodging forward, single-action Colts out and ready. A lump came in Larry's throat as he watched that gallant charge. For Pete was half blind. Pete didn't have a chance. Pete knew it and knew Larry knew it. Yet he was asking no favors. Straight out, Pete was coming for his man, in the only code of ethics he knew.

The second bunch of riders had ridden up out of the cañon, too, and was coming up behind Larry. Beyond Pete the way was open to the horses. The men had fanned out, leaving Pete to cover that particular stretch of ground. Larry knew he could get past Pete without much danger of getting shot. Pete's eyes were that bad. But if the old man missed such an easy target, Jess Parker would accuse him of doing it on purpose, or else find out about Pete's eyes. Either thing would finish Pete as sheriff, and that would be the end of Pete himself. He'd have nothing else to go on for.

Larry ducked low behind the dike and ran, crouching, to the end. Jess Parker was out that way, bellied down behind more rocks, waiting for the shooting to start—Jess Parker who wanted Pete's job.

Pete didn't even see Larry come around the end of the dike, running hard. None of them did at first. They were watching the spot where Pete was due to tangle with the boy who'd been like his own son. Jess Parker was the first one to see. The surprise was so great Jess came up kneeling, firing a six-gun.

Larry couldn't stop to aim; the other men were off to the left, opening up, too. Gun leaping and roaring in his hand, Larry threw lead at Jess Parker and kept going. Bullets filled the air around him. One of them nicked his leg. He was a good target. Jess Parker should have hit him. But Parker was rattled.

Suddenly Jess Parker wheeled, dropped his gun, and went down out of sight behind the rocks. Larry had to pass between that spot and the other men. Out of the corner of his eye he saw Jess Parker flattening down out of sight. The other men were shooting wildly at him. Back beyond the dike, the second bunch of men were riding hard, yelling encouragement. Ahead, not far ahead, the horses were standing.

Passing the first horse, Larry ran to a long-legged black he had often seen Jess Parker riding. The animal was powerful, fast; it snorted and bolted as Larry hit the saddle and spurred hard.

Larry headed away from the cañon toward country that was even rougher, toward the heart of badlands, toward desert where the country was folded, contorted, twisted, and eroded into a nightmarish landscape. But the rougher the going, the better the protection. Two hours later Larry knew he had picked the best horse and had a chance of losing the posse. Raw, bare lava rock, black and hot under the glaring sun, blotted out his trail, and from then on he rode easier.

When night fell after the long, hard day, Larry was walking his horse. Thirst was sapping at man and beast. The night held little comfort. The bright stars were cold and lonely. To the south, Malpaís had a noose ready for him. On the Busted Jug Ranch, old Jughead Taylor's seething hate was a lasting thing. And Kareen—Kareen was worse than hating. Kareen was dead to all that had passed between them.

Two scrubby cottonwoods stood on the parched, bare flats at Sunday School Wells. A jumble of old adobe houses, some of them roofless and gaping, stood around Friar Tucker's Sunday School store.

Friar Tucker, the big, convivial owner of the store—and most of Sunday School Wells, for that matter—would sell you guns, ammunition, grub, and clothes at fancy prices.

He would take mail out to the nearest post office for you, and get your mail in care of his store under any name you fancied. The latest gossip of the owlhoot was on tap at the Sunday School store, and the biggest collection of Reward notices in the country was tacked on the walls. Your standing was apt to depend on the rewards offered for you.

Over Friar Tucker's long wooden counters, you could buy and sell wet cattle and horses, before or after they had been stolen. You could purchase a man's death as easily as you could buy a blind drunk. You could hire hard-eyed outlaws for any purpose for which you could pay. But you could find no women, and Friar Tucker's high prices were cash to everyone. The jolly lord of Sunday School Wells had an aversion to women and never gave credit.

Larry had been to the Wells several times before. Tonight, when he rode in among the clustered adobe huts to Friar Tucker's store, it seemed to him there were more men than usual at the Wells. They were having a good time inside the low, sprawling adobe building that housed the store. Noisy talk, loud guffaws came out the open door. The voices of two men arguing loudly were audible in the high-walled back yard where the wells—the only water in a long day's ride—were safely closed in.

The backyard gate was open. Larry rode in. The arguing men had gone inside. He watered his horse carefully and drank sparingly himself. The water put new life in him.

The back entrance to the store was a hallway running past several rear rooms. Larry heard men talking in two of those rooms as he walked past. The big front room, part bar, part store, had tables on the floor and a solid mass of Reward notices covering all the bar wall space. He was halfway across the room before he was noticed. Then a bearded man at one of the tables loudly exclaimed:

"My God'lmighty! Look who's here! Ol' man Blythe's deputy!"

Every man stopped what he was doing. Some reached instinctively for their guns. Larry backed up against the counter and eyed the room.

The two survivors of the fracas at Navajo Jack's were not present. Several of the men there Larry knew by sight. The rest were strangers. Taken as a whole they were a hard-bitten, desperate lot. He spoke to the bearded man who had recognized him. Ace Hayden was the name, a former Malpaís man who had gone to California several years before.

"I used to be Blythe's deputy," Larry said. "Right now I'm on the dodge, Hayden. Do I need any more sign?"

A sly stranger with a ragged, tobacco-stained mustache dropped one eye and said: "So you're the feller who killed his sidekick?"

A third man, squatty, long-armed, and powerful, sneered truculently: "So you took the posse after the boys who collected from the Malpaís bank an' then got away with the money yourself?"

"Got any proof to back up that lie?" Larry answered him curtly.

"Proof, hell! You're dodgin' your own sheriff, ain't you? Are you callin' me a liar?"

Men stepped hastily out of the line of argument. With his back to the bar, Larry waited. Soft words did a man no good in a crowd like this. Into the cold, taut silence boomed the cheerful voice of Friar Tucker.

"Drink on the house, boys! Bank money don't matter none tonight. Show the young feller hard luck ain't held against him here."

A hearty yell answered that offer. "Judgment day's a-comin'! Tucker givin' free drinks! How come you couldn't trust me a little while ago, Tucker, seein' you can loosen up now?"

Friar Tucker was a tall, paunchy, bald-headed man whose beaming face belied his cold, blue eyes. Now his fat middle shook as he chuckled. "You boys die off too sudden when a posse catches you. I don't have a chance to collect. This is a stranger's welcome."

Laughter greeted that. Larry took his drink with the rest. He needed it. His guard did not relax. Free drinks were not making some of the men any friendlier.

He looked for a man with red hair who might fit the name of Missouri Red. No one in the room filled the bill.

Friar Tucker spoke to him hospitably: "Stayin' around here long?"

A man guffawed. "Friar's already figurin' how much money the customer'll spend."

Larry said: "This seems to be as safe as any place."

"Safe?" Friar Tucker boomed as he deftly whisked the bottle from a liquored customer who wanted two drinks on the house. "You're safer here than you ever was in your cradle."

"Bueno," Larry said. "Next drinks are on me."

At least they were willing to drink up his money. While they were doing that, Larry lifted his voice.

"Some strangers rode over to Cow Springs yesterday to lift my hair. They didn't all get away. I like my hair. Navajo Jack an' me cleared out of Cow Springs at dark, an' later on somebody came back an' fired Navajo Jack's place. Anybody here know what it's all about?"

Some denied knowledge; some said nothing. Larry caught a few sidewise looks, as if a good many of the men knew something he didn't. When no one seemed disposed to tell him anything, he said: "I was mighty near shot up this morning by a posse from Malpaís. They knew just about where to find me. Somebody carried word to Malpaís where I could be found."

Silence greeted that. Then a tall, bearded man who had not spoken so far asked shortly: "You got any ideas about it yourself?"

"I'm not a mind-reader," Larry said curtly.

"Maybe if you was, your health'd stay better," the speaker said.

Friar Tucker broke in again hopefully: "Who's buyin' next? Loosen up, boys! Your money won't do you no good after you're hung."

"Neither will yours," he was rudely informed. "Stop harpin' on a hangin' noose. You'll spoil my liquor."

Watching, Larry had the growing feeling that something was going on under the surface. Something was being kept from him. Every man in the room was heavily armed. Many of them had come together here at Sunday School Wells. He wondered if it had anything to do with the loot from the Malpaís bank, or with Bud Taylor's death. He couldn't see how. These men also seemed to think he had killed Bud and cached the money. But they knew about that fracas at Navajo Jack's. More than one of them probably knew just how Pete Blythe had known where to find Larry. But they weren't telling. It was to be kept a mystery.

Larry was pouring another drink when a newcomer entered from the back and spoke loudly. "Everybody ready to ride? Where's Jess Parker?"

"Parker isn't here, Red," he was told.

"His horse is out back. I lit a match and read the brand. It's Jess's saddle, too, and his initials burnt in it."

Eyes turned to Larry. Glass in hand, he grinned at them. "Parker was in the posse that jumped me this morning," he said. "I got away on his horse." "Red," they had called the newcomer, who, in fact, did have red hair. His sandy face was wide in the cheek bones, running down to a smallish, sharp chin that gave him a fox-like look. So this was Missouri Red—not the big man Larry had expected to find. Missouri Red was a smallish man, wiry enough, but short, unimposing.

He had stopped, listened intently while Larry spoke. Now he edged forward, like a sidling fox. "So you got Jess Parker's horse?"

"I said so."

Missouri Red limped noticeably, as if a bullet might have hit his leg not so long before. He wore a calfskin vest decorated down the front with a row of silver *concha* buttons. One of the buttons was missing. They had not been close enough that day on the Salado road to recognize faces. Missouri Red proved it now by asking: "Who the hell are you?"

He had been waiting on the Salado road for a man he had never seen. Why? "The name is Remington," Larry said.

Missouri Red stared at him. When he spoke, it was softly. "What are you doing here?"

"Minding my own business," Larry said calmly.

Missouri Red grinned. He seemed in sudden good humor. "Mindin' your own business is the safest thing to do around here," he said, and was still speaking as his hand slapped to his gun.

Larry's intense watching had caught the start of that draw. His own draw was a shade faster. Men were still diving out of the way as his gun shattered the peace of the room. The gun just clearing Missouri Red's holster spun to the floor. Stunned, Missouri Red stood there, moving his arm awkwardly, as if he had no control over it for the moment.

Then he began to curse in high-pitched, shrill fury. "You've had the luck of the devil so far! But it's run out now!"

"Who's run it out?" Larry asked, watching the other men. The thing had been so unexpected he was still startled himself. Missouri Red was going to get help. That was plain. But who was going to be first? No man was drawing a gun. They all seemed spellbound.

Behind Larry, Friar Tucker spoke sadly: "This is a hell of a welcome to give a stranger. Hold still, Remington, or I'll have to blow you from here to there."

Larry felt a double-barreled shotgun nuzzling into his back. He lifted his hands. The man standing next to him reached over and took his gun. The tension in the room relaxed.

Missouri Red had been rubbing his numb arm. He snarled at Friar Tucker: "Why didn't you shoot him?"

"I ain't a butcher," said Friar Tucker indignantly. "It'd be wasting good money anyway. That Malpaís bank money now."

"Damn you . . . what's that to you?" Missouri Red limped to his gun, picked it up with his left hand, and snarled: "Well, let's get rid of the ranny before we leave."

Larry had the cold, detached feeling he always got in a tight corner. But his mind was racing. Why wasn't Missouri Red interested in the money from the Malpaís bank? Why? The man knew what had happened to the money. That meant he knew who had killed Bud Taylor.

"You won't get the bank money by fillin' him full of lead," Friar Tucker protested anxiously.

He was backed up.

"He's right, boys. What's the use of killin' the goose if he's got a good egg hid away?"

Missouri Red snarled: "He ain't got any money hidden away!"

"Maybe you know something about it," Larry challenged.

Friar Tucker said: "You boys was all set to ride outta here. Leave him here with me. He'll be on tap when you get back."

The missing loot from the Malpaís bank did the trick. Missouri Red was against it, but what little authority he seemed to have crumbled before that lure.

"I'll lock him up in the hog pen," Friar Tucker stated. "He'll be sittin' there safe when you get back."

The hog pen proved to be a windowless room in a back corner of the building, fitted with a door of iron bars. At any other time it would have been a joke—Sunday School Wells, outlaw headquarters, with a private jail of its own. Men crowded into the passage to see Larry locked up. Friar Tucker elaborately put the key into his pocket. Then they returned to the bar for a final round of drinks.

Before long Larry heard them straggling out into the back yard. Once started, they were quickly gone in a drumming roll of hoofs and a few shrill yells.

Some voices still drifted back from the bar. They presently died away. Larry heard doors slamming. Then steps came back along the passage.

Friar Tucker stopped before the barred door and set a lantern on the floor. In the dim light and shifting shadows he loomed big, plump, and jolly once more.

"Now then," he said, "I reckon we can get down to business."

"Maybe. Where'd that bunch head for?"

"I didn't ask questions, an' the boys don't tell me anything," Friar Tucker replied smoothly.

He was lying, but that didn't matter. "What's this Missouri Red?" Larry questioned.

"Came in from California with Ace Hayden. Never mind that. Let's talk about this here missing money. I had to peel you away from your guns a while ago. But now that we're alone," said Friar Tucker expansively, "you'll find me different."

"That's mighty fine," said Larry. "Unlock this door, an' let's talk."

"As I was sayin'," Friar Tucker went on, without making a move toward the door, "you're in a fix. When the boys get back, Missouri Red'll kill you. He's that kind. Packs a long memory, he does. Now if you could see your way clear about that bank money, maybe somethin' could be cooked up. The boys might not like it, but I can handle 'em."

"How about something to eat first?"

"Sure, right away. A man feels better when his belly's full. I'll get you some grub."

Tucker was as good as his word. He returned with cold meat and bread on a plate, and a tin cup of steaming black coffee. There was a small square opening in the bars for just that sort of thing.

"Gimme the coffee first," Larry begged.

Tucker passed it through. The tin cup was hot. Larry took a gulp of the scalding coffee and reached for the plate. Tucker shoved it through. The light was poor. Before Tucker had any idea of what was happening, the scalding coffee hit him in the eyes and his wrist was grabbed and yanked through the opening.

V

"Back to the Busted Jug"

Tucker's yell of pain met the rattle of the barrel door as he was jerked against it. Using the bottom of the opening for a fulcrum, Larry twisted the arm. Tucker squalled with the pain. He had no gun. His greater size and weight were no good to him now.

"My God, you're breakin' my arm! My eyes is scalded out!"

"Gentle down then!" Larry gritted. "Get out your key and unlock this door!"

Groaning, Friar Tucker groped into his pocket, found the key, blinked through the coffee, and got the key into the lock with no effort. "Who else is inside?" Larry asked.

"No one! I run 'em out an' closed up. Ouch! Easy! You're breakin' it, I tell you!"

"I've got a kind heart like you," Larry said. "Where did Missouri Red take that bunch of border jumpers?"

Tucker only groaned, but a little pressure on the arm made him gasp: "I'm tellin' you as fast as I can! Someone said they was goin' to the P Bar Three Ranch, an' then on to the Busted Jug!"

"What for?"

"They're gonna clean out some cattle."

"They are, are they? Pete Blythe won't stand for anything like that."

"He won't be sheriff long. An' that's all I know." Tucker groaned as he crowded helplessly against the bars, stooping slightly to the twist of his arm.

"Who carried word into Malpaís about me?" Larry demanded.

"I don't know." A harder twist got the answer. "Red sent it, I reckon."

"What for?"

"God'lmighty, I don't know! If you bust my arm, I still won't know!"

"Well, then, who killed Bud Taylor?"

"They say you done it." Tucker groaned again, and that

seemed to be the truth as far as Tucker knew it.

"Step back," Larry ordered. Holding the arm, he pushed the door open and stepped out into the passage. He had to let go of the arm then. Tucker yanked it back through the door and jumped at him, swearing thickly. Larry smashed him in the nose and jumped back.

Blood spurted from Tucker's nose. Tucker went berserk then and rushed without caution. A slamming uppercut knocked him against the side wall. He bounced back, rushed again, swinging wildly.

They battled along the passage, staggering from one wall to the other. It didn't matter that Tucker's arm was still strained, clumsy, that the hot coffee hadn't helped his eyes any. He was the bigger man. He had more height, weight, reach, and fury drove him in and in. Larry kept moving back, fighting mostly with one arm. If Tucker got him down, he wouldn't stand much chance. But there was another side to it, a side Tucker wouldn't have understood if he had been told. Pete Blythe's side.

Old Pete, half blind, carrying on as sheriff with gallant stubbornness, was up against a lot he didn't suspect. Pete needed help now, and only one man could help him. Larry knew he had to help Pete, no matter what came of it. Only he could do it—and it was little enough return for all Pete had done for him—even if a hanging noose made up the reward.

Tending bar, drinking, eating heavily didn't help a man much in a slamming, rough-and-tumble fight. Tucker began to pant, to gasp, to move sluggishly. They were in the store part now. Tucker threw a big fist straight out. Larry ducked under and came up with a hooking smash to the jaw that knocked the bigger man sprawling into a table.

Tucker stumbled, upset a chair, fell down to his hands and knees. Larry could have kicked him. He waited until

Tucker came up, sobbing for breath through pulped, bleeding lips, and knocked him down again. Tucker stayed there.

"Get up!" Larry panted.

But Tucker had had enough. Larry swung over the bar, found his gun belt and gun under the bar where Tucker had put them. Navajo Jack's knife was there, also. His rifle was gone, but Tucker's sawed-off shotgun was there and a box of shells beside it.

Stuffing the shells into his pockets, Larry went out to meet Tucker, who had reeled to his feet, wiping blood from his face.

"I want some more grub an' coffee," Larry told him. "An' then the best horse you've got."

Tucker got the grub in a dirty kitchen, then, carrying the lantern, led the way out back to a small, open-front shed where several horses were tied. He transferred the saddle laboriously to one of the horses.

"Now crawl back in your den, you sanctimonious skunk," Larry directed.

Tucker left. By the time he closed the back door, Larry was riding out of the walled yard, toward the bleak emptiness of the desert flats.

The stars were still bright and cold, as they had been earlier in the evening. The empty night was just as lonely. Larry was deadbeat, in no shape for a long ride, but he felt cheerful. The chance to help Pete brought its own strength.

Nevertheless, at sunrise, Larry was bleary-eyed, haggard, yawning, and about at the end of his rope when he came out of the breaks, down through the purple sage to Jughead Taylor's bunch-grass range.

The early morning sunlight was flooding golden and

warm about him when he reached the ranch house. A man at the corrals stared at him and started for the bunkhouse. Larry climbed stiffly out of the saddle at the back door and knocked.

Kareen came to the door. Color left her cheeks when she looked out at him. Indignation followed. "What are you doing here again?" she asked, poised to close the door.

"Where's your father?" Larry asked. Kareen was small and slender, but her bitter aversion had a flare beyond her size.

"You've done enough! Can't you let us alone? Mitch says you wounded his brother Jess yesterday! Isn't there any end to the trouble you're bringing?"

They faced one another like two strangers—all the hope and tenderness of the past buried, lost.

Larry answered her woodenly. "There'll be no shootin' unless he starts it. I came here to help him."

"Help him?" said Kareen. Her laugh had a shade of hysteria. "You help him?"

"Where's your father, Kareen?"

"Coming behind you!" Kareen threw at him, and stepped out of the doorway.

Jughead Taylor was striding from the bunkhouse, big and massive as ever, formidable behind his black beard and fierce hooked nose. He carried a rifle with the muzzle forward, finger on the trigger, and he was sided by two of his men with handguns out.

"Drop that shotgun, Remington!" Jughead's order was harsh, threatening. "Kareen, get into the house!"

Twenty-four hours of riding had left Larry raw-nerved, irritable. "If I was honin' for trouble," Larry snapped, "I wouldn't ride up in the open for you to throw down on me! I just come from Friar Tucker's place at Sunday School

Wells. A man named Missouri Red left there last night with a bunch of riders. They were headin' for the Parker ranch and your outfit. They're after cattle. By the number of men, the bunch they'll take won't be small . . . an' it'll be your cattle they'll get."

"A pretty story," Jughead scoffed. "My cattle has been left pretty much alone for years."

"You've crowded the outlaw bunch harder than anyone else but Pete Blythe," Larry said. "Your stock is nearest to 'em. They've marked you down for trouble, an' you're goin' to get it."

"The one thing right now is that I've got you," said Jughead with grim satisfaction.

"I'm headin' into Malpaís," Larry said. "I don't aim to be stopped, Jughead."

"Now, ain't that funny? Malpaís is right where we're takin' you. I promised my womenfolks I'd let the law have its way with you, but I'll see that the law gets its chance."

"If you go to Malpaís, you'll follow me in like a stranger," Larry said coolly. "I've run out my rope on all this, you onery old mossy horn. I didn't shoot Bud, but I'll prove it my own way, not before a Malpaís jury with the cards stacked ag'in' me. Savvy?"

"Just so we get you into Malpaís! If a jury don't fix you, I will! Ed, get the hosses saddled."

Then Kareen cut in. "Larry, are you hungry?" she asked.

Jughead grunted angrily.

"I'd feed a hungry dog," Kareen said defensively.

Larry was scanning her face. They had been too close to each other not to read the little signs. Kareen suddenly had become less bitter. Her eyes were troubled now as they watched him.

His faint smile was twisted. "Even a dog gets hungry,"

Larry said. "I could use some coffee, Kareen, an' bless you for thinkin' of it."

Jughead muttered angrily in his beard. Color was in Kareen's cheeks as she went into the house. Bacon, eggs, and coffee she got for him, and Jughead stood, grim and watchful, in the kitchen while Larry hastily ate, and stood up again.

"Thanks," he said to Kareen.

Kareen said nothing. The troubled look was still on her face.

They rode away from the ranch, four of them. It was mid-morning when they entered Malpaís and rode toward the small brick courthouse where Pete Blythe had his office. They were recognized. Excitement went toward the courthouse with them. On foot and in the saddle, a growing crowd accompanied them. When Larry dismounted at the courthouse hitch rack, an angry voice yelled: "First time I ever see a prisoner come in with his gun!"

The crowd trooped into the courthouse after them. The sheriff's door was open. Pete Blythe was just getting up from his desk when Larry walked in and said: "Hello, Pete."

"Where'd you come from, Larry?" Pete jerked out, staring.

Yes, Pete was getting old. Never before had it shown so plainly. Tall, erect, his face heavily weathered and his hair snowy white, Pete was still a fine figure of a man. But his face was deeply seamed, and he had aged a lot in the past week.

Before Larry could answer, Jughead Taylor cut in: "He come to my place this mornin', Pete. I brought him in. Lock him up an' make double damned sure he don't escape. He's gonna pay for what he did to Bud if it's the last thing I do in this life."

206

In the crowded doorway, an angry voice burst out: "He oughta be hung right off!"

An excited murmur of agreement ran through the crowd. Pete Blythe hunched his spare shoulders and faced the scowling leaders who had pushed on into the office.

"There'll be no lynchin' in Malpaís," Pete barked angrily. "The boy'll go to trial the same as any other prisoner."

"No one ever figgered you'd do anything but try to help him, Pete," another man sneered.

"Who said that?" Pete flung out in sudden passion.

"Me. Ben Casey! What's the matter with your eyes? I'm standin' right here!"

Pete passed the back of his hand across his eyes, and then glared at Casey who was standing in the second row of speakers. "Nothin's the matter with my eyes, Casey! An' I'm sheriff here! ¿Sabe? There'll be no lynchin' in Malpaís! Get outta here!"

Casey was a crony of the Parkers. He sneered now and spoke to the men around him. "They lived together. Remington was his deputy. If you don't lynch the dirty dog now, how much chance do you reckon there'll be if anything happens to him while Blythe's got the handlin' of it? Take it outta his hands! Get your justice while you got the chance!"

The angry murmurs broke into loud words of agreement.

"Lynchin's the thing for him! Who's got a rope?"

"Bring him outta there!" a yell from the corridor begged.

"A hangin'll settle all this! He didn't give Bud time to wait for trial!"

Even Jughead Taylor stood darkly to one side and looked his agreement with the idea. Like flame through dry grass, the idea flared and grew in seconds, until the crowd out in the corridor was roaring, and the leaders were being shoved forward.

Pete drew his gun, stepped in front of Larry, and shouted: "Get back, damn you!"

But the leaders still were being pushed forward. Hands were already on guns, waiting for the final spark that would start violence.

Larry stepped to Pete's side and faced them. There was grinning death in his haggard, bleary-eyed face, cold menace about the shotgun he held. It stopped the forward push, silenced the men who could see it. "Hang me, will you?" Larry said to the sullen, angry men he faced. "Who'll hang me? Who's the first son-of-a-bitch to step up an' try it?"

Faced with that question, no man volunteered or drew his gun.

"I'm saying the same thing!" Pete Blythe snarled. "I'm openin' the pot with five cartridges! Who calls the bet?"

Jughead Taylor suddenly erupted in a bellow: "I can see how the wind's blowin'! Still lookin' out for him, ain't you, Blythe? By God, a hangin' is the only way to settle this, after all! Boys, I'm with you!"

Men out in the corridor heard that and cheered, and pushed forward. But the men inside the doorway, who faced Pete's battered old .45 and the double-barreled shotgun, held back, hands off their guns. They knew men would die if the lynching started now. More than one man would die. And none of them was willing to be the first.

VI

"Rustler Paradise"

Larry's lip curled. "You want a lynchin', but you don't want to fight for it, huh? Get out, all of you! If one of you makes a move, I'll cut loose! Who's hankerin' for buckshot in the belly? You, Stevens? You, Edgcomb?"

Stevens, Edgcomb, and the men to the right and left of them edged back. They knew death when they saw it.

"You, too, Jughead!" Pete Blythe rasped. "I've knowed you for nigh on thirty years, but, by God, you'll be a dead man if you lift a hand in here!"

Bristling with rage, Jughead Taylor moved toward the door, also. His voice shook. "They're skunks, boys! Don't get yourselves shot up in here! There's other ways!"

Those inside the doorway had a hard time getting out into the crowded hall. Step by step, Larry followed them to the door, shotgun in hand. Pete kept at his side. Larry slammed the door, shut the bolt, jumped aside, pushing Pete with him, just as a roaring blast of shots tore through the door, just missing them. Shouts, cries, feet scuffling and tramping outside the door were drowned out as other guns cut loose, sieving the door with lead.

Pete Blythe backed aside, gun ready to answer the fire. Grief and concern were drawing Pete's wrinkled face into a sorrowful, although grim, mask. The lynch-maddened bunch beyond the door were Pete's neighbors, friends. He hated to shoot back through the door, where he couldn't miss in the crowd.

Pete's voice was loaded with grief: "Why'd you have to come back here, Larry? Whyn't you hit across the border? You knew I'd have to do my duty."

"I rode all night from Sunday School Wells, Pete. The outlaw bunch are raidin' the Busted Jug today or tonight. Jughead is too stubborn a fool to believe it. All he can think about is gettin' my neck in a rope."

"You went to Sunday School Wells yesterday, an' then rode back here?"

"That's right."

"Why'd you ride here with that story, Larry, after . . . after . . . ?" Pete's voice went shaky, broke off. He faltered on the accusation of Bud Taylor's murder. He gulped and said: "Why'd you get Bud, Larry? There was a reason besides the money, wasn't there? Bud done somethin'. You had to kill him straight out, for a good reason, didn't you?"

"I didn't kill him, Pete."

"But that tally book. I got it here in my desk. A dyin' man don't write a thing like that unless it's true."

"Pete, did I ever lie to you?"

"You never did, Larry. You was like our own boy. God, I was proud of you. So was Ma before she died. It's mighty near killed me to go out an' hunt you with a gun. I . . . I kept seein' you like you was the day you straggled in from Yuma, ragged an' hungry an' mighty lonesome." They were back in the corner of the office, where the crashing, smashing gunfire through the door couldn't reach them. Window glass was breaking, falling to the floor. Larry had to raise his voice to make himself heard.

"You'll have to trust me, Pete. Get me Bud's tally book. I'm leavin' you. I'm half dead for a sleep, but I've got some ridin' in me yet. If I get away from here, come along with whoever follows me."

"You can't get away from here, Larry."

"I'll get hung if I stay here, an' you'll have a lot of trouble that'll probably ruin you. I come back to help you, Pete. I didn't figure on all this, but there's still a chance. Let me have Bud's tally book. You lay low around the office here. They ain't apt to hurt you for doin' your duty."

Pete peered searchingly with his failing eyes, and then, careless of the occasional bullet slamming into the desk, he opened the top drawer, and came back with a small, dog-eared notebook. Larry shoved it into his pocket, clapped

Pete's shoulder, and opened the door behind them.

Winding steps went down to the courthouse basement where the jail cells were. The passage in front of the cells ended in a back basement door, barred and kept locked by a padlock. Larry still had his keys. He opened the door cautiously. The short flight of steps up to the ground level was clear. The crowd was at the front and side of the courthouse.

A look, as his head came level with the ground, showed two saddled horses and a horse and buggy at the hitch rack under the cottonwoods behind the courthouse. They had been there when he rode up. No one had thought to move them.

Not thirty feet away four men were standing at the west corner of the courthouse, looking toward the front, toward the windows of Pete's office. Four men, thirty feet away. Two saddled horses fifty feet away. . . .

One man turned, saw Larry bursting up the steps, shotgun in hand. The man's yell of warning and quick jump to the corner of the building brought the other three whirling around.

"Jump, or I'll cut you down!" Larry threw at them.

They dived around the corner of the courthouse, guns forgotten. But when Larry reached the hitch rack and made a flying mount to a sorrel horse, men were already scattering out and firing at him. The sorrel horse shied as Larry opened up with the shotgun, firing high, on purpose. But the blast of small shot drove the gunmen back out of sight for the moment.

Larry yanked the sorrel's head around and broke with a rush out from under the tall cottonwoods, west toward the rolling range beyond Malpaís, west toward the Bottle Neck ford of the Gila, which would save him running the gauntlet of town to the river bridge.

They stormed after him, gunning him out of town, quirting their horses hard. Water splashed high at the river ford as the sorrel fought across. Guns opened up across the river as Larry spurred up the gravelly rise of the opposite bank. A bullet ripped off the heel of his right boot, and another whipped through the crown of his hat.

He'd had the good luck of the devil so far. Then a bullet struck his leg halfway above the knee. Blood gushed as the sorrel carried him over the crest, out of sight.

Using his bandanna on the wound, Larry drove the sorrel on. It seemed he'd been riding other men's horses forever—walking, trotting, loping, galloping through badlands and range land, doomed, damned, and driven on by the spectral finger of Bud Taylor pointing back from the grave. Hell could be no worse.

The foaming, sweat-streaked sorrel was about done for when it finally plunged down a draw toward the grassy flat where clustered the P Bar Three buildings and corrals. The corrals were empty. At a distance the place looked deserted. Larry had hoped to find the corrals filled, the place alive with Missouri Red and his gunslingers from Sunday School Wells, resting up from the night's ride before they got down to business with Jughead Taylor's cattle.

One sign of life greeted him. A lone rider coming up from the draw toward him stopped, reined half around, as if ready to run for it. Larry's breath sucked in as he recognized the rider. It was Kareen Taylor.

The sorrel stumbled as they met. Head down, it trembled, wind whistling through flaring nostrils. Kareen's hair was in wind-blown tendrils. Challenge, mixed with fear, was on her face. Swift concern appeared when she saw the blood-soaked leg.

"What is it, Larry? Where's Father?" She almost could have cried—*Is he alive? Did you kill him?*—for that was in her mind.

"He's coming behind me," Larry croaked. "Where're the Parkers? What are you doing here?"

"They've gone. Mitch just drove away. Pablo Morales's horse came to the corral this morning with blood on the empty saddle. Pablo was riding the line over by the Dry Creek breaks and Dry Creek cañon. I came over here to help."

"Where'd Mitch go?"

"He went after some of his men. They're going on to look for Pablo. You're hurt, Larry! What happened?"

"I want your horse," Larry said hoarsely. He didn't know bloody fingers had smudged his face, didn't know weakness and strain made his grin ghastly as he said: "I cheated 'em again. Run out from the hangin' noose they had ready. They're comin' behind me."

Kareen was already swinging out of the saddle. She sided her horse by his good leg, head to his horse's tail, and stepped between and turned the stirrup for him.

"You deserve a fair trial, Larry. They can't do that to you."

He hardly managed to get across into the other saddle, taking the shotgun. Panting with weakness, he gathered up the reins and grinned. "It won't make much difference after you're married to Mitch Parker." Back at the head of the long draw, the first of the pursuit burst into view. Larry delayed for a moment, looking down at Kareen. The harshness went out of his voice. "I reckon I won't see you again, Kareen. They'll get me. While I've got the chance, I'll tell you I never stopped lovin' you. How could I have hurt Bud, knowin' it would hurt you? No matter what they think

213

they've proved after I'm gone, just hang onto that when you think about me."

The girl moved as though to show him that she believed him, that she still loved him. Then her pride and her sorrow came over her again, and she drew back. Larry was holding onto the horn of the saddle as he looked down on her, and could now hear the pounding of the men following. He couldn't wait any longer although he felt that he should say something more. He smiled briefly, sorrowfully, and rolled his spurs, leaving her behind him.

The horse bolted ahead as the spurs struck it. Fresher, faster the drumming rush of its gallop swept up the side of the draw to the brush, where bullets would not find so clear a target. Looking back, Larry saw Kareen on the sorrel. She was leaning forward a little, oblivious to the gunfire behind her as she watched him go. Then the brush cut her off, and Larry put her out of his mind. Thinking only made it worse.

The Dry Creek breaks tongued down into the flatter grazing country in a series of ridges and hills, gullied and eroded, bare and bleak, so rough for miles that a man on horseback did well to get through them. Dry Creek cañon, on the eastern edge of the breaks, cut through the first and highest hills, and formed a pathway through the worst of the going. If Pablo Morales had been killed while working the Busted Jug line near the cañon, then trouble was stirring at the cañon.

Kareen's fresher horse outdistanced the Malpaís men. Bearing southwest, Larry entered the breaks south of Dry Creek cañon. He was trying to reach the west end of the cañon by skirting around through the rough country where no one was apt to sight him. The going was cruel and hard, through winding arroyos, up steep slopes, plunging down other slopes. It was true badlands country, killing for man and beast.

He had to look twice when he first saw far ahead a thin,

drifting cloud of dust that marked some kind of activity at the west end of Dry Creek cañon. Mostly Dry Creek ran underground, except after a rain. Here and there in the channel the water worked up in scant pools. One such spot was at the west end of the cañon. There, too, beside the water, a steep-walled pocket enclosed nine or ten acres of bare ground. It was a natural corral, too steep-sided for a cow or horse to get up, almost too steep for a man to climb. Dust was drifting up from that pocket as Larry rode near through the breaks. The bawling of uneasy cattle came on the wind.

He rode near the rim of the pocket, stopping as soon as he could see down to the milling cattle that had been thrown in through the one narrow entrance. While he looked, another bunch of a dozen or so head were hazed in by riders to the south of the pocket. They were clearing the beef off Jughead Taylor's land, pointing it through the cañon as fast as it appeared at the other end, holding everything here by water until the whole lot was ready to travel.

Half a dozen riders were at the mouth of the pocket. Circling the rim, Larry reached a spot where he could look down a steep slope into the cañon proper at the pocket entrance. Mitch Parker was down there, talking to Jess Parker and Missouri Red. One of the outlaw bunch and two of the Parker riders were watching the mouth of the pocket. Two more men up in the cañon were hazing another bunch of beef toward the spot.

Larry swiped the back of his hand across his eyes. The hand was trembling. His blood-caked leg was a thing of fire; his brain seemed to be blazing. Behind him, not far behind, the Malpaís men were coming. Now and then topping a higher rise he had seen their dust far back and caught glimpses of the riders themselves. Like a hunting pack they were keeping his trail.

Down there at the bottom of the slope was the answer to all his trouble. Larry couldn't know what would come of him if he carried out his plan. Yet now he had no other choice. Any hope of ever seeing Kareen again, of even living more than a few hours, lay in what might happen in the next few minutes. Behind him was certain death. Ahead of him death was hardly less sure. But with luck he might make out. And even if he failed, he would be paid off in boothill. The posse was sure to follow him. That's all he wanted at this moment.

He put the horse to the cañon edge, grabbed the saddle horn, and hung on. The horse did not want to go over. Larry gigged him with the spurs. Then the gallant little beast surged forward, bunched his hoofs, and started that wild slide downwards.

VII

"Noose for a Rustler"

By a miracle the little horse made it, plunging to the bottom in a cascade of flying gravel and dust. The men below drew guns when he appeared above. By the dumbfounded looks on their faces when he drew up before them, he saw that Kareen had said nothing to Mitch Parker about his visit to the Busted Jug.

Jess Parker's harsh voice was the first to rise above the bawling cattle in the pocket. He spoke to Missouri Red. "You said, by God, he was locked up at the Wells!"

Missouri Red's fox-like face was haggard, too. He'd ridden all night, worked all day. He answered hotly and irritably. "He must 'a' shot himself out. Look at the blood on his leg. It don't matter how he got here. I'm glad he's here. I got a score to even with him."

Glaring, six-gun resting ready across his saddle roll, Mitch Parker barked: "What the hell's he doin' here?"

Jess Parker made an impatient gesture. "We got him now. Don't worry."

Larry showed his teeth in a savage grin. "So you're comin' out in the open with it? No dry-gulchin' like Missouri Red tried. No sendin' a bunch of killers to drag me outta an Indian's shack on a thin excuse. You got me, but why in hell did you want me in the first place?" he asked.

Mitch Parker laughed. "With you out of the way, we'll cook Pete Blythe's goose quick. That old fool is done an' don't know it. Jess has as good as got the job already. We'll run things in these parts when Jess is sheriff. We'll. . . ."

"Shut up, Mitch!" Jess Parker barked. "What's this talk about a bunch tryin' to drag you out of an Indian's shack?"

"Don't know about that, huh?" Larry laughed. "Ask Missouri Red, then. He didn't show himself, but then he kept out of sight, too, when he bushwhacked me on the Salado road. Where's the *concha* off your vest, Red?"

"What's it to you? I lost it."

"I picked it up where the dirty son-of-a-bitch hid on the Salado road an' gunned me."

Missouri Red blinked, shrugged, and then turned to Jess Parker. "Some of the boys went over to Cow Springs to get him an' find out where he hid that bank money."

Jess Parker swore. "Damn you, I told you to forget about that bank money. It's him I wanted, not the bank money. Soon as we get old Blythe outta the way, there'll be plenty of money for the takin'."

Larry's laugh had a savage edge. "I can read the sign now. Which one of you Parkers killed Bud Taylor an' tore out the last page of writing in his tally book an' wrote on the page?

Red, they've been lyin' to you. I didn't kill Bud Taylor. I didn't get the money. If you were due a share of it, you got cheated."

Missouri Red's fox-like face twisted in a snarl. "You mean you got that money, Jess? You lied to me all along about it?"

"Are you believin' him?"

"Damned if I'm not!" Missouri Red spat. "It sounds like your smooth thinkin'. Your idea of raidin' the bank was good. When Mitch hightailed into the Wells an' said you wanted Remington killed on his way back to Malpaís, I took some of the boys myself an' covered all ways he was likely to come back. I got plugged in that deal myself . . . an' it was only to cover up your grab of the money, huh? You think I'll take a dirty trick like that lying down?" Eyes narrowed, gun out, Missouri Red's words had become a loud yell.

"Don't get hasty, Red!" Jess Parker warned angrily. "When Mitch told me he found Bud Taylor an' the money, an' got it, an' laid it on Remington in Bud's tally book, I seen the first thing to do was to get Remington outta the way quick. Then there'd be no argument about it. If you'd got this fellow on the Salado road that day, you'd've had your share of the money. It's waitin' at the ranch house for you now!"

"When a man lies to me once, everything he says from then on is a lie!" Red snarled.

"What are you gonna do about it?" Jess Parker challenged.

Missouri Red's gun muzzle flicked up, crashing his raging reply. Mitch Parker's shot was too late to stop the bullet that smashed into his brother. But Mitch's .45 sent Missouri Red reeling. A second shot sent the fox-faced little outlaw plunging out of the saddle to the ground.

"Drop your gun, Mitch!" Larry grated.

Cursing, Mitch balanced life and death in one split second, and let his gun fall to the ground. He had lost the drop in trying to save his brother.

"Down on the ground, Mitch!"

The two Parker riders and the outlaw guarding the mouth of the pocket had stared in amazement at the sudden burst of gunfire. Their guns were out. They started toward the spot. The shotgun roared at them. They scattered back toward the milling cattle in the pocket, away from that sleet of small lead.

Glowering, Mitch dismounted. Larry slammed in a fresh shell, backed his horse away, and left the saddle, too. He almost fell on his face when he hit the ground. Mitch was jumping toward him when Larry caught a drunken balance and got the shotgun muzzle up.

"Lie down, damn you!" he gasped thickly.

Mitch took one look at the weaving, wild-eyed scarecrow who threatened him with the shotgun, and went down in the dirt, cursing.

The bunch of cattle coming through the cañon was scattering in panic. The two men behind them opened fire. Lead keened past Larry's head as he opened up with the shotgun over the scattering steers. The blast of shot drove one of the men half out of the saddle. He was clawing at his face as he retreated at a gallop. His companion followed, leaning low to escape the next sleet of buckshot. They could face bullets, but their nerves broke at standing up close to a scattering charge of shot that couldn't miss.

Weaving, staggering, Larry reloaded the shotgun again and lurched over to the bank, and dropped behind a small boulder. There he'd stay. He was too weak to get up again.

Mitch Parker started to rise, then flopped down again as Larry cut dirt near his head with a six-gun.

"I'd kill you if it wasn't for Kareen!" Larry called. "You're a dirty snake, but, if she wants you, she can have you. Lie there! We're holdin' the cañon!"

"You're crazy!" Mitch bawled. "You can't stand 'em off! Lemme up an' I'll see you get out of this safe!"

The three men who had fled back into the pocket out of shotgun range opened up with their rifles now, throwing lead toward the spot where Larry lay. The man he had chased back up the cañon had stopped. Beyond him four riders burst into view, galloping toward the trouble. Every man within hearing would be coming. Mitch was right. There wasn't a chance.

They knew he had only a shotgun. They stayed back out of range and threw lead at the spot where he lay half exposed behind the small rock. It made Larry laugh grimly to himself. He'd solved this thing, had it all settled. But where would that get him now? The posse that had been chasing him had apparently lost his trail. They would not come now. It was all one huge joke to Larry Remington. He would die, and all he could do was laugh. This whole thing was entirely too crazy. From the time he had busted away from the sheriff until the rustler gang turned on themselves, nothing had made much sense. But Larry was not through yet. He had forgotten, years ago, how to quit.

He jacked another shell into the shotgun, settled down with lead whizzing over him, to wait. Maybe he'd get another shot or two in before he died.

Mitch Parker hugged the ground and swore loudly. Dirt scattered over Larry as bullets struck beside him. He rose up to see better, and something clubbed him on the side of the head. He knew the shotgun had slipped out of his hand. He caught a blurred glimpse of Mitch jumping up. Everything went black then.

A booming voice was the next thing he heard. "He's too tough to kill! Look at him wiggle! That blood in his hair's from a crease. The bone ain't broke."

Larry opened his eyes. He was lying on the ground. Jughead Taylor's black beard was above his face.

"Got your noose ready?" Larry asked.

Several men were standing around them. Distant gunfire was audible. Mitch Parker was standing nearby with his hands tied and a rifle held at his back.

"Sure we got a noose," Jughead rasped. "For Mitch there. Fellow who calls himself Missouri Red talked some before he cashed in his chips. Son, the boys are ready to give you a celebration. An' you've done a heap for me today. They was cleanin' out my best beef."

"Damn you and your beef," Larry groaned, sitting up. "Where's Pete Blythe?"

"Leadin' the boys after the outlaw bunch. Pete swears he'll clean out everything from here to Sunday School Wells this time. He's a sheriff to be proud of. An' don't think too hard of me, son. I made a mistake, an' I'm apologizing for it. Kareen stopped me back at the Parker Ranch an' said, if anything happened to you, she'd spend her life hatin' me. An' you're all cut up on the head where a rock or a piece of lead scraped you. You don't look so good. How do you feel?"

"Terrible. There's Mitch Parker. Take him back to her."

"Don't know what she'd do with him." Jughead shrugged. "She told me back at the Parker Ranch she was gonna marry you, no matter what happened."

"Kareen said that? You wouldn't fool me, Jughead. She said it, sure?"

"Uhn-huh."

Larry stared from bloodshot eyes. Then he grinned. "I reckon she is, then. Gimme your hand, Jughead."

About the Author

T.T. FLYNN was born Thomas Theodore Flynn, Jr., in Indianapolis, Indiana. He was the author of over a hundred Western stories for such leading pulp magazines as Street & Smith's *Western Story Magazine*, Popular Publications' *Dime Western*, and Dell's *Zane Grey's Western Magazine*. He lived much of his life in New Mexico and spent much of his time on the road, exploring the vast terrain of the American West. His descriptions of the land are always detailed, but he used them not only for local color but also to reflect the heightening of emotional distress among the characters within a story. Following the Second World War, Flynn turned his attention to the book-length Western novel and in this form also produced work that has proven imperishable. Five of these novels first appeared as original paperbacks, most notably *The Man from Laramie* (1954) which was also featured as a serial in *The Saturday Evening Post* and subsequently made into a memorable motion picture directed by Anthony Mann and starring James Stewart, and *Two Faces West* (1954) which deals with the problems of identity and reality and served as the basis for a television series. He was highly innovative and inventive and in later novels, such as *Night of the Comanche Moon* (Five Star Westerns, 1995), concentrated on deeper psychological issues as the source for conflict, rather than more elemental motives like greed. Flynn is at his best in stories that combine mystery—not surprisingly, he also wrote detective fiction—with suspense and action in an artful balance. The psychological dimensions of Flynn's Western fiction came increasingly to encompass a confrontation with ethical principles about how one must live, the values that one must hold dear above all else, and his belief that there must be a balance in all things. The cosmic meaning of the mortality of all living creatures had become for him a unifying metaphor for the fragility and dignity of life itself. *Noose of Fate* will be his next Five Star Western.

Additional copyright information:

"Blood of the *Dons*" first appeared under the title "Fighting *Dons* of San Saba" in *Star Western* (4/36). Copyright © 1936 by Popular Publications, Inc. Copyright © renewed 1964 by Thomas Theodore Flynn, Jr. Copyright © 2004 by Thomas B. Flynn, M.D., for restored material.

"Bandit of the Brindlebar" first appeared under the title "Last of the Wild Shotwells" in *Star Western* (1/36). Copyright © 1935 by Popular Publications, Inc. Copyright © renewed 1963 by Thomas Theodore Flynn, Jr. Copyright © 2004 by Thomas B. Flynn, M.D., for restored material.

"Valhalla" first appeared in *Short Stories* (9/25/30). Copyright © 1930 by Doubleday, Doran & Co., Inc. Copyright © renewed 1958 by Thomas Theodore Flynn, Jr. Copyright © 2004 by Thomas B. Flynn, M.D., for restored material.

"The Fighting Breed" first appeared under the title "Fugitive Lawman" in *Star Western* (6/36). Copyright © 1936 by Popular Publications, Inc. Copyright © renewed 1964 by Thomas Theodore Flynn, Jr. Copyright © 2004 by Thomas B. Flynn, M.D., for restored material.